CANADIAN FICTION

FICTION MANIFESTES CRITIQUES GRAPHIQUES PHOTOS ENTREVUES

CANADIAN FICTION *Anthology*

Pop Goes The Story

Edited by Rob Payne

QUARRY
FICTION
BOOKS

ISSN 0045-477X
ISBN 1-55082-233-0

CANADIAN FICTION is a twice-yearly anthology of contemporary Canadian fiction. The editor invites manuscripts from writers in Canada and Canadians living in other countries. Unless manuscripts are accompanied by a SAE and Canadian stamps or international reply coupons, they will not be returned. Mail with postage due will be refused. CFM is available for exchange lists or any other arrangements that will mutually benefit literary magazines. The magazine is a member of the Canadian Magazine Publishers' Association. It is published with the financial assistance of The Canada Council and the Ontario Arts Council.

Annual Subscription Rates
Individual: **$34.24** ($32.00 + $2.24 GST)
Institutional: **$44.94** ($42.00 + $2.94 GST)

Address all correspondence to
CANADIAN FICTION
P.O. Box 1061, Kingston, Ontario, Canada K7L 4Y5

Back issues of CANADIAN FICTION are available in film and electronic format from Micromedia Limited, 20 Victoria St., Toronto, ON M5C 2N8 and from Xerox University Microfilms, P.O. Box 1346, Ann Arbor, Michigan, U.S.A. 48106 or 35 Mobile Drive, Toronto, Canada M4A 1H6.

Indexed in CANADIAN PERIODICAL INDEX, CANADIAN ESSAY AND LITERATURE INDEX, MLA INTERNATIONAL BIBLIOGRAPHY, INDEX OF PERIODICAL FICTION, and AMERICAN HUMANITIES INDEX.

Printed and bound in Canada by AGMV, Montreal and Cap-Saint-Ignace, Quebec. Distributed to the magazine trade by Canadian Magazine Publishers' Association. Distributed to the book trade by General Distribution Services in Canada and LPC Group in the U.S.A.

Cover art by David Lester.

Published by Quarry Press Inc., P.O. Box 1061, Kingston, Ontario K7L 4Y5.

Contents

ROB PAYNE is the former editor of *Quarry Magazine*. His writing appears in such forums as *Zygote* and *The Lazy Writer,* and he is currently finishing work on his first pop novel, the marketing-friendly *Generation Why?*

The Infomercial As Oracle

ROB PAYNE

IT'S FRIDAY. *A wild Friday.* I'm sitting at a small, wooden desk sorting through reams upon reams of manuscripts. In between stories, I'm practicing TV commercial poses in the mirror above the dresser. I've got the whiter teeth smile down pat, but my *I can't believe this isn't real butter* elation still needs a bit of work. To celebrate a really exciting story I indulge in Folger's Crystals © post-revelation shock, screaming merrily: "Yes! Yes! Oh God yes, I want another cup!"

When I was in Oxford last year, wandering up and down the curving streets with my Tom Cruise haircut and an English-style Oh Henry © knockoff, dodging students and camera-toting tourists, I encountered a single line of graffiti scrawled on a walled-up window of the old library. It said: "Everyone wants to be Lennon." At the time it struck me as corny — the kind of goop a drunken nineteen-year-old would mistake for deep, enlightened philosophy on the ass-end of a good Friday night binge; but the image stayed with me for a few days, and the more I thought about it, the more the significance of *the act* sunk in. Here, in England's most prestigious university town, old was meeting new. Oxford's most sacred building was being defiled (edified?) by

ROB PAYNE

pop culture, by a strange and urgent message scrawled in the dead of night by some drunken kid desperate to shake off the stony shackles of *high* culture and sullen academia. Here was pop culture bubbling below the surface of a calm respectability, asserting itself like magma exploding through the fissures. And it made me realize that the last form of discrimination unaddressed by the literary community is *pop-aphobia*: fear of relating to the masses on their own, widely known and identifiable terms.

Like so many others, I stopped looking for enlightenment in philosophy or academia or organized religion a long time ago — just couldn't handle the constant oppression. I've come to lean on pop culture for answers: Ricki Lake and Ross Perot, REM and MSG, microwave bagels and that squirrelly-eyed misfit Kenneth Starr. I'm taking the time to read bathroom stall graffiti and subway scrawl and have started carrying around a small notebook and a pen in my jacket. Whenever I read anything interesting I jot it down. Once the notebook's done I'm going to go through it page by page, thought by thought, and see if the words of the prophets are written on the subway walls and tenement halls. I have the feeling Paul Simon is full of shit, but maybe I'll publish the collection, start a bizarre, automatic-weapons-friendly cult in the Hollywood hills, become a spiritual guru.

If all goes well, perhaps I can do a tie-in with the pock-faced guy from North Dakota I saw on TV this week — the guy who collects toilet paper from famous houses and monuments and shrines from around the world. They showed a big room with white and pink and baby blue samples framed behind glass, each labeled with a tiny bronze plaque: the Louvre; Harrod's department store; the Dakota building; the Ed Sullivan Theatre . . . Maybe we can team-up, go online and start a chat group, put together a newsletter and begin recruiting for the cult early, in the right circles.

My Gary Hart-like fall from grace was cemented when I met the ever-enigmatic Hal Niedzviecki one Spring day in Metropolis. He and Jimmy were on assignment and I was eating cabbage rolls and drinking Snapples at the Future Bakery on Queen St. We got to talking and came up with an idea as monumental and life-affirming as the final episode of MASH or the seventh game of the 1997 World Series: we would beat the nay-sayers and uptight literati at their own game — confound them worse than Mr. Roper — and put together an anthology of pop culture fiction, featuring some of the best new and emerging writers. He would contribute and I would edit, and we vowed to share credit for the idea or else battle it out in The People's Court for the beer-swilling North American public to watch. I immediately set to work finding stories, but contacted the ever-shrewd Johnny Cochrane, just in case things went wrong. I laughed, knowing full-well that Hal would be stuck with Marcia Clark (*It's always Marcia, Marcia, Marcia!*) Poor bastard. She'd make me a hero, forcing me to try on the bloody glove O.J. let her keep as a souvenir, then forcing me to prove I could operate a keyboard — all at a crucial point in the trial, when it became obvious Hal was about to win. But it would all end up copacetic in the end, cause we'd all end up on CNN or ABC, talking about defense strategies and the best way to get firm abs and slim hips, drinking mocha lattes and laughing about how great passenger side airbags are when a certain Olympic gold medalist gets trashed and slams her sparkling Ice Capades BMW up your ass, going 140 m.p.h.

And now, months later, the anthology is done and I can leave the house knowing the world is safe for another day — knowing there are writers out there defining a generation, slinking along with Monica Lewinsky and her gleaming collection of semen-encrusted outfits and the brooding underbelly of corporate Disney. So, grab a Snapple and dive in. Slip off your Birks and break open the Doritos. Turn the page and don't worry: there aren't any commercials.

ROB PAYNE

AILSA KAY has published fiction in *The New Quarterly, Prairie Fire, Exile* and *Tessera*. She lives in Toronto.

Vinyl

AILSA KAY

HER NAME IS VINYL. Smooth as raincoats, bright as a beachball, she picked me up; I've never looked back. We have a dog now and two cats. We have an apartment that we decorated ourselves: plastic fruit hanging from plastic trees, plastic flowers overspilling windows, molded plastic chairs at the kitchen table.

I met Vinyl at Business Depot. Mesmerized by the array of labels before me, I was perplexed, enthralled, dazzled by too much choice. I felt a breath at my back. An arm, thin bangled arm, reached round for the box just beyond my shoulder, another arm slipped round the other side.

"Decision time," said the Vinyl I didn't yet know, her voice supple and sexy as melted tiddlywinks. I turned around. She held a package of labels in each hand as she gazed at me, one eyebrow raised. "I'm Vinyl," she said. "You've been standing here far too long." She tossed both packages into the plastic basket I held over my arm and said, "Buy 'em both. You won't regret it."

I hadn't said a word. I couldn't. Would she vanish if I spoke? Would she fold herself, bright and sharp, into origami and take flight?

Would she accordion into a porta-file and pack up? These thoughts and others fluttered through my mind as Vinyl waited.

"I'm Darla," I said, realizing for the first time how dull that was. I was named for a Little Rascal — rapscallion in a short skirt, skinned knees and big eyes. Darla. I'd always felt it held, in its syllables, a hint of coy daring, a hint of "baby, you take my fruitcake I'll knock your socks off!" Next to Vinyl it was outdated and ordinary. I wanted to take her home with me.

"Darla," she said. And her voice redeemed its phonemes. I would be a Texan beauty-queen with this woman by my side. I would be sultry and speak so slowly, whirling a lasso, desultory, about my hips. "How would you like to join me for a cup of coffee . . . Darla?"

I haven't described her, my Vinyl. I should describe her because she is — her form, the space she occupies, the skin that holds her together — she is the most spectacular being I've ever loved. More than that, when I hold her, she's all of creation in my arms. Synthetic, kinetic and when I part her legs it's like disco. Saturday Night Fever. I'm hitting the floor, I'm spinning in the light of her mirrored ball, I've got Abba in my mouth. But this isn't a description. Vinyl is 5 foot 4, her hair is purple and dark. She wears black eyeliner and pale purple lipstick and sometimes she paints her nails. But these are only particulars and they fail.

Vinyl is more beautiful than me.

"Happy birthday to me," she said that first day, raising a bowl of cappuccino to her purple frosted lips.

"Cheers," I said. We knocked our bowls together, froth spilling over our fingers.

Today Vinyl is applying for a job that will change our lives. This morning she pulled her hair into a knot at the back of her head, powdered pale blue shadow over her eyes. She went to her closet and pulled out a sky blue dress. Vinyl wants to be an air hostess.

I argued with her as she smoothed nude stockings over her long pale legs. I sat at her feet, looked into her eyes and told her she's too intelligent to be pushing carts up and down an airplane aisle, miming what to do with a life jacket, pointing to clearly marked exits. But Vinyl is scornful of my elitism. She likes to knock the bourgeoisie out of me, claiming I stake too much on brain potential. For Vinyl, my beautiful

11

Vinyl, there are a zillion potentials. Lift potential, for one. Depth potential, surface potential, love potential, adrenaline. All these she adds up on her calculator of life.

She rubs moisturizer into her perfect hands, her nails unpainted today, her nails trim and clean today: "Darla," she said, "I want to fly right over top of you." And she could. She does every day. "Darla, I want to wear that blue uniform, my hair in a ponytail, my feet in those cute little pumps. I want to wrap blankets around my passengers. I want to make them feel safe when there's nothing below them but a long windy fall. Can you understand that, Darla? I want you to understand that, Darla."

I try to but Vinyl's never made me feel safe. I worry she's changing and if she becomes a hostess of the skies I believe she'll be unalterably altered. I believe she'll begin to worry about the security of our windows, whether they'll blow under pressure. I believe she'll start serving dinner in miniature aluminum trays, only to throw them down the chute when we're finished. I can't sleep, worried she'll take my blanket away from me before I'm through.

When we first started dating, Vinyl was the fire-eater of my party, the deep-sea diver of my lagoon. In fact, she'd done some stunt work and I saw her once somersault, flaming, off the edge of a bridge. Our first coupling was in a deserted train yard, she strapped me to the tracks and made sound effects between my thighs. CHAKA-chaka-CHAKA-Chaka . . . building in intensity to KACHA KACHA KACHA KACHA KACHA. I bucked against her, imagining steam engines bearing down, boiler rooms and stoked fires, men sweating over hot coal. When I came she blew the whistle. She wouldn't untie me until I'd agreed to meet her again next week.

"Darla, I'd really like to see you again." So meek after the fervor of our locomotion. "I don't know why," she said, "but I feel like maybe something's beginning here." I nodded my head, the roughness of the railway tie scraping at the nape of my neck. "Do you feel that way too? Do you feel like love is inevitable?" Again I nodded. "So Friday night?"

Such a fearless proclamation after only one date. Love is inevitable. Like there was nothing we could do to stop it, like all we had to do was ride it. But I never felt safe. Never felt like, in Vinyl's arms, the world could not harm me. If anything, Vinyl's arms were the most dangerous place to be. She might choose that moment to bungee jump from the balcony, to throw herself backwards into shallow water. She might let go, just to see if she could save me before I hit bottom.

I'm waiting for Vinyl to come home. I'm waiting for her to walk through that door and tell me she changed her mind, she'd rather be a hijacker — the clothes are so much better. Cool Armani suits, a grenade in each pocket. A mask. "We'll be pirates of the air!" she would say, throwing me a belt of bullets. "We'll be ridiculously rich and keep at least two French maids in our apartment on the Riviera. Whaddaya say?"

I'd like to understand this new desire of hers. She's tried to explain it to me, her theory of potentials, the aesthetic, the ethic of care. At dinner last night she gripped my wrist so tight I woke up this morning with the imprints of her fingers on my skin.

"I fell out of my pram when I was only a year old. Wandered away and made a life for myself," Vinyl said, telling me the family history I never knew. Had never asked for. "I've been falling out of buses, off bridges, out of twelve story office buildings ever since. And I've loved it. Until you."

I was the cause of it then, the reason Vinyl yearned for the air, the uniform, the compact cart. I told her I didn't want her to change. She said it didn't matter. "Your love anchors me," she said, "I want to live for you." I wanted to cry.

When Vinyl comes home it will be to an apartment strewn with plastic petals. I've melted the fruit in bowls, dismembered the trees and chairs. I'm sitting on the buffet, naked, my hair swirled on top of my head, wreathed in plastic beads, rubber bands, the colorful tags from bread bags. My arms are covered in glow-in-the-dark stars, my legs with a million planets. As it gets darker, I'll light the candelabras I've placed on each side of me and I'll either melt in their heat or glow. In my lap, between my legs, is a long white Boeing 747 — a strap-on. When she walks in the door, I'll raise it. And ask her to fly with me.

13

MARK JARMAN has published in numerous forums, including *Quarry Magazine* and *Front and Center*. He is also the author of *Salvage King, Ya!*

Love Is All Around Us

MARK JARMAN

Once, the snow was so deep
you almost couldn't hear Margaret Atwood

— David McGimpsey

MY CLOSE PERSONAL FRIEND KURT WALDHEIM phones me up — *lonely,* everyone's ostracizing Kurt in his bunker aerie in Alberta's foothills, not as many Nazis as he thought. Can't I come visit? Kurt's got a keg of Big Rock Traditional Ale and the new Radiohead CD, some serious tuneage.

Come on down, Kurt says, come on down!

I hop the Westjet and Margaret Atwood is the stewardess, Margaret Atwood pointing out the four emergency exits, Margaret Atwood asserting that no one has ever really seen those plastic oxygen masks yet we cling to our belief that masks are actually there, waiting for us like a parent, our Lacanian masks waiting to drop.

Margaret Atwood says, Maybe my message is bleak because it needs to be bleak. She says the seat belt parts fit into each other like a hook into an eye — my hook, your eye.

She lights a smoke, mutters, Screw the pilot and his feeble *No Smoking* light, it's a power issue, it's all political in nature. His phony blue uniform and drycleaning bills that could feed a third world village. Her monotone voice rises: If a stewardess ceases to be critical, ceases to judge her world, she'll find herself in one infinitely more turbulent.

I sigh and peer out the plane's tiny window, look down miles and see Margaret Atwood's giant face on the side of an orange United Farmers of Alberta grain elevator. Her giant face is live, mischievous, moving, gnomish. The elevator is like a drive-in movie screen. Her giant face winks largely at me, but then a double hook punctures her giant eye and the UFA elevator bursts into flame, rocketing burning timbers and burning grain across the street of the hamlet, grey charnel smoke enveloping the town and time going sideways under dead light from the stars.

Our stretch Avro Arrow touches down at Calgary airport. Inside the busy terminal we are greeted by Margaret Atwood in a cowboy hat. On the PA I hear Margaret Atwood's voice droning: *Mr. Burroughs to the white courtesy phone.*

Kurt picks me up in his coffee-colored Mercedes and as we pull away from the curb I see her again, head shaven, Margaret Atwood dancing with the Hare Krishnas in a peach-colored sarong.

Kurt takes me to the Ratskeller Klub for pilsner and blood sausage. Margaret Atwood climbs on the stage with a big twelve-string guitar and a Neil Young wig that looks to be made from the hair from a horse's mane or tail. She adjusts the mike, sings, *Hello Cowgirl in the sand, is this place at your command?*

Then kd lang leaps onstage with her Nancy Sinatra hairpiece and, holding hands, they belt out a bitching version of *These Boots Are Made For Walking.* At the end of the song Margaret Atwood and kd lang hug, then start kissing like crazy, tongues and everything, whispering things into the mike like *Sleeping with a man is like being in a river, but sleeping with a woman is the ocean.* Kurt Waldheim looks at me Kurtly while applauding politely. Atwood's husband Graeme Gibson snaps his fingers like a beatnik, but I suspect deep down he feels like Dennis Thatcher.

I duck out, check my messages: Margaret Atwood's recorded voice says, You have no new voice mail; you have no new voice, male.

MARK JARMAN

Message #2 is my mother asking, Why don't you write some nice Jungian ennui like that Margaret Atwood is so good at?

Then I'm chomping burnt ribeye steak and drinking gin and tonic screwballs way up high in the revolving restaurant with Leon Trotsky and Don Cherry. Don is cracking us up with stories about Eddy Shore taking a cat o'nine tails to him, until Leon Trotsky interrupts: Ach, it's that crazy woman again. I look out the window. Margaret Atwood is climbing the outside of the tower like King Kong, like Spiderwoman.

Don Cherry says, That Peggy! I tell ya! Great Canadian kid! Ya gotta love her! But I notice he tosses a twenty down and hightails it for the elevator.

A young woman peers out the window, says, We *did* her, we *did* Atwood, like last semester in, like, English 121.

Which book?

A Jest Of God.

That's one of her best ones. Totally.

Margaret Atwood smashes through the windows, lands on all fours in the broken glass, locks eyes, purrs to me, Love what you're doing with your hair, that Brian Eno-Howard DeVoto-male pattern baldness look. She kisses my bare scalp, leaving giant smears of red lipstick, says, Big party in Hal's Portuguese neighborhood, we'll crash it. She spots Jan Wong eating, gets her in a headlock: Let's do lunch. Tim Horton's, tomorrow. Noogie! Chinese haircut! Jan Wong's glasses fall off, her hair askew and crackling static.

I sneak out with Don Cherry for shinny hockey at the Rec Centre. Margaret Atwood is the referee: striped jacket, scraggly effort at a ponytail. I'm on defense with Don. She drops the puck and Rocket Richard flies straight at me, his eyes lit like a Halloween skull. I can't even see where the puck is, try to stand him up, but he's like a bull; we all fall in a big pile of bodies and she blows the whistle, calls a penalty.

I assume the penalty's to me, but she says, *Rocket*, two minutes for looking so good. A riot starts in Montreal; Brador bottles and smoked meat sandwiches whiz past my skull.

Margaret Atwood places her powdered skull against mine, Atwood's sudden tongue like a pink hook in my ear.

Welcome to the bigs, she whispers. *May you live in interesting times.*

Another bottle slicing by my head. Can I think of a witty reply? I cannot.

Then Margaret Atwood is fading, a statue folded into a blizzard, she is sinking under the ice, she is going west on a jet. It's snowing and snowing, snow is general over Canada. Peggy! Peggy! we call from our wretched snowcaves, shivering, shrinking into our winter skin. Don't go! *Without you we are lost.*

ANDREW PYPER has published one collection of short stories, *Kiss Me*. His first novel, *Lost Girls*, is forthcoming with HarperFlamingo.

The Elbow

ANDREW PYPER

HE'D PLAYED HOCKEY AS A KID and could still recall the sensation of receiving an elbow to the head. But then it was with a helmet.

When he comes to, the first thing he does is try to remember his own name. It arrives instantly: Rick Belle. (Even now he's ashamed of the feminine, unnecessary silent 'e'). O.K., now. Where is he? This is trickier. His eyes blink open to a horizon of unvarnished wood planks caked with powdery mud, and in a close circle looming around his head, a dozen serious hiking boots, the kind with lacing complicated as a seventeenth-century bodice. Light from fake neon signs in the windows visible through legs of soiled denim. *Bud — The King of beers* burns and blurs into *Coor's Light — The Silver Bullet*. The smell of disinfectant not entirely bleaching over the years of wayward urine, smoke ingrained into vinyl chair upholstery and wood paneling, sour regurgitations of beer. Rick Belle is lying on the floor of a bar.

Breathing next. In, out, in, out, in, hold. No holes in the lungs as far as he can tell. But why would there be? The elbow was to the head. Rick Belle knows this, but is still relieved to find that he can breathe without suffering whatever happened when you couldn't.

"You like that, fucker?"

Rick Belle recognizes that this is addressed to him. The voice is unfriendly, and he is aware that he has been the recent victim of an act of unfriendliness.

"Eh? That O.K. with you, fuckwad?"

Fuckwad? Another thing he recalls from his hockey days, the language of midget dressing room and pee-wee bench. And here it is again. *Fuckwad.* Don't certain profanities die out, the weak ones, over time?

"Yeah," Rick Belle croaks.

That's O.K, he hoped to communicate. *No more, thanks.* But The Elbow chooses to interpret it differently.

"Oh, you want a little more, eh?"

Then a completely new sensation, one that lay well beyond even the most involved of hockey fights: a steel-toed boot to the stomach. Now the breathing is an issue. And dinner seems to be on its way back up, rising long enough for him to get a taste before it reluctantly descends: pasta (linguini?) with shrimp in white wine and garlic.

"O.K. *now,* lover boy?"

With the breathing still in question, and given the unhappy results of his last response, Rick Belle decides to remain silent and instead gives movement a try. Maybe if he can just raise himself on hands and knees he'll be allowed to scrabble out of here. As for where "here" is, no progress.

"Jesus, man," the voice above him rattles through a throat of calcified tar and scar tissue. "You look like an old grizzly wakin' up to take a shit!"

Around him, laughter from the hiking boots. In addition to his obvious physical sufferings, Rick Belle's heart sinks. But he does remember something from The Time Before the Elbow. Drinking. There had definitely been drinking.

"Look at *that!*"

"Ohhhh, *poor* baby!"

"Holy *Christ!*"

This from the hiking boots, one of them squealy, hand-clapping, female. Again, no question about it, it is he who is the subject of these exclamations. Why now? What fresh hell was this? Something's

19   ANDREW PYPER

up, he knows this, beyond the troubles already tallied. Then the new data arrives. Oh *God*. He'd lost control of his bladder. But if it weren't for the visibility of the seepage he wouldn't mind — he had gratefully felt the relief of something unwanted being released — but he also knows what this means in the larger scheme of things. He'd had the piss beaten out of him.

Lover boy?

Hadn't The Elbow called him that? First thought: this whole thing was a case of mistaken identity fag bashing. Second thought, this one more likely: all this lover boy business had some direct connection to the drinking. The kind of prodigious, willful, reckless drinking that visited Rick Belle on occasion. Not a symptom of a *problem*, the manifestation of some chemical or genetic predisposition, but an expression of something deeply felt, an arousal of the spirit. His desire for drink was nothing less than a yearning to convene with the whole human world, a reaching out to another, every stranger in the room, a better tomorrow, the past. Sometimes it nearly worked. Other times it didn't come close.

But now is the time for sober thoughts. The entertainment value of his lying prone on the floor of a bar and his clear status as the defeated party could only buy him so much time, he knows. Where he came from, his condition would have prompted a 911 call and the immediate restraint of the perpetrator by reasonable bystanders. But here it was different. Here it was *fun*.

Maps. Longitudinal lines and latitudinal horizons. The whole of the world passes through Rick Belle's head like a grade eight geography class slide show. Each continent and their different representative colors flashing back at him from the National Geographic fold-out atlas of his adolescent bedroom wall: purple for Australia, pink for Asia, blue for South America, etc. He can't see himself on any of them. A bar with muddy wooden floors and people who mercilessly stomp on others for unclear reasons — that could be anywhere.

But wait.

English! They're speaking English, of a sort. And didn't The Elbow mention grizzlies? Where did *they* live? Canada, the U.S., that's about it. What else had The Elbow said to him?

Fuckwad!

Eh!

That nailed it. He is in his homeland. Rick Belle is lying on the floor of a bar in Canada, in a part of that country where someone might have some acquaintance with grizzly bears. The North.

But these speculations are interrupted by a new assault. Or is it help? Whichever it is, he definitely has hands upon his person, half a dozen of them perhaps, grabbing onto the back of his pants, his shirt collar, cupping under his arms. Rick Belle is being carried aloft, resurrected (this word occurs to him), the urine pooled in his underwear now rushing hot down his legs, his head lolling on his neck in a way that makes him appreciate its tremendous, disproportionate weight. Kindness. He is being delivered from his trouble, he'd been judged to have had enough, cooler heads were now prevailing and he was to be removed to a safe place. Right? This is how it is to go, isn't it?

Laughter. Of the vicious, at-someone-else's-expense kind. No, there was to be more.

"Can you sit up for feeding time, lover boy?"

Feeding time?

Rick Belle isn't hungry.

But there he is, being propped up on a leather-backed bar stool, a plastic bib strapped too tightly around his neck. Pink. And with the remains of it's previous wearer's dinner captured in the trough at the bottom.

"Hope you got a big appetite, 'cos you're goin' to eat every one of your lovey-dovey words, lover boy. How's that sound?"

Rick Belle shakes his head and the pool of creamed corn, chicken bits and mushroom sauce slosh around a foot under his chin. But once more the intent of his communication is misinterpreted.

"Oh you *are* hungry, eh? All's we have to do is find you a menu. Belinda? Where's a friggin' menu?"

An only slightly distressed waitress emerges through the circle of hiker boots.

"Kitchen's closed," she says.

"Closed? But lover boy here is *starving!* Well we'll just have to make do, won't we?"

The Elbow puts his finger to his chin in a pose of consideration,

ANDREW PYPER

then lunges around the room from table to table, checking the empty plates. When he returns it's with a platter of half-consumed french fries glued to their places by congealed, near-black gravy.

"*Here* we go, lover boy! Open wide!"

And the thing is, Rick Belle *does* open his mouth, lips parting and tongue clacking about within. Not in anticipation of the entry of food, but to beg for his release. He holds onto the possibility that if he strikes the right note he could make them see how *much* he wanted to leave, how *sorry* he was, the *amends* he was prepared to make. And just when he thinks he's come up with the right words, his mouth receives the first of its pre-frozen, deep-fried then cooled to a degree below room temperature, beef jelly glazed potato sticks.

"That one's for *Your eyes are dark as night*. And *this*," The Elbow slides a drooping, impossibly long fry from its resting place, "*this* one is for *You're so refreshing*."

The fry is lifted above him, flaccid and obscene. Rick Belle will have to tilt his head back to receive it. He will have to co-operate if this offering is to be consumed, and it's clear that it must be. Eventually The Elbow will insist, he'll do whatever has to be done because he's a man who can't stop once he's started something, especially public demonstrations involving a tourist who has overstepped the line.

And this is what Rick Belle is. A *tourist*. Sticking out like a sore thumb on holiday in a cotton golf shirt (canary yellow) tucked into grey dress slacks with a neat crease down the front. A point-and-shoot camera the size of a bar of soap dangling off his shoulder. And his shoes! Brown leather sandals, the ones with fussy interlaced straps over the top, a loose encasement at the end for the toes and a metal buckle against the heel that made a clinkety dog tag sound whenever he took a step. At the sight of his appearance, his self-recognition as *tourist*, but mostly at the discovery of his footwear, Rick Belle feels the hot mucous of tears cresting in his eyes, streaking down his cheeks to land on his distended stomach and splash off the country club coat-of-arms sewn to his breast.

"A lit-tle *wi*-der. Now, that's a good fellow."

The fry is lowered, and Rick Belle's tongue guides it in, coiling it onto the back of his throat.

"There!"

Rick Belle chews, is watched chewing, sees himself as those standing around him must see him. A child. A grown man. A *tourist*. Rick Belle, child, receiver of a blow to the head, a grown man whose story was now being returned to him.

And with this return, a discovery: Life Before The Elbow had been difficult to remember in part because there was nothing there to remember. Nothing terribly special at any rate. *Events*, yes. There were things that had happened to him: graduation from a school that allowed him to find a job, the keeping of a house, or a condo anyway, a glassed-in cube in a chunky green tower where he lived for some time with a woman, now gone. A woman whose name started with a K and whose face now appeared against the black screen of his closed eyes as an oval pincushion wearing a wig of brown hair. Why did the pincushion leave? There had been *reasons*, of course. A list of well-considered reasons (they had gone so far as to write them down, three or four pros against a long, withering column of cons) which included irreconcilable *belief systems*, a desire for different *spaces*, conflicting visualizations of a *personal future*. Both of them knew that what all this really meant was that she wanted to have babies, but not with him. He was "a great guy" who "deserves better than this," but Rick Belle doubted both of these assertions. He just wanted her. And while he can't remember the face of K, he can still hear her voice rhyming off her justifications as though she were now speaking them directly into his ear.

Rick Belle has to shake his head to rid himself of this voice, a violent shiver that draws new laughter from the hiking boots. He tells himself not to meet their eyes. Blinks up past their beards and mole-dotted shoulders at the TV chained to the ceiling over the bar. It's the twenty-four-hour music video station showing Marilyn Manson wearing a Gauthier bra and drinking a glass of blood. Rick Belle would laugh at it himself — a glam rock thingy mincing and tongue-sticking over the airwaves even up here, wherever he was — but his mouth is too full of potato and he's afraid he would choke.

"Mmm-mmm *good*," says The Elbow, chewing along with him.

But Rick Belle's eyes are still fixed on the TV. He recognizes something in it, the blood drinking, the little network logo permanently set in the bottom corner of the screen. Something to do with what he does for a living. Then he realizes that it *is* his living. He pitches this stuff, it's the product he's paid by commission to move. Rick Belle sells television air time on MuchMusic — he knows that if he were permitted to throw his hand back to his ass and pull out his wallet he could produce a business card with his name on it to prove it. He can even recall the difficulty he'd had with a juice-in-box manufacturer and this very video, something to do with the blood looking too much like their new Raspberry Rave line. But in the end he'd sold the fuckers, Rick Belle thinks and allows a pasty smile to move across his lips. He'd *sold* them.

"You having a nice time there, lover boy?" The Elbow asks him, his level of amusement draining threateningly away.

But Rick Belle doesn't care what they do to him now. His life is coming back bit by bit and he's giving it some thought. But aside from his job and status as the dumpee ex, what else was there? Surely there was more, and there was if you included his position on the squash ladder and the new Volvo coupe he couldn't afford but had out on a two-year lease for the hell of it. But none of this stays with him — he has the overwhelming sensation that that's not who he is.

In the space of the few seconds The Elbow has allowed him, he continues to rifle through the slim file of his life, and as he strings the details together what pains Rick Belle the most is the absence of *triumphs*. A private breakthrough of a modest scale would have been enough. The acceptance of an award, say, handed to him by an official as he crossed a stage through a wash of applause, or winning the affections of a woman he would have otherwise thought outside his range. Proud tears glistening in the eyes of parents, arms outstretched to take him in. What's missing is the one thing that couldn't be taken from him, no matter what. And time. That was missing, too, because he wasn't young anymore, either. He couldn't remember the exact number of years since his birth (a figure that startles him when encountered in print), but Rick Belle is aware that he is a man of an age where certain things — true love, spiritual enlightenment, accomplishment of the highest kind — could no longer be reasonably pursued without embarrassment. Not yet an old man, but compromised. And so it had always been with Rick Belle. He'd sought compromise years before it was required.

"What do you think of your lover boy now?" The Elbow is saying to a dark-haired woman standing outside the circle of hiking boots, and with his words she steps forward to look at Rick Belle, her face a police composite drawing come to life. "Eh? You still think he's kinda cute?"

"No," the woman says, her voice empty of either sympathy or meanness, and for the second time it occurs to Rick Belle that her eyes *are* dark as night.

The Elbow gives him a long look now, head bent over at an angle to meet Rick Belle's purple-hooded eyes. And the room waits for this look to complete itself, the hiking boots a blank-faced chorus in the periphery, and the only sound is the smacking of Rick Belle's tongue clearing his mouth of the spongy glue that threatens to close it shut forever.

"So, you enjoying your trip so far?" The Elbow eventually asks him. The hiking boots cough and whinny, bending over to show him the tops of their heads. The dark-haired woman places her hand on The Elbow's bicep and sticks her teeth through her lips.

But they all give Rick Belle enough time to reach around to the back of his neck and pull his bib off, spit the remaining indigestible matter in his mouth onto the floor and lift himself from his chair. He wobbles on his heels for a second, an underwater sound in his ears, his camera spinning from its strap and clacking onto the floor, but he stands, remains standing. The hiking boots part and he steps through them, walks to the door, pulls at the handle for a moment before figuring out that it's a push, and in this moment The Elbow calls after him once more so that when he finally lurches out all those passing in the mud street can hear.

"Come back *soon* now, lover boy!"

Left or right? Which way to his hotel? Rick Belle hasn't a clue, so chooses left just to keep moving and immediately bumps into a withered old woman wearing lumpy lipstick the color of hollandaise and a "*Hi! My Name Is*" tag pasted to a chest which the years have stretched so far down her front it could no longer be called a chest at all but has instead become that senior citizen mid-zone where belt and belly and ribs have come to share previously distinct territories.

"Ricky? Is that *you*?" the old woman bubbles out from shallow lungs, and with her words, the sound of his given name spoken by a

ANDREW PYPER

stranger, the final details of his situation come to him.

He was on the same bus tour as this ancient name-tag standing before him. The same "all-inclusive adventure package" as his mother, left back at the hotel following a slippery dinner at the Caribou Room. Hadn't she always wanted to see the North, been reading up on it, poring over glossy pamphlets showing can-can girls, riverboats, prospectors, grinning Mounties? It was the Yukon she had talked about, the gold rush, the cruel lessons of greed. And now they were here. Some mud street outpost accidentally blessed by a half-dozen overpriced hotels and filthy bars. That's where he is, travelling with his mother and a busload of other fogies from stop to stop, the whole while being aggressively perked up by a stout blonde tour guide Rick Belle believes must be some kind of born again Christian. They sit beside each other near the front looking out at the passing fireweed and stone and wiry bush, speaking of the possibility of rain or the cleanliness of visited bathrooms. Sometimes she places her vein-ridged hand on his forearm and falls asleep.

Why isn't his father with her instead? A flash of ill-fitting dark suits, suffocating flowers, a funeral director whose frequently bared teeth could have done with a good flossing. His father is gone.

So, once she'd swept the lawyers, distant relatives and casserole leavers out of the house she'd asked her son to go with her and he'd been glad to accept, the last several years of accumulated vacation time becoming a private embarrassment. And the trip had brought him to this bar, to a stool he'd found next to a woman he hadn't noticed at first but who became something fairly close to beautiful as the scotch-and-waters came and went and he turned to start up a conversation in which he felt his contributions were at first witty, then charming, then bold. But before the effect of these efforts could be evaluated, he'd been pulled aside by a dirt-creased fist on his golfshirt and he'd made the mistake of going on the offensive, trying for a roundhouse punch at the assailant behind him that never made it, for well before contact could be made there was a crack to the side of his head and his life, such as it was, had been wiped clean.

"Are you alright, Ricky?"

What the hell did her name-tag say? Why did the tour guide bother handing them out at all if arthritis prevented any of their wearers from writing legibly anyway? Then it comes to him, not from reading her breast but from a crackle of memory: Margaret. She'd befriended his mother early on, in Anchorage, fed him Scottish shortbread she'd brought along in a round tin, insisted on adding a 'y' to the end of his first name. She was nice.

"I'm fine, Margaret."

"Ricky, what happened to you?"

"I met some people."

He tries to gesture behind him with his hand but it refuses to raise itself, so instead he shrugs. Margaret nods at him, or at least twitches her chin up and down in a manner of nodding, her face a wrinkled plate of help.

"Ricky, do you need — ?"

"Can you tell me which way the hotel is?"

The old woman shuffles close and takes him by the arm, squeezes her swollen knuckles around the soft flesh above his elbow, and walks him back the few blocks to where they are staying. On the way Rick Belle wonders if his mother is still up. If she is, he will talk to her.

ANDREW PYPER

MATTHEW FIRTH is the author of *Fresh Meat* (Rush Hour Revisions) and co-editor of *Front and Center*. He has recently completed a second collection, *Therapy*.

Nostalgia

MATTHEW FIRTH

FRIDAY NIGHT THE TELEPHONE RINGS ABOUT 9:30. I'm unwinding over cold pizza and cold beer, watching Friday Night Football on TSN. I am mildly interested in the Blue Bombers versus the Alouettes.

Three rings and I answer.

"Richard?"

"Uh-huh."

"It's Laura."

I pause. Think, Laura who?

Her voice registers: Laura from the realm of the recently divorced. Laura from university days. Days long since passed. Ten years ago we drank hard together, but we never slept together. It is a lingering regret that still crops up when I bump into her.

I last saw Laura about six months ago in Limeridge Mall. I was lost in the muddle, searching for The Bombay Company. She appeared by my side magically and directed me to the store. She was stunning, of course. She had a certain radiance in the dim shopping complex light. Laura was then two months from the beginnings of a ruthless divorce. I learned about her marriage collapsing several months later from a mutual friend over drinks in Hess Village. I barely batted an eye when I heard the news. At the time, my attention was riveted on a middle-aged woman slumped at the bar on my left.

"You busy tomorrow, Richard?"

I don't answer immediately. I'm still hung-up on a missed sexual escapade from some time back in 1987.

"Richard? You there?"

I grunt.

"Because if you're not too busy tomorrow, I've got a proposition for you . . . "

I mute the television. Tracey Ham scrambles silently on the astro-turf in Montreal. I caress the bottle of Red Baron in my right hand.

"I've got nothing planned," I respond, oblivious to the consequences.

"Then I have a favor to ask . . . "

I have passed the point of no return. Whatever Laura asks now I am obliged to indulge her. It is my reward for not listening, for being more concerned with a meaningless mid-season football game.

I, too, was married once. Straight out of university I married another girl I drank with. She came to university from Chatsworth, a small village split in half by highway six, about twenty kilometers south of Owen Sound. She made the two-hour trip to take Phys-Ed. Then it was supposed to be a teaching degree, followed by a hasty retreat back to small-town Ontario to live out a life of normality. But the proverbial cart was overturned after only six months. She got swept up into the thick of things and lost in the undertow. Her Phys-Ed degree changed to French, then to Women's Studies, and finally to the cosy confines of Sociology, where she eked out the minimum requirements for a three-year degree. Teaching plans were abandoned. So was the retreat to Chatsworth. She decided to stick it out in the city, an outcome I had something to do with.

We ran in the same circles, drank in the same bars, puked in the same bushes, once in a while fucked in the same bed. We settled into this familiar pattern, until I was poised to graduate and she was still parrying from one program to another. Threatened with abandonment, she latched on to me like a lamprey.

We were married six months after I graduated in a chapel just

MATTHEW FIRTH

outside Chatsworth, on a road that meandered to Meaford. We divorced fourteen months later in a lawyer's office in Hamilton, on Main Street East, five lanes of one-way traffic cruising by outside the window.

The Blue Bombers are kicking off to the Alouettes. Ham's scrambling led to an interception that was promptly converted into six points. Trevor Westwood, looking impish behind the single bar below his chin, sends the ball sailing back to Montreal.

Laura's voice cuts through my reverie. "Because I've been invited to Charlene's wedding tomorrow and . . . "

I am still paying more attention to the game. The Alouettes bring the ball back to their own thirty-seven. Ham trots out onto the turf, a new series of plays churning in his head.

Charlene's wedding? It hits me suddenly. I don't want to think about how unwelcome my face will be at *that* event, or how uncomfortable I'll be when I knock shoulders with Charlene's dad, my ex-father-in-law, at the bar. As in the past, he'll have no more than half-a-dozen words for me.

"Sure."

It comes out somewhat slurred, even though I'm only on my second Red Baron. I may be anticipating the twelve or fourteen drinks I will have tomorrow at Charlene's father's expense.

My only wish is that the reception is not in the same dreary community centre where Charlene and I celebrated our nuptials: a terribly trite barn-like structure that possessed all the elements of scary small-town Ontario. A Union Jack and a horrid portrait of some long-since-dead local Orangeman hung on the wall. Dinner was served by a slew of featureless faces, who, along with the kitchen staff, shared no more than three surnames among them.

"The wedding's in Toronto," Laura says, disrupting my flashback, washing away the hick-town cliches.

But at the same time, the Alouettes are pressing and I feel a sudden need to absorb myself in the game. I feel affinity with Ham and his plight. I want him to answer with six points of his own.

"I'll swing by, pick you up at noon," Laura suggests.

I mumble something back at her. Laura thanks me and I fumble the phone towards its cradle.

I wonder for a second how she knows where I live.

Then, it's back to the game. I un-mute the television. The Alouettes have come up short. Their few loyal fans bellow for them to go for it on third-and-two. Ham looks over to the coach for guidance and then to the scoreboard, checking the time remaining. The first half is winding down. There is sufficient time for gambling later, the coach concludes, shuttling the field-goal unit out onto the field. The crowd boos. I finish my beer. Ham looks expressionless, resigned to his duty.

Charlene is wearing a cryptic-looking, nicotine-yellow dress. I don't know how she got into it, but I have no worries about being the one to determine how she'll get out of it. That honor this evening belongs to another.

The ceremony is high Anglican in downtown Toronto. The weather co-operates. It is a wondrous September afternoon.

From my vantage point at the rear of the church, I examine the backs of heads in front of me. I recognize farmers' haircuts and slightly shrunken suits. The women are adorned in colorful hats and all manner of dresses spanning broad backs and shoulders. From back here I cannot see my former in-laws. They are surely crowded into the front pew, their thick palms splashed with sweat, brows dewy and moist, praying — no, yearning — that Charlene is second-time-lucky.

At the reception — at a swish country club within city limits — I feel sorry for Laura. She should have declined the invitation and spent another Saturday night with another Harrison Ford movie. She looks slightly sick and it's not the wine. Amazingly, with more self-control than I could ever muster, she has limited herself to two glasses and will be able to drive us back to Hamilton.

But the entire thing is obviously too much for her on the heels of her messy divorce. Drink firmly in hand, I think for a second why divorces are always described as "messy." It sounds as if blood and other bodily fluids are spilled: a perfect image to clog my head at my ex-wife's wedding.

All my efforts to cheer Laura are lost in the tide of saxophone from the band. She doesn't want to drink. She has refused my invitations to dance. She appears committed to gazing blankly around the room, her head crowded with images of revelers celebrating a new union. I realize soon enough the futility of my quest to distract Laura and decide to concentrate on getting good and drunk instead.

The showdown with Charlene's dad never transpires despite countless trips to the bar. On manoeuvre number eleven or twelve — when I have long since given up on politely asking Laura if she'd favor a cocktail — I meet up instead with Charlene and question mark directly. I never did read Laura's invitation, or listen to the vows, so I honestly have no idea what his name is.

"Richard, this is Charles."

There's my answer: Charles. How regal and distinguished it sounds. Charlene and Charles. They even look alike, the narcissism running amuck.

I'm not sure if Charles realizes that this is *the* Richard, but he greets me gracefully and loiters for a moment before striding off, leaving me alone with my ex-wife for the first time in ages.

We have very little to say to each other, which is just as well. I refrain from complimenting Charlene on her dress, choosing instead to flatter her hair, something I recall she always appreciates. I am, despite my drunkenness, alarmingly non-confrontational. I am not at all bitter or envious. I offer no sarcastic remarks. No coy slugs at Charles rise in my gullet. I behave completely out of fashion. For some inexplicable reason I am simply not an asshole at all. This confuses me terribly and I stumble for words.

But as quickly as she appeared, Charlene vanishes back into the crowd — a smoky yellow apparition, off to make more small talk.

"There goes my ex-wife."

I actually stutter this ridiculous phrase to myself and hear it come back at me. Thankfully, glancing around me, there is no one within earshot.

With my drink in hand, I realize that we are finally finished. I no longer hold a place in Charlene's life. She is moving on. It is over. A few muttered phrases and promises endorsed by the church have trumped the court's authority.

My head bobs and sways as I sputter incoherent nostalgia to Laura on the QEW. She is sober at the wheel. She is uninterested in my epiphany, my realization that Charlene has moved on with her life. I try not to sound too liberated or sanctimonious, recalling Laura's pain. But then again I never liked Laura's dick-head husband. He's a lawyer from Ottawa — which should say it all — who condescended to socialize with Charlene and me half-a-dozen times. After that he was forever "on business," an excuse that didn't sit well with me. How is a lawyer "on business"? The feebleness of the excuse bothered me more than any thing else. This, and Laura's predicament. It was clear back then that she had no future with the prick. Years later, she is crammed into a compact car, using all her resolve to stop from begging me for silence.

On the curb outside my apartment of all places I slide my hand down the back of Laura's dress and dig lightly into her ass with my drunken digits. Her left hand is braced defensively on my clavicle. She will endure a few moments of my come-on, giving me the opportunity to realize my vulgarity, and then gently push down on my collar bone, easing me away.

This is exactly how it happens.

I kiss Laura's cold throat three or four times, feeling absolutely nothing from her. I try to ease her ass into my groin, gauging only resistance. Stupidly I persevere, rubbing the small of her back with my palm. This is it. Laura's hand on my shoulder shifts and she inhales deeply. She is on the verge of explanation, but I save myself the humiliation. I back off, defeated on my home turf.

But what the hell do I want from this anyway? A mercy fuck for me? A comfort fuck for Laura? Do I really think this is even a remote possibility? How is it that I behave like a perfect gentleman with Charlene and Charles and then a lecherous boor with Laura? Surely I have only added to her grief.

But then again, why is Laura so untouchable? She has always been this way. We've danced this dance before, years ago, mind you, back in university when we were both pissed, but even then she shrugged me off. There was always something condescending about it. Something that said I never had a chance. That she was — and would be forever — completely unattainable as far as I was concerned.

All of this flashes through my mind at the moment of rejection. Laura's behavior rankles me more now than it did years ago. Back then her attitude was too easy to dismiss. Then, I really felt nothing for her.

MATTHEW FIRTH

I was just trying to get laid. But tonight I want her in a different way. I may be pissed, but I actually believe I want to comfort her, that I am capable of such an act.

Instead, I get a patronizing kiss on the cheek as Laura turns away from me. A few seconds later I am offered a mere glimpse of Laura's sacred, unapproachable body as she slumps into her car: a sliver of leg displayed amidst the folds of her black dress. Ten seconds later she is pulling away from the curb without so much as a wave.

Inside my apartment the answering machine offers no wisdom or succor. My stomach lurches — booze sloppily mingled with a plate-full of midnight sweets. I spy yesterday's pizza box at the summit of a heap of garbage in my kitchen. In my best black suit, my tie still snug against my neck, I gather the refuse and trudge towards the cans in the alley at the side of the building. I deposit the waste and then cast a skeptical glance towards the city's star-less firmament. There is no comfort there either.

On the verge of stupid despondence, I start shuffling back to my flat, my bladder bloated. I am drunk and alone again. But I refrain from muttering any more cliches about women, circumspect that I might embarrass myself before the raccoons pawing split bags of garbage.

JIM NASON has appeared in such magazines as *sub-Terrain* and *Quarry*.

Allen Ginsberg Died and I Didn't Feel a Thing

JIM NASON

THE POSTER IS BEIGE with an inner frame of green-lime-and-banana cock-and-balls. Allen Ginsberg: Bard of the Skeletons: Friday November 15, 8:00 p.m. The audience is an odd mix: an older man reading *The Globe & Mail*, beautiful blonde, brush-cut androgenous twins, each in tight matching mauve cashmere sweaters; a bearded, bald, fat man chanting. An endless Guru-cum-poet-buzz keeps the room stirring. The older people saunter in, a more refined *this is how Ginsberg would have us be cool* walk. The students rush to the foot of the stage like a tele-vangelist cult. The stage is set — table with orange cloth, a granny's-den flowered chair. There's a royal blue backdrop, an enormous painting of male nudes in the center, a cross between Attila Richard Lukas and Alex Colville without that iron line of normality.

I look for my friends who were inspired by Ginsberg. All dead now. I pray that someone, other than me, survived the revisioning. Artsy queers into lots of drugs and sex had no idea that AIDS would wipe us out like the wave of a bottomless ocean. Instead there are bookstore clerks, twenty-years-old, black baggy clothing, hair green or purple. And the liberal aging swingers of the seventies who never swapped partners more than twice and never really did anything dirty.

The ceiling is round, glass. Eight Chandeliers — crystal and light droplets hanging. He has been silently commanded to the altar. A young man, head to toe in grey, places a hot drink gently, like a wine chance at high mass, next to the microphone. Ginsberg sings Blake's Tyger, Tyger exaggerating the meter. This is where it began. The vision from Blake. The audience is frenzied. Ginsberg sings, I fought the Dharma but the Dharma won. The older, meditation clones shift proudly in their seats. One smiles. Another squeezes her meditation beads.

Question period is long. One middle-aged drunk man invites Ginsberg to the El Mocambo. "I am tired. I am old," says Ginsberg. "Next question."

Ravings, neuroses beyond therapy. "Don't stop to think of words," he says. The barbaric yawp listens. "America, I'm putting my queer shoulder to the wheel . . . " They smile, nervously. I feel tired.

The crystal above Ginsberg sways. The room stinks of wet clothing.

Eddie gets up to see why the puppy is crying. We named her Annie, short for Anniversary. An insane moment of sentimentality that will live for eternity. He squats naked in the moonlight by the blindless window, sets her down on newspaper to pee. Eddie is long and pale. He is gentle with her. When she is done her tiny yellow wetting, he picks her up, sets her at the foot of the bed, crawls in bed beside me, snuggles his nose between my armpit and rib. "How was Ginsberg?" he says.

"Almost dead," I answer. Turn over to face the window.

Tonight the stars will fall on me. Each cosmic prick a reminder. "If you think it's so easy," Ginsberg says, "you stand up here, read naked, poetry."

HAL NIEDZVIECKI is the editor of *Broken Pencil* and author of *Smell It* (Coach House). He has a book of non-fiction forthcoming with Penguin and is currently completing work on his first novel.

Rat King (King Rat)

HAL NIEDZVIECKI

"THERE ARE TWO KINDS," Elsberg says to the doctor. "There's the Rat King, that's a giant rat who lives in the warren and emerges only to defend the brood. That kind of rat doesn't really exist, I mean they don't think that kind really exists. And then there's the scientifically proven King Rat. That's five or more rats whose tails are tangled together in a giant knot. They can't be separated. The King Rat develops a single identity. It can live up to two years. Scientifically proven. They've got a dead one in a museum. A museum in Holland."

The doctor nods politely. "This won't hurt," he says.

Elsberg pulls up his pants. "I've got *The Book of Rats*," he says. "Signed by the author."

The doctor opens the door of the examination room. Elsberg starts to walk out. The doctor puts his hand on Elsberg's shoulder, stops him.

"I'll have to do another test, I'm afraid. At the hospital. The receptionist will make an appointment for you. Don't worry son, I won't hurt you."

Elsberg grins.

"Are you alright otherwise?" the doctor asks.

On the bus, Elsberg can't decide whether he should sit or stand. There's a certain level of discomfort endemic to just being alive, to just living. Elsberg puts a hand in his pocket. Moves his fingers. He's not all there, not as deep as he wants to be. It's a long ride. He isn't necessarily paying attention to where he should get off. The bus ejaculates forward in wheezes.

He feels weak. He decides to sit down. He decides to quit his job as an usher and go back to school. He decides to pursue a degree in something he hates, just to prove he can do it. A woman stinking of hair spray and hot dogs wedges into the seat next to him. She talks under her breath, then yells a series of expletives.

"Ah, excuses," Elsberg says. "I'm just a little upset, my stop, here . . . "

He climbs over her lap. She curses the bank, credit cards, somebody named Pauly. Elsberg pulls the cord that lights up the sign telling the driver to stop at the next stop. It's all very organized. It's all quite well thought out. Exhaust wind. The kind of silence that shrieks.

What tea is the tea that is good for him? There is a cure. Is there a cure? Fruit is a gleaming pyramid. Elsberg picks up an apple. He remembers a TV show: shoppers in the grocery store suddenly turning into zombies and ripping their own eyes out. He looks for the exit.

"You have to pay for that," someone yells.

Elsberg unlocks the lock and lets himself into his apartment.

Two rooms.

Goldfish. A heap of mail by the door. He kicks it. There's something in everything, he reminds himself. He sits down, picks up a pad and pen. He writes it with shaking fingers. Illegible. It's good, he thinks. He rips the piece of paper off the pad and crumples it. He gets up. He has to calm himself. He has to be calm. He sent something to a magazine, and now he is waiting to hear back from that magazine. But all Elsberg gets in the mail are offers and catalogues and personalized invitations. He paws through the pile. Ten letters, fifteen letters, then a week completely devoid of promotional offerings. Suddenly, thirty urgent communiques from Publisher's Clearing House. The envelopes stick to his hands. He has to shake to get them off. The one he is looking for is horribly thin.

"I have a letter from a famous magazine," he tells Louis. The turgid fish bobs. He tears open the letter, trying to be gentle just in case.

"Thanks, but not for us," he reads, connecting ripped pieces to each other. "There seems to be a limited vocabulary at work here. We want art. Still, we cared enough to send this note." Elsberg reads the letter several times.

"The Editors," he says. He thinks back to the doctor, how impossible it is to be a doctor. He should have told the truth. "I've never even seen a rat," he says.

She said to call her and tell her how things worked out. "We may never have babies," he says.

"We'll never even have sex," she says.

"Well," Elsberg says, "I guess I wouldn't know about that."

"I guess you wouldn't."

"Rats are breeders," he announces. "Rats multiply ferociously. At a ferocious rate. There are ten new rats born per every one-hundred rats. You know how many rats that is?"

"You and your rats."

"That's more than a billion rats. They live underground. They live in the sewers, in the subways. Rats eat rubber, can you believe it? If they're starving, they'll eat their young. The only mammal known to do that, besides humans that is. Anyway, they've sure got enough of them." He laughs nervously.

"Shut up with the rats," she says, louder this time.

"Listen," Elsberg says, "I have dreams now like on TV. It's exactly like that. There's something and then there's something else that's not that thing inside of that first thing. King Rat on the floor of my apartment. In the other room — you can't, would you, you wouldn't be able to hear the scratching. Listen, I've been — you know, I'm upset, there's a test in a hospital. I finally got that letter I've been waiting for. Can't tell yet. Good or bad. Names are nothing. Everyone's got one. King Rat. Or else: Rat King."

"Don't do this to me," she says. "C'mon Elsberg, snap out of it. I can't deal with this right now. Jesus, El, I'm your sister, not your fucking psychiatrist. Look, okay, forget it. I'm sorry. I shouldn't have — I know you must be upset. I'll come by, okay? I'll come by with Harvard. In the meantime, watch TV, or just take a nap, okay? Close your eyes and we'll be over before you know it. Elsberg, you're a pain in the ass, you know?"

Harvard is a lawyer, his sister's boyfriend or fiancee or ex-husband or something. There may have been a wedding. Elsberg hears the silence over the line, his sister breathing through her nose the way she does when she's angry or upset. The pops and jigs and crumbles of static in between silence, inside the silence. He hangs up the phone before it can get into his ear.

To get a little perspective on this, what's wrong with Elsberg is what's wrong with the rest of us. He locks the door so it can't get in. His sister might be a widow. There's a widow on TV. She's dressed in all black, arms hugging a tombstone. A hand digs out of the moist earth. Elsberg imagines being buried alive. No sound. The TV's sound turned off. He doesn't need sound to hear, you have to imagine or else you'll never really see. The woman jumps back. Oh! Her mouth in an oval.

"Rat!" Elsberg yells. "It's only a rat!" Behind her the zombie creaks out of the spilled ground. The sky flashes lightning. Elsberg feels a splitting in his crotch, a pain like collapsing intervals — moments lost to seconds — commercial. Commercial.

Can you say urologist? Can you say cystoscopy? There is a certain tea. Elsberg sleeps in an armchair. He wakes up, blinking. The muted gray of morning. There's a pain, potential trapped in the wet innards under his skin. He opens the door, walks into the front room. The mail in a formless heap. A fish belly up, eyes in blank bulges.

"It's nothing," Elsberg explains as he carries the corpse to the bathroom in a tiny net. "It just happens. There'll be some pain, but it won't really hurt. Not really." He flushes Louis down the toilet, watches the fish orbit and then slither into the pipes. "I have a limited vocabulary," he whispers.

"The hospital show hospital is supposed to be a poor hospital," he tells the receptionist. "But it isn't like this. It isn't shabby."

A nurse writes something down.

"Of course, there wouldn't be rats in the hospital," he hurries to say. "There wouldn't be. But — does the building have a lower level?"

They dress him up. Robe, mesh cap, booties. Everything off below the waist, they tell him. They take his pants. Elsberg feels the air swooping up the bottom of his gown. Someone says something about a procedure. Elsberg flaps his arms in voluminous folds. They lead him to a small waiting room.

"Have a seat."

Two men and a woman, all dressed in the same green garb. They dart furtive, morbid glances at him, then stare back at their booty feet. Nobody looks like this, Elsberg thinks. The hospital show hospital. Nobody. A test, the doctor said. But for what?

The nurse arrives with a clipboard and asks for Mr. Jawolski.

A fat man stands, crosses his arms, coughs into a loose fist. Elsberg watches him disappear. Needle in your dick. An elderly fellow is led in by another nurse.

"Have a seat."

He sits next to Elsberg. His head bulges out of his green mesh cap. "Ed Varney," the man says. "I used to be in sales at Tyson Toyota. Retired now. What do you do, son?"

"I'm a writer," Elsberg says. "Also I'm going back to school. For business." He wants to tell Ed about pain, about fear. He wants to put his head in Ed's lap, feel warm skin.

"Married are ya?"

"Uh . . . no," Elsberg says. He glances around the room. Green robes, the anonymous protrusion of bodies. "I'm engaged."

Speed Culture

HAL NIEDZVIECKI

IT'S TWO DAYS BEFORE THE CONCLUDING EPISODE of the moron cartoon Beavis and Butthead. I'm sitting in a *This Morning* radio studio waving around my Beavis and Butthead pseudo-remote control with sound effects (a present from my brother) and listening to a Carleton University professor of media studies explain why the show is ugly, stupid, violent and, worst of all, morally bereft.

When it gets to be my turn, I can't help myself. First thing I do is hit the *Shuddup, Assmunch* button. I follow this with the key that vomits up Butthead's he-he-he laugh. There's a brief moment of stunned silence, then comes one of those rare moments when I'm actually proud of my own shrill rhetoric. I tell the Professor (and Avril Benoit who looks on with her patented expression somewhere between bemusement and horror) that his concern about the ethical nature of Beavis and Butthead reveals his generation's inability to truly come to terms with the shifting culture landscape of North America. That's when it hits me: pop culture is dead.

First of all, I say, nobody who is a true member of the TV generations (roughly anyone born after 1965) watches television for its advocacy of family values and societal rectitude. To the contrary: we watch TV for its capacity to disgust, to horrify, to reveal and even penetrate the thin veneer that covers up the heart of darkness deep in the jungles of the capitalist cultural experience. But, I go on, there's a larger issue at stake here. There's the way academics and bureaucrats and arts administrators and, basically, anyone who is not actively engaged in the creation of what can be loosely termed art, seeks to perpetuate the myth of pop culture. Our Carleton media prof must condemn ridiculous cartoons like Butthead & Beavis and the eponymously hilarious South Park (currently my favorite TV show) as synecdoches representative of the evil vice that is — heaven forfend — pop. And pop culture must be bad, because it is the opposite of high culture, which must be good.

Well, the Carleton professor spluttered.

Thanks for that, Avril cheerfully said. Coming up next, Farley Mowat joins us to talk about reincarnating the spirits of murdered baby seals!

Actually, there never really was any such thing as pop culture, just the on-going clash of generations. And I was at best semi-articulate that morning. So, okay, I take it back. Pop culture isn't dead. It can't be, because it never existed, it's one of those collective conspiracy things like alien landings and Quebec City cultists and multi-mono-media. The whole idea of pop was conceived as a way to differentiate generational conceptions of the function of culture in society. The initial model went like this: aesthetic culture — culture to be respected, analyzed, and patronized for its educational capacity — versus low culture — culture to be dismissed, ignored as if it didn't exist, relegated to the gutters where it would hopefully languish and disappear. Low culture wouldn't — couldn't — be appreciated on any level; it could only be consumed like cotton candy.

But things didn't work out that way. In fact, once the awesome behemoth that is consumer culture spread its scaly wings to their full span, every kind of culture was affected, and changed forever. Not the least of these changes was the collapse of the fence that critics and academics and effetes had erected to create mythical dialectics like pop culture versus high culture, alternative culture versus mainstream culture. These categories never really existed in any meaningful way and now, for better or worse, all things cultural must be and are evaluated on the basis of their status as, first and foremost, pleasure instilling products that differ from, say, the automatic foot massager, only because of the way they stimulate our mental and emotional capacities (however limited those capacities may be). In other words, everything cultural is to be considered pop culture now, because nothing ever really was pop culture. And if this argument is circular, that's perfectly all right because, thinking about culture is, essentially, a circular business in which one returns to the same tired old themes whether we're talking about South Park (a ghostly creature named Hankie the Christmas Poo drives a small boy longing for acceptance mad) or Hamlet (a ghostly creature drives an older boy longing for acceptance mad). The fact is, cultural production now occurs in a no-man's land without maps or rules or boundaries, the sort of place you can wander around forever and end up exactly where you started. In other words: pop culture really is dead. Still, the majority of our pundits remain stuck reiterating a pop culture mantra that is so profoundly out of touch with reality, it's like the Dalai Lama advocating the use of nukes (which he apparently did, so there).

It's time to start again, re-establish our capacity to dialogue on arts and culture in North America, preferably without the rhetorical strictures imposed upon us since the fifties by strait-jacket academics frightened of the immoral impetuosity of what they choose to call pop culture and what I would prefer to call something else — though the right term hasn't yet presented itself, something between mass culture and immediate culture and entertainment culture. Something catchy like Speed culture, you know, something marketable that will please the sales department and make publicists lives a whole lot easier. Yeah I can see the cover of the book now. Speed Culture, with a run away train packed full of hipsters and a punk-jazz band and cartoon characters like Wonder Woman and that fat kid from King of the Hill. And it'll be hurtling off the cover and no one will know what it's about and it will be the next big thing; it'll be cool and fresh, a mixture of cultural criticism and opinionated personal confession and communal reference points directed toward a whole new way of appreciating our society, a society in which everything can — or must — be viewed from an overarching perspective of the irony of our lives being nothing more than sitcom moments that refer us back to, you guessed it, our lives.

Remember that book by Geof Pervere and some other guy, *Mondo Canuck*? I perused it a couple of months back once I finally managed to extract it from the over taxed Toronto library system (I visit my local public library along with the immigrants and the winos and the other fools who believe in having access to books regardless of bank account statements). *Mondo Canuck*'s unstated premise seemed to be that the larger number of people who were exposed to some tacky, feckless cultural happening, the more important a pop phenomenon it must have been. And, inversely, the less important the actual significance of the event on the cultural and social environment of Canada — that is, on actual people's lives. There's an unsettling tone to the book, as if the author's are high up on the mountain looking down at our seemingly endless capacity to be duped by the cultural iconography of Anne Murray and the Dionne Quintuplets.

The unseemly smarminess of the book is essentially the discomfort of generations who simply do not know how to come to terms with the irreversible revolution in cultural mores in society. The fact is, for better or worse, there is no longer a good kind of culture and a bad kind of culture. There are horrid, awful, idiotic happenings that pass themselves off as cultural activity, and there are smart, fascinating, creative bursts that reaffirm the role of culture as, perhaps, the sole bright spot in the millennial morass we are perpetually stuck in. But bad and good art comes, like giants, in many different forms and sizes — from mass market to underground, from personal to abstract, from the highest pinnacles of thought to the basest outbursts of instinctual idiocy.

The question of good and bad culture is no longer one of the deluded masses not knowing what's good for them. We have, more than ever before, a participatory culture, a pick and choose environment. We can take in what we want and cast the rest aside; and we don't need the pundits and the professors to preach to us anymore than we need our elected officials telling us how we could better live our lives. Having spent several decades shut out of the so-called high arts by any number of complex demographic and social reasons, we, the people, have done for ourselves, creating and appreciating a whole spectrum of aesthetic experiences that amalgamate and challenge and transcend artificially-imposed divisions. Left to fend for ourselves in the steel cage mud wrestling grease pit spectacle that is mass culture, we have fragmented and spread out, moving from punk jazz to rap poetry to zines like *Infiltration*, "the zine of going places you're not supposed to go." Yeah, we've even infiltrated high culture, subjected it to the dizzying speed of life, adapted it to ever changing technologies, to the realization that our lives are made tolerable and yet ever more complicated by a culture that does not observe us from a distance, but rather depends on us, lives and dies on our capacity to identify the vagaries of existence in a work's plots and concerns and rhetorical devices.

So we have demanded college courses on the sexual implications of 90210 and turned political sex scandals into movies and movies into political sex scandals. Not surprisingly, our efforts — particularly those of creators who do belong to the TV generations — continue to go largely unnoticed, dismissed in the papers as fads and fantasies, and disregarded by the arts bureaucracies as uncategorizable and potentially threatening to the establishment they exist to defend. Meanwhile, going full speed ahead, the American, Joe Queenan, writes a book in which a cultural critic dedicates a year to exploring such white trash fare as the Olive Garden and Deepak Chopra. *Red Lobster, White Trash and The Blue Lagoon* (as it is called) demonstrates both the immense appeal of low culture in all its seething sentimentality, and our capacity to distance ourselves from it, to want something more and better and substantial. Here we see an evolution, of sorts, or, better yet, a progression. Give us our speed culture: make us laugh and cry and think, all in half-hour bursts, because despite all this talk about the new leisure class, nobody seems to have any time for anything anymore. So take us with you, move us fast, we want to be on the train, not waiting at the station to see what unloads.

The seething masses and their tendency to move from passive consumers to agitated producers has forced so-called high culture into the position of trying to sex up its product, marketing old master travelling exhibits like summer blockbusters and throwing in the occasional TV theme song into the repertoire of the symphony. I remember the outrage of a woman who attended a Christmas concert of the Messiah at Massey Hall put on by a usually serious professional ensemble. However, this was the annual sing-along, and it featured the conductor dressed up to imitate a drunken Handel. The woman was infuriated, somewhat embarrassed by the extent to which high culture has increasingly come to parody the so-called pop culture it supposedly has nothing to do with; though in actuality the two opposing aesthetic approaches feed off and learn from each other and, in the irredeemable capitalism of North America, are irrevocably pitted against each other for our ever scarce entertainment dollars. The woman complained to me and I smiled and shrugged and said: I'm just the usher.

Which is true, in a way, my presence here as the author of this essay being to usher you across the twelve lane highway of speed culture, noting, as we go, the quality of the road kill, the sumptuous paint-jobs of those new bowl-shaped bugs, the way the tarmac goes hot and hazy under our feet as we slide dangerously between hurtling vehicles, trying, in vain, to make sense of what doesn't make sense, and, in fact, only ever made sense when it was believed that the arts were for the experts, the geniuses, the rich and the famous. Now, with homemakers compulsively collecting hippo figurines, TV programs devoted to literature hyping graphic novelists, mail order catalogues offering exclusive opportunities to own grisly Nazi memorabilia, and every tenth high school kid publishing a booklet full of occasionally transcendent free prose poetry, things just don't make sense the way they were once supposed to. Hey, don't push me in front of that pick-up. I'm just the messenger, the guy in the orange vest futilely flapping a red flag and begging the traffic to slow down for us pedestrians.

But culture isn't slowing down. It's speeding up. Only media journalists and fools think that we retain our capacity to evaluate the aesthetic experience on the basis of the social values and demographic pretensions of the art-world meritocracy.

Among the stodgy defenders of the existence — and evil — of high culture is another Carleton professor — what's with these guys? — one Tom Henighan, who uses his book, *The Presumption of Culture,* to articulate his old-style vision of a Canada of ballets and symphonies, a

Canada where culture is as moribund and ineffective as the Senate. Henighan argues, first and foremost, for the perpetuation of aesthetic culture — something he describes imprecisely as "serious culture" and "high culture" (though we know he really means the theater and classical music and galleries and literary publishing houses). Anyway, he argues that the only way to defend Canada against trashy U.S. pop culture invasion is by retreating into a protective shell of high arts, funding only those institutions that guarantee to present aesthetic culture, while withdrawing all direct funding to the artists themselves.

As you may have guessed, Henighan is an old-style champion of cultural divisions that no longer exist. But he's more than that. He's also a cultural puritan who shows what happens when we cling to our antiquated, generational implanted vision of what culture is in now, and what it will become. Henighan trumpets the worst, most insular aspects of North American culture, the very things that have all but forced individuals to reclaim the aesthetic experience from the hands of institutions and bureaucrats. But that's only half the rebuttal to Henighan's theories. The other half would be a lengthy survey of the mind boggling combination of do-it-yourself projects by fledgling collectives whose work in the cultural no man's land relentlessly subvert the precepts of high and low both, calling to our attention the hidden machinations of Spice Girl chocolate bars through grainy super-8 shorts and performance moments and giant oil portraits of liquor bottles even while subverting the precepts of the gallery by personalizing and having fun (the new artist doesn't condemn, but revels).

Still, Henighan denies the intelligence and need of the human spirit, a deep rooted savvy that has allowed us to survive in this cultural desert of Shania Twain and E.R. He denies the capacity of cultural paradigms to evolve. He would never acknowledge — despite his desire for the so-called high arts to reach the greatest number of people — that we are all collectors and commentators now, all in charge of revitalizing our culture so that we can rise above our role as chagrined debutantes (a role he and his cohorts perpetuate despite their best intentions, of course). Witness the evolution of television, from sappy and exclusionary to self-referential and ironic (similar to another highly developed cultural form that we participate in: advertising). We've gone from Leave It To Beaver to Seinfeld, from Wild Kingdom to When Animals

Attack, from Donahue to Jerry Springer. We, collectively, have raised the stakes because we are participants, cultural interlocutors who insist that the way we actually are should be a big component of our aesthetic entertainment. Guilty pleasure being better, after all, than no pleasure at all.

One more point about Henighan and those who think like him. Their ignorance — however well intentioned — allows the arts media/establishment to better ignore the next wave of artists and writers and thinkers who will, one fine day, knock them off the bow of their yacht. The insistence on the old school dichotomies of pop versus high and underground versus mass puritan art critics marginalizes everyone who creates culture as an amalgamation of social elements, as a towering Babel of ideas all told in languages made instantly understandable by communal reference points like Captain Kangaroo and New Coke and Ernest Hemingway.

But I'm not just some naive patsy who is telling you all this in order to perpetuate an amalgamated speed culture that is neither here nor there. My vision is of a participatory culture that doesn't exclude through useless categories and inflated prices and meaningless art-speak. I'm thinking of the kind of thing Toronto artist-activist Sally McKay does. Here's someone who recently crept out of the visual arts underground with a solo exhibition at the Art Gallery of Ontario, a show notable for its accessibility, and vision of a speed culture in which even those who never get off can still catch a glimpse of something meaningful through the window. Sally's work shows what alternative or underground or indie culture (like pop, these are meaningless, irrelevant terms that so far lack a more appropriate lexicon) continues to do best. Her work consists of taking mainstream fodder and investigating the myth behind what, when you come right down to it, is mostly just useless crap. Among other things displayed at the AGO was an extensive collection of Fisher-Price kiddie phones accompanied by a folder of artificial news clippings from magazines and newspapers reporting on the worth of her rare and valuable collection. Now many would argue that this kind of so-called art is not even deserving of the few precious months it occupied a small room in one of Canada's most prestigious galleries. But I hold that McKay's

HAL NIEDZVIECKI

work is at least as valuable as the rarefied and expensive paintings that surrounded it. Not only is McKay taking our hand and telling us it's alright to be guilty consumers of speed culture, she's also showing us how, in fact, our speed culture depends on us to assign it value. Where would manufactured trinkets be without our wonderful, bargain basement obsessions, our capacity to hold all forms of cultural experience by the scruff of the neck and give em a sarcastic but affectionate little shake? When I asked Sally about her iconoclastic yard-sale approach to art she told me the that it was her intention to "demonstrate the way in which we are together in our commodified culture, not alone. And that that's where the fun comes in." She also told me something that I found incredibly prescient and compelling given the average North American's iconoclastic position as both a helpless consumer and an empowered creator of speed product. I said something like: "Don't you wish you could be creative in a way that doesn't have to be about the market-place, that doesn't have to always refer us back to mass culture?" And she said: "I wouldn't be interested in that. Beauty is boring. Art on its own isn't that interesting." Neither is pop culture.

SWITH BELL is a Toronto writer. Her work has appeared in *Blood and Aphorisms*.

The Walking Papers

SWITH BELL

I LOOK AROUND AND WONDER, *how would I do it?*

They make it so hard for you in airports, with crowds of people everywhere, leering against arcade games and feeding at snack counters, lining up right out of the restrooms. There is no privacy here. If it's not people watching me — people in their travel track-suits with their gym-bag luggage who don't know it's not polite to stare — it's the security cameras recording reel upon reel of me in transient despair, filed and saved for when future generations appreciate the kitsch of airport security footage.

Efficiently I hand off my travel papers to the flight attendant, and am rewarded with a deep papercut. My blood drips onto the floor, shocking red.

This plane could crash, I think. But as I eye the emergency-procedures documentation in front of me — this caricature of how panicked passengers would react — I am discouraged that the crash looks soft, the escape slide bouncy and fun, the life raft like a tropical cruise. There are no casualties in this cartoon, and I am stifled by the ubiquitous safety of the airline.

The man in the adjacent seat is looking past me out the window. I catch his attention. I roll my eyes at the inadequacy of the assurance literature and inflict my observation: *This could crash.* He looks suspiciously uneasy and I find myself hoping he is a hijacker.

When the attendant comes by offering drinks, I ask for a rye and cola because I like saying it: *cola.* It makes me feel a bit like I am a time-traveller from the fifties or whenever people were arcane, inane. I am lonely for food and ask him politely if he will be serving lunch on this flight. He responds by laughing at me and then throws honey-roasteds in my lap like I'm some kind of circus elephant. By the end of the flight I have finished four more of these silver-bubbled snacks and another rye and cola. I think the man in the next seat despises me.

This weekend trip is a two-tiered flight from Kingston, *the limestone city,* to Philadelphia, *the city of brotherly love.* A victim of my own greedy curiosity, I am meeting my father in his country — my father, who I have not seen since the Reagan administration. And I am a mess. I have no idea how this weekend rendezvous will end. I would rather it was already over, so that I could look back from my emotional hangover and not remember a thing.

There are only a few things I know about my father, and they aren't good. About myself, I know that there are just two things I cannot bear: obtuse people and fat people. (Actually there are three things: I'm still very apprehensive about Siamese twins, or conjoined twins as we're supposed to call them. I think it must be the worst torture to be constantly attached by flesh to another person; I am sick enough of being around myself all the time without having to be around someone else.) I am sadly unforgiving about certain realms of human failure. Given my strongest areas of repugnance, the only nice thing I can say about my father is that he has just one head.

This whole weekend came about because he found my phone number and I was still drunk the morning he called. I drawled on the receiving end,

"Sure I'll visit. What's a weekend? Just make sure you get me a hotel because I'd be freaked out staying with you."

Maybe that should have been the first warning to change my mind, that he freaks me out. I should not jet to see people who give me the creeps, not to mention are fat and feeble-minded. But I'm pretty easy when I'm drunk.

"Who *was* that?" Miguel had asked, half-asleep. "That was the weirdest exchange I've ever heard. You sounded like you were talking to swine, but I couldn't tell if it's because you're still wrecked, or if you were really talking to swine."

Conscious of my breath, like gaseous vodka, I replied evenly, "Curly Larry. My father. My birth father."

"Since when do you have another father?"

I guess I wasn't really sure myself, so I just shrugged lamely and redirected my attention to a pummeling headache. Maybe the question should have been, *Since when do you have a father named "Curly Larry"?* The name, of course, is one of those monikers given to bald barflies, a name so offensive it gets wide enough recognition to spread disenchantingly to family. His official name, Leonard Hurst, meant nothing to me. Whereas *Curly Larry* could at least make me wince.

I fell back asleep, an apathy colored with nightmarish Americana: Snapple, Tasty-Cakes, cheese-steak hoagies and Pepsi, hairless men concealing their bodies beneath a thick stratum of fat. I was awakened at last by Miguel, urging and laughing, "Talk *swine* to me."

I met Miguel six months earlier at a bar in Kingston. I had knocked my pint over and he told me to wipe my wet hands on his shirt. He was wearing a light blue, ruffled tuxedo shirt that was open at the neck to display prominent Italian chest hair. I had such a low opinion of him that first encounter. I didn't even realize he was in costume.

The plane lands and I wander the airport searching for the fattest man. When I finally spot the winner I approach and say, "I recognized you at once. You haven't changed at all." He has though, of course. He is bigger. His shiny skin has less hair.

He is too stupid to tell me how beautiful I am or offer any other catch-phrases that would lower my guard a little. I am a slave to psychology and can be toyed with through text-book tactics, if only he would try. I know this about myself and have campaigned, accordingly, to avoid friends who study psychology. I am wary of analysis that I don't pay for. I like to maintain some control through such means as sessions per week, prescription load and, in the event that I disagree with my assessment, through switching psychologists. Although I have spent over half my life with analysts, through some subconscious anomaly I am terrified of being understood. I look at my father, this tugboat of man, and try to glean some indication of my higher meaning. Through retarded chatter I feel myself vying for his attention. *I hate myself for this.*

My mother left Curly Larry two years too late — after she had married him and become pregnant. We moved to Kingston, in Canada, and he stayed in our old home; nothing changed for him, there were just less people around. Except for holiday cards, he forgot about us. But for me it was different. In my head I would scream for him to love me. But he couldn't hear, and my disappointment made me even more silent. I cried at everything when I was young: looking at the moon would make me sob; driving on the highway would leave me moping; and the aloneness of night made my cheeks raw from tears. I thought I was crying for him, for how much I missed him. But I was crying because I didn't have the courage to ask for love out loud.

He takes me first to his market. That is what he does now, he runs a farmers' market. It's situated outside a Mennonite settlement in the ironically named Intercourse, Pennsylvania.

Curly Larry tells me proudly about how he swindled the property and its woolen mill, how he shirked various contracts to save money. I picture him getting the Mennonites to do his renovations in exchange for a half-hour a day on Compuserve. However his office tells the real story. On his desk are three televisions of varying size and quality, about ten empty bottles of Pepsi and Snapple, an open jar of French's mustard, a crushed box of donuts and a 600 mg canister of salt. In the corner is a leather recliner that has over seventy-five different massage settings and combinations; its remote control can also manage the televisions. Behind his desk are empty beer bottles, displayed like he is some kind of college freshman. The rest of the office is sprinkled with the skeletal casings of fast food and grocery products.

The market is the size of a city block and perches threateningly over the wide river. At one end of the building, where his office and travel agency are located, the river goes through a series of lochs and changes its name to Assyunka, an Indian word for *place to get fat.* That's what he tells me, anyway. And he's not just trying to be funny.

I am left alone while Larry chases down the lady from the bagel stand who hasn't paid her rent this month. Easing into the massage-chair, I program myself a strange session of kneading and chopping. I am surprised at how wonderful it is. I wander out to the adjacent travel agency office and pick up some brochures on Greece, where I am meeting Miguel this summer. Taking them back to Larry's office, I read travel itineraries so that I do not have to remember where I am. The phone is right in front of me and I want to call Miguel and tell him about the Mennonites from Intercourse, and ask him what he thinks about having a massage-chair and three televisions in an office. I want him to laugh at Curly Larry with me, so that for a second I can separate myself from my birthright and feel ok again. I don't call; he won't be in.

Finally I deploy Larry to the hotel. He has let a woman friend book it for him, thankfully. I am in the Marriott Regatta in West Philadelphia, a beautiful hotel. My daunting suite has two rooms and a bathroom, three phones, a stocked bar, a coffee maker and ironing board, and a stunning view of the twenty-four-hour Wawa across the street. There are lots of ways for me to do it here: electrocuting myself in the hot tub looks best.

He leaves and I go downstairs for a whirlpool bath and a sauna. When he comes to get me for dinner a few hours later I am already drunk. We eat in Intercourse and I order a double Glenlivet before dinner. It doesn't feel so bad this way. I no longer pretend to be interested in his market or his satellite dish I know he only got for porn. I remember back to when I used to withdraw books from the library on fatal food and drug interactions, planning to poison him dead. The plan has been so long in my head that I wouldn't even feel bad now, or guilty, if it worked.

We go to a bar after dinner and his friend Jim from the fish stand in the market talks me to death. He tells me how envious he is of our relationship that we can drink together in a bar like this. I tell Jim I haven't actually seen my father since the Reagan administration, then excuse myself and throw up in the bathroom. I hate fish and I hate Americans. *Most of all I hate myself.*

SWITH BELL

I had my first drunk at fifteen, an experience which grew naturally into weekend bingeing and lifestyle choice, and then became the remedy for boredom, until it progressed into a self-medication for anxiety and then, finally, the bottles themselves evolved into talismans to ward off delusional fears. For a while I was convinced that I drank so much because I was crazy; now I'm starting to wonder if maybe I'm crazy because I drink so much. If I'm going to be honest with myself, then I think the reason I drink at this point is so that, for a few faultless hours at least, I don't have to be responsible for my own mind.

The second time I met Miguel I was also drunk. I was also funny, and so was he. By accident we were sitting together at a table just as all our friends got up to dance. We talked probingly about books and studies. He was not only well-read, but well-read in the same aggregate of books in which I was well-read. He had long-finished his Honors degree in psychology; although I noted his area of expertise, I misjudged early on that it would ever affect me. In my analysis of him, Miguel changed from a ruffled-tuxedo-shirt-boozer to a profane and pedantic hedonist. Immediately we were conspiring to fuck up people in the bar: I would flirt with witless men while he snuck behind them and tied their shoelaces together; he would charm sophomoric women whose full cocktails I swiped to share later. One of the women started talking to him about Robertson Davies, and after I had shanghaied her drink he cut her off, proclaiming, as he followed me away, "Robertson Davies is an erudite buffoon." He was the person I had been waiting my whole life to meet.

Although my morning hangover folds me over the toilet, twice, I keep drinking. I remain unaware of my surroundings, of what I am doing. I covet the eclipsing effect of too much drink which ensures that I will forget Intercourse quickly enough when I am home again. I am growing more impatient for the end.

The whole day passes in shopping like some dreary cable retail channel that I can't turn off. At night I dress up in black evening wear and we pick up my grandfather for dinner. Three generations at the fanciest restaurant they know. I cannot really complain, the food and the wine at the Legion Inn are excellent. However the menu is full of misprints and explains the food in capitals as if to toddlers. I order "Boston fried CLAMS in a white whine sauce; FILET MIGNON with cornmeal-crusted arti choak hearts and garlic potattoes; Triple chocolate layer CAKE wiht a peppermint drizzle." I coerce Curly Larry into ordering two-hundred-dollars worth of red wine and then proceed to talk all night using big words, confident that neither he nor his father will understand what I am saying.

I learned that trick from Miguel. He is the only other person I know who thinks that vocabulary can also be the subject of conversation. He would quiz me: "Can you use *saprogenic* in a sentence?" And I if I was unsure I would always answer:

"Yes, once again you've mistaken your *saprogenic* cruelty for personable wit." I would usually be close enough because all the words he knew I liked had something to do with being acidic or produced by putrefaction. Later when I looked up *saprogenic* in my dictionary, I wrote in margin, *n.b.: good adjective for SWINE.*

Back at the Marriott, Curly Larry reads the sign at the front door, "WELCOME TO SEENS BAR MILALA." He asks me what kind of bar would have such a stupid name. I can't bear to respond. I leave him at the door and cruise in to crash Sean's gala bar-mitzvah in the Regatta Ballroom. I am no novice to crashing formals; only a month earlier Miguel and I had slid into my own graduation formal through a side door, without tickets. I was actually held for questioning, which, at two-and-a-half bottles of wine, I responded to well enough. My congeniality seems to come out and cover up my dark cynicism when I'm not part of the planned guest-list.

No one bothers me as I enter, so I cross the ballroom, double-fist myself at the bar with scotches and sit down at a table. Everyone at this bar-mitzvah is either geriatric and dressed in gold glitter or thirteen-years-old. My table consists of the latter.

"Who are you?" asks a bow-tied teen.

I pull from my drink and tell him I'm Sean's ex-girlfriend.

"How old are you?"

"Almost fourteen," I answer, knocking off my right-handed scotch.

They all look at each other like I'm a dirty criminal.

"You are *not* almost fourteen," says the first boy. "You are about thirty, probably."

"Thirty?" I shriek incredulously. "I'm barely twenty-one, you *swine*." Finally we all get to talking on more pleasant terms and they don't rat on me. I ask a sexy sixteen-year-old to dance and he complies. Feeling his hand sliding down off my back, I panic and wonder, *how did I get to be crashing a bar-mitzvah and asking jailbait to grope me?* I look around the ballroom and see hundreds of ways to do myself in.

But this isn't the right ending. Not like this.

I escape to my room and vomit up all my liquor and all my CLAMS and all my FILET MIGNON. I keep flushing the toilet but the bile will not go down. I am so desperately alone.

I order room service: cashews, coffee, toast and ice cream. When it arrives twenty minutes later I have made a pile of empty travel-sizeds on the kingsize next to me. I can barely walk to the door to tip the guy. I just don't know what to do with myself. I am so alone and I hate myself for being here, in this suite, in this city, in this life.

I try making a crank-call to Kingston, to my housemate Marina. I screw up the punchline, and she's heard me tell it before anyway. "Are you ok?" she asks from so far away.

"I'm not sure that I am," I respond. I tell her that this trip is not nearly as engaging as if I was Holden Caulfield running off to New York City. I want to hug her. I need some reassurance that I am not really fat and stupid like my father, like that heinous swindler. It's not helping and I hang up. Next I try crank-calling a few more friends, and I still can't get it right.

Finally I call Miguel's number. A man answers and I ask, "What do you call a boomerang that doesn't come back?"

"Who is this?"

"What do you call a boomerang that doesn't come back?" I insist.

"What?"

It's not him. It's after four in the morning and I know he hasn't come home. I feel dejected and answer slowly, "A fucking *stick*."

"Oh," he says. "Aha."

"Is Miguel there?"

"No. I don't know where he is."

"Can you tell him I called and I'm coming back tomorrow?"

"Coming back tomorrow. Got it," he says.

I look around and wonder, *how should I do it?* I am almost serious now. Obviously the best way is the pills, the least painful. I am wallowing in my own melodrama, planning my next move as if in a miniseries. The pills and the rest of the liquor. Just swallow it, watch some lousy American television, and have the best and last sleep of my life.

I pass out before I can kill myself and wake up in a mess of black silk and vomit. I dress and pack and wait for Curly Larry in the lobby.

There is a hospitality survey on the coffee table and I fill it out, high marks down the line. I doodle on the back for a while and then toy with Curly Larry's request that I write a poem for him. He hasn't asked me about my life all weekend, but has somehow gleaned through an aside of mine that I write poetry. I am surprised that he has retained anything about me.

Larry arrives and, seeing the scribbling, asks, "Did you write my rhyme yet?" I laugh, first with him, then at him, and tell him no. He shakes his head and takes me to the airport. In the car he tells me how much he loves me, how important I am to him, how he will always be there for me. I feel the hospitality survey crinkled in my pocket, with its verse written sarcastically on the back. I want to read it to him in response:

> Fat man, I don't want to know these things
> About your grade six reading proficiency
> your cheese-steak hoagies all day
> your breath like dumpster babies
> your mind like pudding.
> You're my ungainly guardian, I won't grant bail
> The only thing the world has to say to you
> is thank you, Fat man, for shopping retail.

As we pull into the airport lot I consider that this may be the last time I ever see him. It's one of those things you can never account for, never go back to make the last parting better. It feels familiar and I wonder if the last time I was with Miguel will also turn out to be conclusive. Everything is set on ebb and I cannot get back. I stare at Larry with a mixture of miscalculated curiosity and contempt. He returns my leer with a witless love that I can do nothing about. I would let him buy me,

I could do that and I don't think it would make me feel any worse. But he is too thick to offer me money. No money? What is the *point* of him if he doesn't give me money?

I am running from him to catch my plane, to catch some part of me that I have left behind in Canada. *What is the point of me?* I wonder. I have to forget all this and go home to find it. I will never come back here again.

On the flight home I read a *Life* article about Britty and Abby, the Siamese twins with one body and two heads. *They are popular with their classmates and lead a normal life,* says the copy. But they have *two heads!* How can they lead a normal life? *Nobody* leads a normal life. I read the story and get hooked on these girls, one who wants to be a pilot, the other a dentist. They can't even see how absurd they are.

Because they are *exhaustively* absurd. They are *ridiculous.*

On the flight home I am responsible for finishing off the airplane supply of scotch. I am laughing to myself and talking fearlessly to the sky. The first half of my goodbye is over, and I am OK. I think about how Miguel is the only one I ever dated who didn't mind how much I liked to drink, or what I did when I was drunk. I had asked him what he couldn't deal with from me, and he had said that everything I did was wonderful. He added, "I don't even mind that you turn into an entirely different person when you drink."

Floored, I probed, "I turn into an *entirely different person* when I drink?"

"Well, yah," he had responded, as if people had been doing their Masters on the subject.

"And is it bad? Do I turn into a bad person?" I had wanted to ask: *Do I embarrass you?* And more than that: *Do I seem like I have feelings when I am that person?* But most of all: *Am I happy, then?*

I have lived under the auspicious dogma that whatever I can't remember can't hurt me. I thought that forgetting everything would simplify the goal of having no regrets. I thought that misery was sober people.

He considered me and answered sheepishly, "No, you're not a bad person at all. In fact you're quite remarkable when you're drunk."

Silent pause, thinking.

"By corollary you're quite afraid, quite earnestly *sober*, when you're sober," he added quietly.

Upon arriving home I have to start, and finish, all my term work within three days. I am quiet about the journey to my roots, instead sharing my time with the computer and Becker's coffee. Every once in a while I can no longer resist the temptation of the phone that still hasn't rung for me, and I dial Miguel's number. But I lack the courage to do anything except silently hang up.

At the end of the week I run into him when we are, unremarkably, both drunk. I barely know how to look at him, how to understand how easily he passed me over. Near the end of the night he approaches all casual as if he hasn't missed a beat. I must give off this vibe that tells men I have no understanding of time and its passing, or of their absence in its wake. But I have to tell myself that Miguel is not my father. This could be different, I could be different if only I could remember that.

He takes me out for a walk and my hair gets kinked in the rain. My hand keeps moving within an inch of his arm, wanting to touch some part of it, grab it for security. We sit down on my front porch, a few blocks away. He moves his face so that the light falls most flatteringly on him and says, in the grave manner of someone who has the authority to make life-altering decisions, "You are wonderful."

I scrutinize his face for about one second because it is all the courage I have. I am afraid that if I look any longer I might find sarcasm, irony , or worst of all, pity. I want to ask him to say it frankly to me: *I'm in love with someone else; I want to be able to be in love with someone else; I want to be with someone who has the potential to love me back; I want to get out of here.* But I know why I don't ask him that. I can't bear that he doesn't think I'm so wonderful after all. I look back up at him after a lull, trying to meet his eyes as if to show how I value him and admire him, as if it will make a difference. Yet all I say is, "You're wonderful, too."

Inside I am sinking in a sentimentality that is not shared, a tension which shows up as conversational paralysis. We are quiet, looking in our laps. I don't know what to say, whether to say that I will try to understand, or not understand at all. Do you make conversation about being dumped? Do you analyze it while it happens? Do you ask what went wrong? Do you fight it?

SWITH BELL

Do you fight it?

I touch his face and it feels hot like my own hammering heart. I let my fingers linger in his hair, then reluctantly withdraw them. *I must finish my reluctant withdrawal,* I will myself. I stand up and go inside, alone except for my weighty walking papers.

I watch Oprah the next day and her show is about the conjoined freaks, Britty and Abby. I wonder, at length, what keeps them from ending it all? What are they waiting for? Their life isn't going to get better, just more complicated. Why do they fight for it?

Britty proves herself to be the queen of non-sequiturs and Oprah is baffled by her guest's stupidity. Abby sticks to her lesser half in a sort of degrading loyalty that makes me consider commitment as the highest form of suffering. I bet Abby would give anything to get the walking papers from Britty, or likewise to have the opportunity to give them. That kind of freedom is beyond not only their emotional potential, but their whole biological budget. Unnaturally they will stay together despite the simple fact that they are two people. They are accidents of nature, too absurdly trapped with each other to behold their own monstrosity.

I sigh.

But they are kind of nice because they can't see it.

Against my better judgement, I start to like them. There's something to be said for a world where a two-headed girl can dive and swim and shop at the mall. I watch the whole show, right to the end. And every Siamese moment is worth it. I can wait. I can manage. I think to myself,

I want to be happy. How will I do it?

HENRY FERRIS lives with his wife, Dolores, and their daughter, Ashley, in Vancouver B.C., where he teaches Computer Science at University Hill Elementary School. His poetry and fiction have appeared in over twenty journals, including *Queen's Quarterly, Grain, The New Quarterly*, and *Rampike*.

The Donahue Show

HENRY FERRIS

TRENT AND I SMOKED UP before going to The Donahue Show — a few steps down a convenient alleyway off 24th Avenue, five quick puffs on the magic dragon — and the stone hit me, that slo-mo warp blossomed in my brain, unfolding itself, unfurling, the way it does, just as we walked round the final corner of the Rockefeller Center and took up places at the edge of the thrumming knot of humanity that was the ticket holder's line. The entire surrounding scene had a stillness, an off-kilteredness, which spoke to the quality of the marijuana.

Our fellow Donahuers swung around to inspect the two of us. People in the shade under the awning, a circle of plumpish matronly-types talking together, the six or seven men leaning against the chrome columns of the building, the three sleek girls in cut-offs sitting on the dusty curb — everybody took a good long look. A hundred curious faces, all at once, a wall of eyeballs wheeling about to meet my gaze . . .

I shot a glance at Trent. His own eyes were bloodshot, watery, weak. Anxiety poured off him in translucent little waves — he was just odd-looking and uncomfortable enough to make people notice. I turned away and smiled at the girls, slow and deliberate, and they grinned right back. "They're onto you!" I whispered. "They can sense your fear! Use your force-field before it's too late!"

He nearly laughed out loud, and the dead-tight wires of his body loosened up a bit. Around us, the crowd's attention fluxed and shifted and ebbed away as people found other things on the street to stare at.

"Don't sweat it," I said, "no one ever actually died of paranoia, right?"

"They do all the time. The government covers it up."

I gave a loud chuff of laughter that drew a second collective glance from the orbed wall. Facing them, eyeball to eyeball, I laughed again — unlike Trent, being in groups of people didn't often make me uptight. I put a hand to his shoulder. "It's worth it. It's worth some psychic stress to see Phil . . . to see Phil tear their little minds open."

Trent pried himself up off his shoes and met my gaze for a moment.

"I just hope that the guest is someone good, someone like Salman Rushdie, you know, or George Will or Paglia or Hilary Clinton." He was calmer, now, but I could still see the white noise of the drug in the voice of his eyes.

"I wish," I said, shaking my head. "Trust me, the way the show's gone lately, it'll be something dumb, some Ricki-Lake-level ratings trash . . . homosexual housewives from Venus, or metabolically-challenged people who ate themselves whole and gained a hundred pounds in the process."

Just then the woman ahead of me in line, large and metabolically-challenged herself, hesitated and swung about to talk with us. She'd overheard something. "I know what the topic is," she said. Poised, holding the moment, she flashed an in-the-know smile, waved a hand towards the stainless-steel-and-plexiglass edifice of the building towering there above us. You could tell that she thought this was indeed a good one, a show of shows of shows.

A non-caloric feast of light.

"Actually, I guess it's not really a topic, it's a guest." And at this point her smile evolved, seemed to grow oddly smug. "It's Rush. Rush Limbaugh."

It sank in. Paranoia forgotten, eclipsed, Trent let out a little whoop of pure gladness, I turned my palms up in the low-five position and he slapped them, hard, ringingly, once and then again, a rictus of joy written on his face. Neither of us could believe our luck. We were in an uproar, yelling into the mirror of each other's expression: "Oh, glorious day!" "It's a classic!" "It's good versus evil!" "The devil himself has come to town!"

Our informant stood there, smoothing her hands over the pleat of her red-and-copper sundress and growing more and more mystified with each passing second. You could tell that she wasn't at all sure who the evil one was supposed to be here, Phil or Rush or, even more likely, one of us — and now I pegged that earlier look, that syrupy I-told-you-so look of the hare-brained Rush devotee. Without being told, I knew for certain which side of things she was on. The insight had a calming effect.

Quieting down, apologetic, I stuck my hand out and she took it. "I'm Dave, and this is Trent . . . We're huge Donahue fans . . . We came down from Toronto to see him in action . . . This should be a pretty good show, hey?"

She gave me a slow, pendulous nod. "I'm Carah Lee. It should be good — so long as it doesn't get *too* political, you know?"

In unison, Trent and I returned the same off-speed nod. "Yeah, yeah," I said, "I *hate* it when that happens, when they get *too* political and all." As I repeated the line I felt Trent quiver and rattle in the space beside me and I knew he'd slotted it in the comedy file — we'd be quoting it for weeks to come. I looked at him: he was grinning outright, a stretch of lip and cheek as big and luminous as the moon.

Someone next to Carah Lee asked her a question and the two of them began to talk. Trent and I stood quietly for a time, blissful, fully content with our luck. In the silence I could feel the drug doing its funny things to the delicate mechanisms behind my eyes. After awhile a woman dressed in a navy-blue dress suit and a no-nonsense expression came out of the building and walked over to talk with the two uni-formed men standing near the door. People began to surge forward, ever so slightly, the last few men peeled themselves off the building, the girls got up off the curb in a tangle of tanned legs and a cloud of pheromones, and as they stood there, wiping zinc-colored dust off the seats of their shorts, the tallest one caught my eye on her and gave me a smile sweet enough to burst the ventricles of my heart. It was perfect.

In my excitement with everything I had to resist a dizzying urge to blow her a kiss.

This was it. What we'd all been waiting for. The show of shows of shows was about to begin.

In the studio, wedged into a small space on the hardwood bleachers, we watched the buzz and bustle of activity taking place all around us: people searched out places to sit; two women were onstage moving furniture and doing their level best to duct tape an eeling mess of wires to the floor; and there were green-shirted technicians scurrying hither and thither, checking on the lights, on the TV monitors, on the nine different stationary cameras, checking everything. Twice. A third time. The essence of meticulousness, perfectionism.

I exchanged a wave with Carah Lee as she crossed by towards a front row spot six or seven seats below us. The girls were nowhere to be seen. We watched as Carah lowered herself down and said some pleasantry to the African-American fellow in the spot next to hers. Trent didn't breath a word, but I knew his rhythms and just how lighthearted it made him feel to have her safely out of range of an awkward conversation. Relieved, comfortable, he crossed his legs and slouched down towards the bottom of his seat.

Elsewhere, Carah Lee's excessive friendliness was the rule. There were any number of people striking up conversations amongst themselves. Strangers, mostly, excited, animated, touching, squeezing hands, getting acquainted, suddenly eager to wish each other well now that the all-seeing cameras were bearing down upon them. Soon Trent had to sit up to field three or four introductions from voluble neighbors. Falling all over themselves, really. Ready to join hands together and skip off down the yellow brick road of peace and harmony.

An elderly woman pointed at the camera directly in front of us. It loomed there, a black thing built of sheetmetal, ground glass, levers, cones, rock-hard science. There was something about its form, something about its crepuscular lines, that put me in mind of Darth Vader or perhaps a Praying Mantis. It was aimed outward upon the crowd, at Joe-and-Sue Public. There could be no doubt: here, the audience was the show.

A few minutes later a cameraman started panning the room,

and a wave-like chorus of "Ohhhs" and "Ahhhs" went up as people saw themselves appear on the monitors. I watched closely: I still hadn't spotted the girls, even with all my moving and twisting around and feigning interest in the blue-paneled false-front pseudo-architecture of the room. I had begun to suspect that they were sitting directly behind me — I could feel their eyes corkscrewing into the small of my back.

Suddenly, in ultra close-up, our every pore and ingrown hair revealed, there we were on the monitor. I looked at us. From the outside. Two Gen-Xers, tall, of a height, one dressed in bargain-basement black and the other in a raggedy wool sweater, one as handsome as the other unlovely. College students. Probably socialists. The kind of people that tear a country down around the ears of the hard-working, God-fearing people who gave everything to build it up.

When he saw who was onscreen Trent stiffened and looked askance, pretending to be oblivious, doing his very best to ignore what could not be ignored. On the armrest his fingers were jittery, aflutter. To divert things, to rescue him, I peered straight into the purple eye of the lens and gave myself an enthusiastic two-handed wave.

But it didn't work. The camera didn't move — they were fiddling with some ratchet or sprocket on the back of it — and after awhile I began to squirm a bit myself. The pot was definitely having an effect. An hour-long minute passed. And another began. Each second had become freeze-framed. Time had assumed a new geometry, a new telemetry, looping around itself, and in the whorl of it I was suddenly awkward, I couldn't think of what to do with my hands, there was a stiffness to the red pattern of muscle under the skin of my face.

And Trent in even worse straits. Finally he leaned in close, shaking his head with real feeling. "I feel like the proverbial bug, here. A really stoned, paranoid bug."

My nod had some force behind it. "I know the feeling, fellow bug. Plus, time seems to have just stopped or something — another three or four thousand years of this and I'm going to have to speak to Phil about it." At that we shared a good long chuckle. I liked how it made us look onscreen.

"Yeah," Trent said, keeping his voice low, "It's not a good time to be stoned. My granny always warned me not to look into the mirror when

I was on LSD, but she never told me about dope and TV monitors . . ." This time our laughter sounded out at full volume, a little wild, a hosanna of pure enjoyment.

I was feeling better, nearly Zen — as usual, humor was the road to the center of things. The picture now zooming in and out, the hard gleam from the Klieg lights, the mindpressure from that lidless exophthalmic wall — it was nothing I couldn't handle. Something weirdly benign. Manageable, anyway.

Finally, mercifully, they fixed or maybe unglued the whatever-it-was and the camera swung away from us, resuming its search-and-catalogue scan of faces. Trent let out an operatic sigh of relief. A second refrain of exclamations floated up towards the rafters. And, without looking to my watch, I knew that time had reasserted its constancy, that the seconds and minutes and hours would be ticking off as rhythmically as ever, once again matching the drumbeat of the encircling universe.

It was a half-hour or so later, boredom setting in, growing unrest in the seats, when a short vibrant Mary-Lou-Retton of a woman snatched up a microphone and addressed the crowd. "Hello there," she said, her merry voice swooping through the speakers and a glossy oversized smile splayed across her lips. She was wearing faded black jeans big enough to belong to a man and one of the *Phil Donahue For President!* t-shirts from the souvenir stand. Though I could see no pom poms or school uniform or any marching band, I knew her for who she was: our cheerleader had arrived.

"Welcome to the Donahue Show!" It was a shout of joy, of epiphany, and it brought Trent and I and our fellow Phil-worshippers out of our seats, whistling and clapping and stamping our approval. She clapped along with us, the microphone pressed under one shapely arm, every tooth gleaming, every line of her body crackling with positive vibes, until that exact moment when the full force of the applause had begun to ebb and slacken off. And then, after an exuberant full-circle swing with the cord, she caught the mike and lifted it to the bee-stung halo of her lips.

"Are you feeling good?!" For a second time the house came down around our collective ears. My hands had begun to smart. I fielded a glance from Trent and he gave his head a toss — it was overwhelming. Pure unadulterated Hollywood. After awhile the applause died down again. I won't say what happened next, but it should be enough to know that I stopped counting knee-jerk ovations after the seventh.

Her name was Helen Peabody and she was the executive producer of the show. She spent five or ten minutes going over the show's basic routines, pointing out the backlit applause signs, the bathrooms and the neon-green exit signs, making happy little jokes all along the way. She did have a list of pink-and-fluffy rules: If we wanted to participate we should raise our hands and wait for Phil to notice us, and if handed the mike we should stand up before starting to talk, and above all, we should be careful not to hog airtime — after all, everyone should be given a chance to speak their mind.

For fun, for us to practice, she interviewed people out of the crowd, asking where they were from, if they were married, had children, a dog or cat, a pet goldfish. Watching her, the sizzle in her smile, the busy dramaturgist's hands, the eyes full of bubbles and light, we all fell in love. As cynical as the drug made me, I still couldn't help myself — it was like trying to resist a chocolate eclair or a bowl of Froot Loops.

After awhile she bounced back down to center-stage and spun around to face us. All at once that incandescent smile turned down at the corners. It was time to be serious for a moment, to take stock of weighty things.

"As you may or may not know, the Donahue Show has been on the air for over twenty years, and there are six months left in its run. In my opinion it's been time well spent . . . It may sound like something Walt Disney would say, but I like to think that the show has helped make the world a better place." Her voice had dipped into a softer range. Every word echoed with a musical sincerity. Rapt, motionless, we all just sat there. "We feel that the show opens people's minds to contemporary issues, to new ideas, to new lifestyles. Shows like this help teach us how to accept our differences, how to accept each other . . . And, I guess, how to live together."

The ninth — or was it tenth? — round of applause thumped out of our battered hands. A wave of communal spirit swept over the crowd. People shared glances, found ways to almost touch. A pretty woman in

HENRY FERRIS

a sepia-colored dress pressed against me from twenty feet away. You could see it happening all around. It struck me that TV land was a lot like Oz or Narnia or Willie Wonka's Chocolate Factory — here there were no politics, no enmity, no fist-fights, everybody just loved everybody else.

Helen's brow cleared, and, as if on cue, so did everyone else's. She looked at her watch and smiled, her teeth so white and beautiful they might have been capped with little sheaths of light. "Phil's going to come out and talk with you in about five minutes or so — and like I said before we'll start taping at one o'clock. Does anyone have any questions? . . . Anything at all? . . . Any more goldfish jokes?" An arm playfully extended, she held the microphone out to us, let it dangle on its cord.

No questions were forthcoming. No one could stop grinning long enough to formulate one. Sitting there next to each other, elbow-to-elbow and knee-to-knee, united, brethren, we were content to bask in the warm glow of communal spirit that was leaking out of every heart.

And then it was ruined.

Helen clapped herself on the forehead in disbelief and took up the mike one last time.

"Oh, right, I almost forgot to mention today's guest!" The mistake had her flustered, pink-cheeked. She straightened up, put her shoulders back, took a deep lung-stretching breath. "Today's guest" — Her voice lowered two or three notches — "is the one and certainly the only" — she dipped into the pit of her stomach to punch it home — "Ruuussshh LLLimbaughh!"

A ragged but heart-felt cheer went up. A well-dressed wall-street man off to my right leapt to his feet in appreciation. Then it was a wobbly old woman and what looked to be her grandson in the second row. In twos and threes others followed suit, launched from their seats as the volume rose higher and higher. From the corner of my eye I spied Carah Lee and the man beside her clapping like mad, clapping for every bit they were worth.

And then, a nanosecond later, came the boos, the howls, the jeers, the catcalls, and all else was drowned out as Trent and I added our voices to a dark-throated chorus of hate. There was real hostility in our voices, in the stretch of our faces, ringing in the stomp of our feet.

Overt, spine-tingling hostility. Below us, her aplomb completely vanished, Helen marched up and down the no-man's-land of the third aisle and waved her arms in a vain effort to quiet things down.

And suddenly, just like that, upon mention of one name, we had found ourselves divided in half, split down the middle into two diametrically-opposed political camps, more than willing to go to war.

Phil looked like Phil; Rush, like Rush. Two good suits topped off with big glowing heads. They sat facing each other across the white oval table the technicians had set up center stage right, mano a mano, superliberal versus archconservative, the new good versus the oldest and deepest evil. It brought a thrill to see the two of them squared off and ready to go at it. It felt momentous, historical — as if something would indeed be decided here today, once and for all time. I decided that, come what may, every single minute of the wait had certainly been worth it.

The monitor showed a close-up of Rush. Trent ducked his chin and whispered at my ear. "It's not that he's fat, it's okay to be fat, everybody gets fat at one time or another — it's the *way* he's fat. The way he just gloats in his economic advantage. You know he'd eat the whole world if he could." The image wrestled a chuckle out of me, I couldn't help myself.

Onstage Phil was talking to Rush, one hydrocephalic head to another. "Well, things are going just fine for you! Just fine! ten to twenty million people tune into the show every night, every single night. Ten to twenty million . . . As they say in the business, those are some pretty good numbers, some unprecedented numbers. The radio show is bigger than ever — almost as big as Howard Stern. And the third — or is it the fourth? — the fourth? — the fourth book is on the top of the *New York Times* bestseller's list."

Phil lowered his voice, whispering now, that photogenic smile out, those Hollywood teeth casting universes of light. "The pundits are saying you may be onto something, here."

Rush was laughing silently, the way he does. His eyes glimmered, his bulbous chin twitched up and down, his shoulders jiggled, the whole expanse of his body was involved and gyrating in a not-so-little earthquake of flesh. Watching, you half-expected the blue silk suit to pop like a balloon. It took a couple of moments for him to recover enough to speak.

"I just tell it like it is. I point out the obvious. That's what people tune in to hear. Plus, I occasionally point out mistakes the administration has made." At that, the woman directly in front of me let out a strangled laugh — a sound with nothing in it but anger. One of the "stage-managers" searched out the source of the noise and shot her a very dirty look. To my left, the flashing sign asked for quiet.

Phil swivelled his chair away, facing a point equo-distant between Rush and the crowd. It took me a moment to realize they had switched cameras.

"Well, well, well, Mr. Limbaugh. It's obvious to us that things are going quite well for you at the moment — and for that matter, for the party you so ardently support. This last election didn't turn out too shabby, did it? A historic, a *historic* Republican victory in both the House and the Senate, so over the past six years they have managed to keep complete control of both institutions." On a cue from offstage Phil pivoted ever-so-slightly back towards the original camera. "C'mon, Mr. Limbaugh, confess, fess up, tell us the truth — that's gotta feel pretty good, doesn't it?"

Rush had on a big, planet-eating grin. There could be no doubt as to how it felt. It felt like being able to devour music, like drinking light, like tasting the translucent flesh of God. It was so good he could just barely contain himself.

"It was an unprecedented event, Phil. Unprecedented. A real landmark in American politics. One of those defining moments in the development of our nation — of the entire world, for that matter. The American people said it loud and clear — the Democrat's reign of incompetence had to come to an end before the entire country fell apart. I think — "

" — Not to interrupt, but on your show, on the record, you have claimed some responsibility for those same election results — yet you have also said that you do not determine public opinion, you do not persuade your audience of anything they don't already believe. Unlike the far-left media establishment, you aren't trying to convince anyone of anything, nothing at all." Pausing, holding the moment, Phil looked outward upon the crowd, his eyes like blue tractor beams. Trent and I shared a look of glee — this was the Donahue Show at its very finest.

"So I have to ask you — *we* have to ask you, once and for all . . . are you in any part responsible for the Republican electoral wins?"

Across the table, a vibrating ball of agitation. Rush was wagging an index finger and snapping his head side-to-side — the question was so ridiculous, so preposterous, so utterly lunar, one barely knew where to start. "Look, look, you're taking what I said completely out of its context. On the show you're talking about, the show following the Republican win, I simply made the point that we — that all right-thinking Americans — who had gone out and voted were jointly responsible for what had taken place. That should be pretty obvious, Phil, that the voters are responsible for an election result — "

" — I think, I think, the exact quote is, what you said was . . . " Phil stopped for a moment, laid a finger behind his ear to better listen to his earpiece: "You said that it was, and I quote here, 'a night to rejoice, due in no small part to yours truly.'" That statement, to many people —"

"— All I meant by that was that I had voted the right way, with the rest of the American people. I didn't make anyone out there vote the way they did. They did it themselves. I don't have any telepathic abilities, I can't control people's minds" The Carah-Lee types thought that was funny, and a ripple of laughter purled through the seats. "People just went out and voted their conscience. They went out and voted against forty years of taxes and big government and corruption and self-serving Democrat incompetence."

Another wobbly cheer went up. The Republicans in the crowd gnashed their teeth and slammed their palms together in ecstasy while the people who felt neutral did nothing and the scattered islands of Democrats whistled and hissed and howled in a splenetic effort to ruin things. An ugly mood was brewing in this particular melting pot. Handshakes disregarded, camaraderie forgotten, people edged away from each other, exchanged offended looks with strangers. There were foul expressions on any number of faces. When I let out my own gravelly boo, my partisan contribution, Carah Lee spun around and took a fix on me like she had radar antennae hooked up to the back of her head. Our eyes crossed that little distance and locked solid for a moment: hers gave nothing back but malevolence.

After a few moments the room calmed down. Trent and I hid in the bottom of our seats, waiting, expectant, hyper-attuned — it was high time for Phil's rebuttal. I could see it coming. He would point out how ludicrous Rush's position was. He would demonstrate that Rush did shape public opinion, was in fact trying to do so right now, in a sneaky reverse sort of way. He might even ask how Rush, like Bob Dole, could think that certain Hollywood movies made people kill each other and in the same breath insist that the Limbaugh show had no effect whatsoever. You just knew it: a killer question was coming, a rhetorical hammer-blow. The Wizard of Talk would win the day with the wonderful things he'd say.

But it didn't happen. The next thing to cross those lips was an unrelated question about Dr. Foster's failed nomination for Surgeon General. And it quickly became a trend: whenever the debate heated up, whenever things began to get lathered up and vociferous, Phil backed off. Way off. All the way off. Time after time, over and over and over again, he gave Rush huge chunks of airtime, let him have the all-important last word with which to explain everything away.

To my mind, over the next half-hour or so, the debate became a rout. A virtual butt-kicking. My disappointment knew no bounds. I felt like Dukakis in November, Gary Hart the morning following Donna Rice, like Hilary Clinton after Health Care Reform had drowned in a puddle of blood. Sitting there, listening to Rush put his insane spin on things, seeing that gleeful know-it-all smile, I was sick, dizzy, heavy-headed, I could taste the fluorescent poison coming off the lights. It seemed as if our side had lost the war, and everyone and everything good and beautiful was now forfeit the Father of Lies.

During the third commercial break Phil left the stage to come out into the crowd. Microphone in hand, smile in full efflorescence, he took up a spot less than twenty feet away, cracking a quality joke or two as he waited for the camera's red indicator light to flash. It was audience-participation time. In spite of the jokes, an unruly, riled-up mood prevailed in this particular audience — everyone's little red button had been pushed. There were hands going up here and there, one woman in the top row was waving at Phil to notice her, and two or three other people had risen to their feet: Joe-and-Sue Public were eager to speak their minds, to set the celluloid record straight.

And then the bulb flared red. Phil picked a hand from the grasping mass, a hand that turned out to be attached to the wall-street man.

"You wanted to say . . . " Phil held the mike up to the man's chin.

"Yeah, uhmn, I ah, I just wanted to ask Rush if he thinks Clinton is the worst president this country has ever had. If he's the worst."

Rush liked the question. His grin looked replete, satiated, as if he'd just gulped down a galaxy burger or swallowed a universe. "I've said it before, and I'll say it again. Mr. Clinton's character is highly suspect. He is a weak man, an extremely weak man, a man with no moral code whatsoever. He is simply the wrong man to be running the government. If we don't stop him, he's going to destroy this country." Once again, like an exclamation point, a jagged refrain of cheers and boos rang out.

And now *everybody* wanted the microphone. Phil was running all over the room: two or three normal-enough-looking folks wanted to know if Rush would run for president in 2000; a woman in ripped jeans thought he'd make a superb congressman; a frail old lady took a death-grip on the mike and, in a lungy, bullfrogged voice, insisted that Rush was the only man who could save the country from the fiscal and moral mess it was in. Only a few people, among them the woman in the sepia dress, had anything at all negative or challenging to say. More and more, with each lovingly rendered comment, it looked as though Mr. Lucifer had full control over the assembled minds.

Trent wasn't happy. He hadn't said anything in quite some time. As the love-fest continued he kept glancing over at me, trying to catch my eye; once he gave me a little prod with his elbow; it grew clear that he wanted me to speak, to question this point or that, to rise up and breathe a little left-wing fire. As usual, he wanted me to talk the talk for both of us. Sheepish, more than a little fearful, at first I ignored his little encouragements, and I passed up on a number of chances at the mike.

But then Rush said something else, and this time my anger brought me to my feet, ready to go, ready to speak my piece. Uncertain, hesitant, I took a half-step towards the clear space of the aisle. And suddenly, smoothly, like something we had choreographed in advance, Phil moved up beside me and held out the hollow leaden tube of the microphone.

HENRY FERRIS

And that's when it happened. The drug declared itself in a blinding flash of paranoia. The camera took shape there straight ahead, imblackened, menacing, Vaderesque. I could feel all the eyes on me, all those unblinking eyes, Trent and Phil and Rush and Helen and Carah Lee and the wall-street man and the missing girls all staring at me and beyond that the television audience in all their goggling numbers, and the wall had become a tunnel of eyes, I stood in a tunnel a mile high and miles deep, a tunnel of a hundred-million extruded eyeballs, all of them moving in horrible concert, looping about to stare straight at me.

It was terrifying.

I literally couldn't speak. Not a word. For a long three-count I just stood there overtop the microphone, all those millions of people watching me. Feeling their undivided attention. Their mindforce. It was all I could do to keep from bolting for the door, to remember to draw a breath.

Phil, after waiting patiently, finally gave me a quick nod that meant to get on with it. But there was no way I was going to be getting on with anything. Nothing was forthcoming. I was locked in place, frozen solid, and the only way I was going to say anything was if we were all willing to wait the four or five hours until the THC wore off.

And that's when it happened.

Trent rescued me. I couldn't believe it. In one big heave he just stood up and made a waving motion for the mike, and as I sat down I had never been so glad in all of the years of my life. Phil was there beside him, lickety-split, holding the black foam end of the microphone up to his chin. I could feel Trent's terror, I could see the shyness permanently inflected in his eyes. I knew what courage it had taken for him to rise up to be counted. An incredible, heroic thing. The move had taken so much it seemed as though something good must come of it.

It had better. The show was almost over.

"And you wanted to say . . . ?"

"I wanted to say something to Mr. Limbaugh." Trent lifted his chin, stared directly into that hyperoptic tunnel, and found Rush's eyes.

"You, Mr. Limbaugh, are the least responsible journalist I have ever seen. The very worst. You have broken every single commandment of journalism at every single opportunity. You make up statistics. You make up "facts." You cite discredited and irresponsible studies. You quote yourself to make points. You edit pieces of video footage so they will match your arguments. No credible journalist would do any of these things — every single one of them is a cardinal sin."

An ugly roar went up — the Rushniacs were not at all happy about Trent's choice of words. Oblivious, focused, he kept right on going, shouting now, bellowing, fighting and winning against a growing swell of dissenting voices.

"I mean, spin is spin, and lying is lying! You, sir, are a liar! The rules exist to protect us all! Those standards are there to prevent exactly what you're doing . . . "

I think, in those next ninety seconds or so, I have never been happier. As I hid there beside him I saw that somehow Trent was doing really good here, really good indeed, in actual fact he was winning the whole debate, he was becoming the highlight of the show.

In fact, I'm sure everyone there could see it: Trent was winning. He was carrying the day, the week, the century, the millennium. Under his own power. By himself. And it was thrilling to behold.

And as I sat there in wonderment, watching his every movement, listening to the euphonious sound of his voice, it suddenly seemed to me that he stood in a nimbus of light, and when I looked closer I understood that this light was coming off of his body, rising from somewhere deep inside him, from some luminous hidden pocket, and every sinew and fiber and cell was aglow with it, every inch of his face and hands and exposed skin shone bright silver, and as my heart hammered within me I saw that his eyes had changed, his eyes were blazing with life, with exultation, with the incandescent rapture that sometimes comes to those who are truly right and brave in what they do.

MICHELLE BERRY is the author of *How To Get There From Here* (Turnstone Press) and *Margaret Lives in the Basement* (Somerville House). Her first novel, *Home*, is forthcoming from Key Porter.

Hunting For Something

MICHELLE BERRY

TOM HUNT HAS JUST OPENED a religious supply store on Main Street in the city. The sign out front says,

Hunting for Something?
Religious Paraphernalia and Supplies

Tom took the money he received from his mother's will and quit his job at Mack's Factory where he had worked for twenty years as a machine welder. Tom misses working with fire, the quick scent of fuel, the hot-blue of the flame, but sitting behind the counter at Hunting for Something he's come to fully appreciate running his own business. He opened the store last week, on Wednesday, and it's now Friday and he's doing a booming business. He can come in at any time, he can leave at any time, he can take a walk at lunch up and down Main and wave to the other store-owners, he can watch the TV he installed behind the counter, he can be his own man. At Mack's Factory he was told when to stand up and sit down. He was told when to sneeze. Tom Hunt is completely satisfied with his new calling.

Tom was a little concerned that the word would get out that he isn't Christian, that he comes from no denomination, that his mother, rest her soul, never thought to baptize him or take him to church. He wondered for awhile if that would hurt business. If his customers, mostly nuns and priests, would stop coming if they thought the store was run by an atheist. But Tom isn't atheist, really, he's more secular. He likes to think of himself that way — a man of the world. He's open to all religions and, at the same time, no religions. Tom accepts people just the way they are, be they pure or be they sprinkled with a bit of zealousness — it's all the same to him. He has no responsibility to anyone, and doesn't care to, and so whatever people believe in doesn't bother him at all. If anything, Tom thinks, his openness can only help business, move it along.

Besides, he's been open over a week and, so far, no one has complained. One nun did tell him the TV was on too loud, that Oprah was guffawing much too heartily, that the store should be quiet and blessed, but Tom just took that as a kind of jealousy for being able to live life normally.

It is Friday afternoon, just after lunch, and Tom is sitting high on his stool behind the counter, letting the Thai food he just ate rest heavily in his stomach. The garlic and pepper scent on his breath irritates him. He has brushed his teeth in the little bathroom behind the store three times, but still the smell lingers, the taste lingers. Tom sits on his stool and blows into his cupped hands and smells his breath.

He watches an ad on TV for car polish and then one for diapers. A fat baby, naked but for a tight diaper, holds his hands up to shiny cartoon star floating high above and tries to catch it. Tom supposes that catching the star may symbolize the leak-proof quality of the diapers, but he isn't sure. He's never had kids, nor a wife, and he's never wanted anything of the sort. His life has remained uncomplicated and controlled. Nothing to take away from him, nothing to give. Tom mutes the commercial and waits for the talk show to continue.

The bell above the door rings and a man wearing blue jeans and a black leather jacket steps into the store. The man looks around and picks up a few items as if noting the prices. He moves around the

MICHELLE BERRY

store. Tom begins to feel slightly nervous because he isn't yet used to approaching people, making a sale. He would rather sit on his stool and look at the floor, give people their buying privacy. But all of the store owners on Main street have told him that it is better to talk to your customers, look them in the eye, make contact. They have told him that their businesses thrive on the personal well-being of their customers.

So Tom says, "Hello. Can I help you?"

The man looks up, startled. He looks quickly at Tom. "I didn't see you there," he says. "I didn't know you were there."

Tom smiles. "Well, I was. I am."

"Yes," the man says. "Yes, you are."

"Can I help you with anything? Are you looking for something in particular?" Tom wants to say, *are you hunting for something*, but he thinks he might giggle if he uses the store's name in a sentence. It took him weeks to come up with that name and now it seems so obvious — religious supplies — Tom Hunt — Hunting for Something? Tom shakes his head.

The man shrugs. He runs his hand over a statue of Jesus on the Cross and then lets his palm rest on a Bethlehem Snow Globe, cupping it. Tom wishes the man would shake the globe and see the sprinkles, see the snow, like diamonds, fall down upon the desert city. He knows the man would buy it if he just shook it. Tom marvels continuously at that globe. He has seven stored upstairs by the foot of his bed. Seven he just didn't want to sell. And he shakes them each before he turns out the light each night. Shakes them up and watches the desert get cold.

"I was looking for something," the man starts. But then he stops talking and glances down at his boots. Tom looks at the man's boots. They are black leather cowboy boots. The design on the boots matches the design on the back of the man's leather jacket. Tom has only been running this business for a little over a week but he was getting used to the nuns and priests, the black outfits and clerical collars — he certainly didn't expect to see a man dressed like this walk into his store.

"You were looking for something?" Tom says, hoping to jog the man's memory.

"Yes," he says. "Something."

"Can I help you find it or would you rather just wander? You can just look, you know. You don't have to buy." Tom shakes his head. He can't get used to selling. Personally he would rather be left alone when he walks into a store. He would rather be completely ignored. But it's bad for business, he knows, to tell people not to buy, to discourage people from purchasing his products and tell them to just wander around touching things, leaving fingerprints on everything.

The man smiles nicely but says nothing, and continues walking up and down the aisles of the store.

Tom turns back to the TV. A talk show about aging and baby-boomers. Something about how the cosmetics industry is making a killing selling carcinogenic make-up to help women stay young. Tom tsks. He is constantly reassured as to why he stayed single, unmarried, unhitched. He need only look around at the other half of the world, look closely at their fear. He shakes his head back and forth.

Tom looks at his store. He looks at how tidy everything is, arranged by size, by price, by category. Everything is finely dusted and washed, the windows gleam, the carpet is vacuumed. He is proud of all his hard work, of the hours he spent painting the store, making it just right. He is pleased with the way he priced the products — stickers on the base of most things so that the price doesn't leap out at you, so that you have a chance to appreciate the beauty of the object before you know how much it costs. Tom likes that. He thinks that customers will then have a harder time refusing to buy the item.

"Oh my," Tom heard one nun say to another yesterday. "Look at that pose." They were staring hard at a small miniature of The Last Supper. "Just look at the beautiful eyes." The nun bought the minia-ture, even after she turned it over and gasped at the amount. "Oh dear," she said. "But it's worth it, isn't it?" and Tom wrapped it in crepe paper and packed it in a gift box. He made sure the nun thought that what she bought was special, that what she had spent her hard-earned money on (and Tom doesn't know if nuns earn money the same way other people do) was worth buying, was something she'll cherish.

What's the cost of a little gift box in the grand scheme of things, Tom thinks. What's the cost involved in making a customer want to come back to the store? It hurts no one and takes barely anything out of Tom's pocket. As a matter of fact, Tom thinks, if he gift wrapped everything for everyone he could up the price, cover his costs, so to speak, and make some money. Buy a bigger TV. Mount it above the security cameras where everyone who entered the store could see. Tom's been in the malls and clothing stores, the popular stores, and he knows that a little loud music and a flashing TV brings in customers.

Tom scratches his head. Some dry skin sprinkles on the counter. It makes him think again of the snow globe.

Tom knows that his enthusiasm for his store will soon run dry. It's bound to happen. He's seen it happen up and down Main Street. In the twenty-years that he's walked this street to and from Mack's Factory, he's seen at least one-hundred store changes. He's seen people come and go. It's all because they burn out. That initial feeling of success and satisfaction runs dry. They start losing money, losing patience, getting robbed and then . . .

Getting robbed?

Tom looks at the man in the leather jacket standing before him. He sits up straighter on his stool.

"Excuse me," the man says. It seems he's been trying to get Tom's attention for a few seconds. He is standing directly in front of Tom and staring intently into Tom's eyes.

"Yes?"

"Are you alright?"

"Yes." Tom feels sweaty. Too much pepper in that Thai food, he thinks.

"I was just wondering," the man begins.

But then the door opens and two nuns and a priest come laughing into the store. The bell above the door jingles as it shuts behind them. The man, interrupted in mid-sentence, stops talking and looks again at his boots. Tom wonders for a minute if the man has stepped in something outside of the store and is surreptitiously wiping it off on his nice, clean carpet. He sniffs loudly but doesn't smell anything foul.

"Can I help you find something?" Tom leans towards the man, feeling slightly annoyed. He's missed half his program and now the store is busy. The man is a nuisance. Just bored. Has nothing to do. Here to bug him, pester him. "Do you want to buy anything?"

"No," the man looks around, looks lost. The nuns and priest wander loudly around the store, touching everything in sight. One nun is wearing white gloves and she slyly rubs a finger over several surfaces as if testing for dust. "I can't find what I'm looking for. I've been looking. I just can't find it."

"But you haven't said . . . " Tom begins.

And then the man turns on his booted heels, quickly, and rushes out of the store.

Tom looks back down at the TV. He looks at the woman whose entire face peeled off after she wore a mud-mask for more than the allotted twenty-minutes. He looks at the burned marks on her chin and cheeks, at the scabbing, uncomfortable, painful red blistery parts. It baffles his mind, this, Tom thinks. Just baffles him.

The nuns and the priest buy candles, matches and several "Congratulations on Your Conversion" cards. one of the nuns takes a pocketful of candies from the complimentary dish Tom has placed nicely on the counter. She takes a handful and fills up her pocket. Twice. Tom gives her a friendly smile. He knows she'll be back.

The store is empty again and Tom hasn't moved from his stool. His breath still reeks and his stomach aches. He is filling up with gas. He's getting too old to eat Thai food, he thinks. He should be having soup and crackers for lunch, something easier to digest.

When Tom's mother died it surprised Tom how much money she had saved. Tom, having lived in her house on her pension until the day she died, had also managed to save quite a bit. Now that he thinks about it, all those meals of Kraft Dinner or baked beans, he can see how cheaply they both lived. After he buried her, Tom put all their money together, sat down with a financial planner, researched store options and bought this empty building. Lock stock and barrel. He bought everything. And then he quit his job as a welder. He converted the upstairs into store rooms and a small apartment, moved in, painted the downstairs and then walked up and down Main Street for a month trying to determine what was lacking in stores, what the needs of the people were. He didn't immediately think of Religious Supplies. It wasn't obvious. He thought first of a flower shop, or a variety store, or an underwear emporium. But all those things were available in some way or another up and down Main — the variety store sold flowers, for example — and so Tom searched far and wide for the most lucrative business he could find. Something that would never go under.

And he found it. Other than funeral homes, there is no other business, in Tom's estimation, that people desire more than a Religious Supply Store. Where else do the faithful turn to buy their prized objects? Where else do the clergy buy their clothes? Their rosaries? Their prayer books, hymn sheets, figurines, statues, candles, etc.? Tom saw a niche that was waiting to be filled. Of course there are other Religious Supply Stores in the city, but Tom was sure his would be the cleanest, the most accessible and, most importantly, in the best location — Main Street. Where else? The seminary is located over on Monroe and there are four churches just blocks away.

And Tom plans to branch out, fill the needs of the other religions and cultures in his society — Hinduism, Buddhism, maybe even some Jewish or Muslim supplies.

Tom gets off his stool and stretches. The talk show on aging is over and there are more babies in diapers chasing cartoon stars. And then he sees the man with the leather jacket again. He is standing across the road peering over at Tom's store, smoking a cigarette. No, a cigar. Tom is sure it is a cigar the man is smoking. The man puffs once, twice, looks at his cigar and then looks at Tom's store and then down at his boots.

Can it be possible that the man is staking out his store? Planning to rob him? or perhaps he is looking to injure Tom, just for fun. Tom has heard of gangs of men who terrorize store owners, beat them up, and then collect protection money. Protection from themselves, Tom supposes. Tom saw a show once, Oprah, or Jerry Springer, or maybe it was Cops, about a gang of young boys who terrorized a variety store owner until she shot them all one day when they came in to buy milk for their breakfast cereal. Tom doesn't want to get that paranoid. Besides, the man is alone and looks harmless enough. He is clean cut and his boots and jacket aren't anything out of the ordinary for the city or for Main Street. Tom has seen some priests who have looked more threatening than the man across the street. The man continues to puff and Tom continues to look out of the store and wonder.

The day ticks on. Tom is disturbed in his reveries several times. He watches two more talk shows and a soap opera he's been following all week. But each time a customer leaves Tom looks out again at the street and at the man leaning on a light pole. The man doesn't move. He just stares. And he smokes cigar after cigar after cigar. Tom is sure the man will get sick if he continues to smoke so many cigars. He is sure of this because once, when he was a bit younger, Tom smoked six cigars in a row and ended up vomiting on the card table during a poker game with some people from work. That was the first time he had been asked out and he was never asked back. Tom has always been a bit of a loner, a quiet man, and this suits him fine. He doesn't need friends to have a good time. Tom knows that if he wanted to he could make plenty of friends, but it's in his nature to be alone. He likes being alone. He likes the feeling of space he gets from being solitary in his mind. When too many people are talking at once Tom feels like his head is going to explode. And the strain of keeping up an interesting conversation, of holding his own side, is more than he can bear. That's what he likes about TV. Someone else carries the conversation and there are no uncomfortable gaps. No silences. No white space or nervous fidgeting times. Tom can just sit back, his arms crossed in front of him, and look down at the TV behind the counter, at the world in the box.

Out of the blue, it is five o'clock and time to close up the store. Tom is always surprised at how quickly the day goes now. When he was a machine welder he would be checking his watch every hour or so, having to listen to Fred or Nick go on and on and on about their exploits, their families, their boats or cars, but now, owning this store, he has time to watch TV, to let his mind wander, and when it wanders he loses track of time. It's a wonderful feeling, time passing quickly, the sun on the front of the store gone now and the inside lit up by a warm glow in the Spring sky.

Tom moves towards the front door to turn the OPEN sign to CLOSED. He locks the door and pulls the blind down. He turns off the TV. He turns the lights on in the display windows (to lure potential customers at night) and he turns the lights in the rest of the store off. Emptying out his cash register in the dark, Tom catches movement at the front window. He sees a glint of something metal, something reflected in the waning sunlight. But then, when he looks up, there is nothing there. Tom looks across the street for the man in the leather jacket, but he is gone. Tom shivers. The store is silent without the TV on and Tom's breath seems loud and guttural, almost unnatural.

He thought working with fire was dangerous, but the thought of being stalked, intruded upon, robbed, watched, is filling him with dread.

85   MICHELLE BERRY

Weigh the pros and the cons, Tom thinks. And the cons are imaginary — the pros are real. He hasn't yet been robbed, but he enjoys his store, he loves this kind of life. This solitariness. This emptiness. And look how much money he can sock away in the bank tonight. Tom counts the money and places it in his bank bag. He zips up the bag, rolls it and puts it under his belt buckle and shirt. Then he takes his coat off the peg at the back of the store, puts it on, zips it up, and leaves the store, startled for a second by the jingling bell above him.

Tom walks to the bank quickly. It unnerves him to carry this much money on his body. It makes him feel exposed, naked, vulnerable. He has never really felt worth anything to anyone but his mother, but carrying money like this every evening, to place in his bank account, always makes him feel worth a million bucks.

Tom waves politely up and down the street at the other store owners who wave back as they close up shop. He feels like a king surveying something of which he owns. Awnings are rolled in, sidewalks are swept, displays in the windows are taken down or locked up. Everyone is going home for supper. Tom makes it to the bank, deposits the bag and walks back down Main Street towards the store, intending to head up to his apartment, price some more figurines, have a late supper and watch TV in bed. The thought of his seven snow globes glistening with the light from the lamppost outside his window makes him feel sleepy. But, as he nears the store, he can see the man in the leather jacket standing just in front of the door, looking in. Tom stops. He watches the man. The man places his hand on the doorknob and turns it. Then the man shakes the locked door hard, kicks it a bit, and rests his forehead on the cold glass.

Tom doesn't know whether to approach the man or turn away. He thinks he might be safer if he went to the Pizza Factory, had a nice dinner, and came home later, but then he wonders if, left alone, the man will do damage to his store. Or perhaps he will hide and, when Tom strolls back along Main Street, the man will jump out at him. And, on a pizza-full stomach and a couple of mugs of beer, Tom might not be able to protect himself.

Why pick my store, Tom thinks? Why mine? Unless the man knows how lucrative this business is, unless the man has robbed this kind of store before . . .

But all his money is locked safely in the bank. Tom doesn't even leave five dollars in the float. The tray is open so that anyone peering in can see that it is empty. His store is locked up for the night. And Tom is free to walk away. Let the police deal with a man banging his head on a window. Tom can go eat pizza and relax.

He turns.

But for some reason he turns back. He walks up to his store, up to the man, and says, "Can I help you with anything?" It's as if in owning a store, a religious store, Tom can be confessor and forgiver. As if he's invincible. Tom suddenly feels the weight of the woman with the burned and peeled face on TV this afternoon crash down upon him. He feels her sorrow, her guilt, her sadness, her fear. Tom wishes he could reach out and stroke the woman's cheek, tell her that faith will make everything better, but then Tom smiles at his idea because it's the idea of a salesman, a store owner. If she is faithful, he will sell more religious supplies. Faith. What is it really? Tom thinks.

Swivelling on his booted heels, the man in the leather jacket doesn't have time to disguise the pained expression in his eyes. Tom is stunned by the look. The man quickly glances down at his boots.

"What's wrong? Can I help you?" Tom tries again. His shoulders and neck and arms are tense. He hasn't felt this nervous since he was a small boy and the other boys at school would turn away from him on the play-ground. Or turn towards him and taunt him and kick him and beat him.

"I'm looking for something . . . "

"Yes?" Tom was once looking for something, looking to be saved, but he found it here in his store. Complete isolation, omnipotence. A store owner. He can sit high on his stool and look down at the world. He can sell or refuse sale. He can talk to the priests, to the nuns, or talk to no one at all. He is saved, he supposes. He is safe.

The man stands with his arms dangling by his side. "You closed the store. I'm looking for something . . . "

"It was five o'clock," Tom says. "I close the store at five o'clock. I'm open again at nine tomorrow."

"But you were busy all day," the man says. "I couldn't come in when you were so busy."

Tom raises his eyebrows. He knows there were moments in his day when the store was completely empty, moments when the man could have walked across the street and entered the store and bought whatever it is he was looking for.

"What do you need?" Tom asks.

"I need," the man says. "What you have."

"What?"

"I need what you have."

"I don't understand."

The man shrugs. "Neither do I."

Tom looks closely at him. "Are you alright?" Tom asks. "Can I take you to the doctor?"

The man laughs suddenly. His mouth open, his laugh echoing around the now-empty Main Street.

"The doctor," the man says. "That's funny."

"Look," Tom says. "I have to go home now. I have to go up to my apartment and eat supper and watch TV. You can come back tomorrow if you need something from the store."

The man stops laughing and looks up at Tom's blackened apartment window. "You live up there?"

"That's not important," Tom says.

"Okay," the man says. He stands back from Tom and looks at him. "Okay, here's the story. I've done something bad. Very bad. And I'm looking for something." The man pauses and looks over his shoulder. "Something that will take it all away. Something that will . . . " He stops talking — sighs. "Something that will make everything better."

Tom stands completely still.

"Something," the man now whispers. "I'm looking for something. Can you help me?'

All Tom wanted was to open a little store, have a nice income, settle into his advancing, lonely, quiet age like a mother-hen. He wanted to roost. No more talking, always talking, to the other welders at work. About their wives, their kids, their vacations, their ups and downs. No more taking care of his elderly mother. Fetching her soda crackers and licorice sticks. Nothing. No one. Tom wanted to sit on his stool behind his counter loaded with rosaries and votive candles, silver crosses and Jesus figurines, and think about nothing, absolutely nothing. He assumed that the religious who entered his life, walked in and out of his store, would be quiet and contained, would have no problems that needed discussing. Nothing more important than a rip or a stain in a clerical collar, a broken crown of thorns. And now, in one day, a week into the job, this man in front of him has made him again be beholden to someone, again have to take responsibility for another man's actions.

Tom sighs.

The man before him sighs, mimicking Tom. "Something," he whispers. "I'm hunting for something, I guess, something to make everything better." He laughs politely.

Tom looks into the man's eyes. He searches that painful expression, those sad and lonely pupils, and he says, "Come in then. We'll find whatever it is you are looking for."

"Thank you," the man says. "Thank you."

Tom thinks suddenly that life is about balance. About the balancing, tilting, careful weighing of what is important and what is not.

After opening the door of the store, listening intently for the jingle of bells above and turning on the lights, Tom leads the man in, places a hand on his shoulder and walks him forward into the cleanliness, over the fresh-vacuumed carpet. He feels a bit like God. Or Jesus. Leading the injured forward. The sick. The needy. "I found what I was looking for, I guess," Tom says. "I guess I really did. Didn't I?" Tom smiles. "Maybe you can find what you are looking for, too."

The man walks slowly up and down the aisles of Hunting for Something, his hands in his leather jacket pockets, his eyes staring intently down at all the items before him. And Tom watches the man move. He sits up high on his stool, the TV flickering below him, and he watches the man wander slowly up and down his store. The black sky outside is awash with stars. It startles Tom that he can see so many stars shining high above Main Street in the city. And then a feeling of somethingness creeps into Tom's soul. A somethingness which quickly replaces the nothingness that was there before. Maybe, Tom thinks, maybe this is the way of the world.

MICHELLE BERRY

PHILIP QUINN has appeared in such magazines as *Broken Pencil* and *Quarry*. He is soon to release a novel, *The Double,* and a book of short stories.

That Great Mouth Correctly Hurt

PHILIP QUINN

AUGUSTUS AND EMILY CARR BLACK ARE STANDING on the Gerrard Street bridge which crosses the Don River. From the sidewalk, they can see the older section of the Don Jail and the river of cars heading north and south on the Parkway.

A cool evening breeze tugs on her black peasant dress like a spiteful child. To turn her attention to what? The vibration of the cars in the cement? The ghost faces painted by the earlier rain onto the pavement?

The river moves slowly with the weight of a full moon and thousands of other lights. Her blood. And of course, her boy-man, that wait, as he struggles with yet another phantom.

"That shit with Gillian Mania has fucked me up. She sent me back to the school . . . I went there. I saw her in the window . . . remembered how it had been. I don't know who I really am, she's right about that . . . only who I can be . . . possibly anyone. I . . . I . . . no . . . I can't say it . . . no . . . the controls are too powerful."

"What?"

"Can't tell yah. Can't. Can't."

"Have to now and no phony accents."

"There is a special someone I've always wanted to be."

"That's better . . . Ray's son? Or my son?"

"More . . . I want to be a woman."

"That's not entirely unexpected."

"No, an actual woman . . . Jackie. Will you help me?"

Jackie? Trying to retrieve bits and pieces of JFK's skull from the back of that Lincoln Continental. And Augustus? Trying to retrieve bits and pieces of his own blown apart skull by becoming that graven image. Even though her own image of Jackie was more up-to-date. While leafing through *Publishers Weekly* magazine, she'd come across photographs of Jackie in her role as a Doubleday book editor, attending special Manhattan literary events. Her face too tight from the many lifts, and even the mouth thinner and less powerful.

Still, why not see where his latest preoccupation would flow.

The next day, she took him to a shop on Queen Street that sold vintage women's clothing.

After searching through a large bin, they finally found a classic pill box hat. But white. However, she knew of a place on Spadina that could dye it. He paid the fifty dollars and decided to carry it like a pet instead of in the box.

Next they took the subway car across town to the Goodwill and Salvation Army stores on Parliament Street. They looked through all the clothes until they found this double-breasted woman's suit with wide lapels. It was green but again she knew it could be dyed. There was also a collection of women's wigs and he selected two dark brown pieces that could be brushed into something that would sit on his now completely shaved head.

He paid seven dollars for all of it and again insisted on carrying the clothes, hair and hat in his arms like the lightweight remnants of a favorite aunt who had simply faded away. They walked further north until they found a Chinese grocery store which sold plastic red roses. He bought his bouquet.

A week later, Emily Carr Black shows up at this hotel room with the hat, skirt and jacket dyed the proper shade of pink. The lapels on the jacket were, of course, colored black.

Taped to his full length mirror is that blown-up photograph of Lyndon Baines Johnson taking the oath of office in Air Force One. Jackie stands beside him.

"Show me how to do the mouth."

He hands her a gold tube of lipstick and puckers his lips as if for a kiss. She paints them heavy but sad. He dresses, putting on his favorite black bra and panties, garter belt and black nylon stockings, then the pink skirt and jacket after spilling ketchup on the front.

Before the mirror, he sets the hair pieces on his head, then holds them in place with the pink pill box hat. He puts on a pair of white gloves and assumes a high heels power stance, but with his head properly bowed and that great mouth correctly hurt. She hands him the plastic bouquet of roses.

"What do you think?"

"Well, Jackie. You haven't worn well. But that was to be expected. There is one question I've always wanted to ask you. Why after that first shot, didn't you push him down into the seat instead of leaving him hanging there for that fantastic Zapruder head shot?"

In his soft little girl's voice he answers:

"Vanity. My stupid vanity. He was bleeding. And I didn't want to get blood on my favorite suit. And, of course, there was that Marilyn thing."

The problem with Augustus playing the role of Jackie was that by its very nature it was extremely limited. For example, he had no funeral to organize — even if he had Boris's hearse — and, of course, no Caroline or John-John to look after, even if, occasionally, he saw little Gywnne.

He could hope for a future Aristotle Onassis, maybe meet him in some Greek bar, allow him to paw the goods in return for being promised a yacht ride on Lake Ontario. But really all he could do is "ride the car," so he rented a VCR and an assassination videotape containing the Zapruder film. Over and over again, he studied the ten-second sequence of 'shots' until he had it down pat.

Motorcycle cop. Old Glory flapping on the hood of the Lincoln Continental. Jack's right hand waving. Then he goes into a blocking position, hands clenched in front of his face, as if he's playing another game of touch football. Jackie bends her head down to ask what's wrong. Grabs with right hand his left arm, moves her head in front of his, then Jack's furiously nodding yes. She wraps her arms around his humpty-dumpty head then pushes off with her left hand. Jack falls forward.

Then begins the great modern dance that has spawned such derivatives as break dancing.

He acts it out on the floor of his apartment. Jackie crawling onto the back of the Lincoln Continental, doing this rapid hand tap, trying to play tag with the secret service agent and make him it.

But he realized that the tight pink skirt was too confining, the dance really wasn't his dance. And there was the tribal violation of playing the pre-Onassis, still virginal, still beloved Jackie. The grieving and courageous widow. And if he got a little excited from wearing the clothes and brought himself off, he saw the white stain on the pink skirt as just more brain tissue.

So just as quickly as Jackie found him, she left him, buried him and so he had to reach out again. For other rays of light.

PHILIP QUINN

CHRISTOPHER TAYLOR is a Vancouver journalist.

Diary of a Cultural Exile

CHRISTOPHER TAYLOR

LA Airport, Nov. 1

AS I LEAVE NORTH AMERICA for the jungles of southeast asia, I wonder about the nature of the culture I am leaving: the culture that has captured the imagination of the planet, with its magical melange of assault weapons, decaf espresso, and O.J. Simpson defense lawyers. Perhaps, while abroad, I will learn to yearn for the testimony of Police Criminologist Dennis Fung: nostalgic for a culture, whose instinct is to accelerate into a Kato Kaelin. This is North America at terminal velocity, in low-speed freeway chases, the whereabouts of Latino housekeepers, or the exact melting time of bowls of spumoni ice cream. I do have a culture, I do I do I do, and it involves unemployed houseguests and their six-figure publishing advances. This is what would come out of the cyclotron, clarifying, clarifying, the ghee of American society. Culture confined to a former Hertz spokesman and his discarded knapsack. I say this from the departure lounge of the LA airport, where I am not far from Judge Lance Ito. We are sharing the same smog.

LA Airport, Nov. 1

If — as the saying goes — a butterfly beating its wings in China will create mudslides in Santa Ynez, my airport dinner of breaded sole could conceivably play a crucial role in the trial strategy of prosecutor Marcia Clark — or, for that matter, the credibility of Det. Mark Fuhrman. It sobers you: your hearty minestrone, your casual choice of beverage. Responsibilities amidst the salad bar condiments. I eat deliberately. This is my last thought before I am extricated from a culture.

LA-Jakarta, plane, Nov. 2

I am wondering if Generation X was a product of the US military, as much as deformed Cambodian children or LSD guinea pigs in Canadian neurological hospitals. Rather than exposing unsuspecting millions to insidious bacterial agents or sarin nerve gas, releasing controlled doses of The Brady Bunch or Gilligan's Island. It's a grand, Burbank-friendly experiment in biological warfare: snatches of sitcom dialogue sprayed over the populace to see the future effects. The Hot Zone of slapstick comedy, biohazard experts approaching scripts in space suits. Worse than anthrax, or Ebola. The brutality of war.

Jakarta, Java, Indonesia, Nov. 2

Theater idea: an updated version of Jean-Paul Sartre's "No Exit": the play that made famous the adage, "Hell is other people." Scene: the baggage claim of the Jakarta airport. Players: Guatemalans, convinced the world is an LA barrio, testing the current of stun guns for camcorders; a stuttering Dutch man endlessly repeating the tragedy of his parents-in-laws' pig-raising business; and a German named Norbert in furniture design, who spends his days in bars talking of either the injustice of the world economic system, or of his twelve-year-old whore.

Jakarta, Nov. 3

While channel surfing from Aaron Spelling's Models Inc. to a Qu'ranic lecture on Indonesian television, I have become fascinated by local programming wars. Do they have the equivalent, for instance, of Fox stealing mosque coverage from CBS for an exorbitant sum, luring over Terry Bradshaw and Pat Summerall to jazz up the halftime show? The nightly call to prayer going up against a poorly dubbed version of vintage Charlie's Angels? A challenge for Brandon Tartikoff: to prove that enlightenment and ad dollars can mix, goddammit.

Jakarta, Nov. 3

I am the Silkwood of sitcoms, body irradiated by my pseudo-culture, emerging from my Boeing 737 a scrubbed-down Meryl Streep, setting off sensors with ions emitted by memory of cheesy dialogue and physical comedy set a southern Californian apartment block. The half-life of Mr. Roper or Don Knotts rivaling that of uranium-235. Sitcom melanoma, from being in the cultural mines too long: we should leave it in barrels, far from any active ecosystem. Episodes of Chips and other lethal microbes, buried in the muds of North Pacific ocean floors, or sealed within the mountains of South Dakota.

Pangandaran, Java, Nov. 5

No doubt because of syndication costs, Indonesian programmers tend to run generic American shows never seen in America, a continent and a cultural theory distilled into its elements of guns and bad dialogue. These shows are so Zen, overproduced koans with extras and hairdressing staffs: usually hosted by Michael Landon, they look into such gripping topics as youth penal systems, and the travails of convicts on fishing trips. Things that the Indonesian government would like to have us believe is representative of Western culture, like minors throwing up over the sides of boats.

Pangandaran, Nov. 6

I have made an important discovery, in that no matter how far you are from cell phones in the backs of airline seats, how far from the land of focus groups and reaction dials, you will never escape the infomercial. There will always and forever more be revelation in cassette form, complete with complimentary salad spinner and day planner. There will always be faceless chimney sweeps whose productivity went up 50%, teachers who can now solve math problems more quickly because of having achieved Nirvana, people who have made the potentially treacherous transition from pro football to enlightenment. This is the Fran Tarkenton nebula, a world populated by syrupy salesmen in cardigans, buttering up viewers with the unstated suggestion that you, too, could be that spokesperson, and speak in pseudo-erotic tones of motivating principles and Highly Effective Habits.

Probolinggo, Java, Nov. 8

Note to Biblical scholars: I think Paul on the road to Damascus must have had an Indonesian driver. I say this because I too almost became a Christian on the road from Mt. Bromo to Probolinggo, the site of this particular conversion being the chassis of a 1979 Toyota. Heartfelt appeals to Christ, Buddha, Don Rickles — anything to complete the journey alive in a minivan (with 40 people) whose engine was overheating directly underneath a dignified Javanese lady, she of the noble carriage and the severe steam burns.

Night bus to Bali, Nov. 9

"Porno. You know porno?" the local Elvis with the moussed hair exclaimed, as he unfolded some faded picture of a white model morosely holding her breast, cut from a Nixon-era Penthouse. He obviously saw this treasure as subversive, cutting edge, putting him on the same mental wavelength as the Western masses. Our psyches laid out for inspection alongside the stereo ads, encoded in the pouting lips and the come-hither expression he's committed to memory. I began to wonder if he was so wrong. Maybe I should carry around those photos to gain a better understanding of myself, to uncover the deep secrets of my skin: a collective heritage, in the neon lipstick and the breast cupped for the camera. Seeing it like pious children in the former Yugoslavia see Mother Mary in the hillsides, or amongst the heavy artillery pieces; I will see that image materializing before me, eager to impart its knowledge, privates assembling in all their brightness. Our

CHRISTOPHER TAYLOR

Elvis as a Javanese John the Baptist, clearing the way for the lord, making his paths straight, on the night bus to Denpasar.

Kuta Beach, Bali, Nov. 10

In Bali, the richest of cultures in culture-rich Indonesia, what I was not expecting to see was a neon green Fry Guy walking jauntily through a traditional temple gate. To set the scene: I stand before a McDonald's mural at that multinational's particularly profitable franchise on Kuta's Legian St. Beneath the split gate are artists' renditions of a Big Mac; a double cheeseburger; a particularly heartfelt Filet-O-Fish. To the right is that clarion call of capitalism, Ronald McDonald, his red bouffant hairdo framing a multi-level Hindu temple. There is Hamburglar, his usual black-and-white-striped prison garb now with a climate-specific floral trim. He is offering a handful of fries to an obviously grateful local resident, emaciated baby slung over her back. I see Grimace on the neighboring island of Lombok, lounging with Mai Tai in hand, floral soft cap, and yellow flared sunglasses. To the left of the gate there is Irian Jaya, invaded by the Indonesian military twenty years ago (its incorporation recognized by the UN soon after), where a pair of Fry Guys prance in baby blue hightops, purple and orange surfboards slung over Fry shoulders, flouncing by a smiling native busy on a sculpture. The country is distilled to its essence: a large Komodo dragon; the spectacular Buddhist temples of Borobudur; and, of course, the flagship Jakarta franchise, with its two-story inflatable Ronald McDonald: Big Brother, in a red-and-yellow-striped jumpsuit.

Kuta, Nov. 11

I'm wondering about the Southeast Asian equivalent of the Elvis cult: whether some Indonesian singing sensation, enamored with polyester, prescription drugs and/or peanut butter and bacon sandwiches, is consistently sighted in the produce section of local supermarkets fifteen years after his death. Whether Asian tabloids put crudely doctored photos of said star into the receptive arms of his professed latest mistress. Whether the region breathlessly follows theories of how he died only days ago, in the throes of a diabetic coma, or perhaps hopelessly irradiated after an alien abduction. An Asian Graceland, in which said star is still said to lurk: ghostly behind picture windows, hints of jewel-encrusted bodysuit appearing on a German tourist's film negatives.

Uluwatu, Bali, Nov. 13

As I look out over the rocky coast of southern Bali, I think of a Toronto dominatrix who had herself incorporated. I like the idea of tax shelters for the sadomasochistic, it's so . . . Western. A culture crystallized, in a leather harness written off as a business expense.

Ubud, Bali, Nov. 14

One thing to keep in mind here is that Indonesians don't understand English unless you use the same misspellings and mispronunciations as they do. Our words are modern Patty Hearsts, abducted and surviving in a strange environment, like polar bears at the San Diego Zoo. You see these hardy sorts primarily on T-shirts: "High Energy for a World Style"; "Floral Concerto"; "The Best of Danger"; "Keep On Thrash Line." They make no sense together, are surviving on their imagined import and a fabricated meaning, a life out of context. They are words chosen for their sexiness, the bathing suit competition of the English language, disparate words and catch phrases overheard and thrown together with no other qualifications than bust size. A grammatical Amsterdam, words put behind bars and made to stand in suggestive poses, the red light district of syntax. A politically incorrect parade, surviving on outposts like Ubud in the forests of central Bali.

Ubud, Nov. 16

As I consider the Guaci Molle offered on a local menu, I feel like a backpacking Winston Smith, taken away to the dreaded Ministry of Grammar for language retraining. Two plus two equals five, and proper conjugation is a plot of enemies of the state. Two Minutes Hate for capable spellers. Big Brother Likes Mispronunciation. Newspeak, alive and well and thriving in Balinese snackbars.

Lovina Beach, Bali, Nov. 17

Did you know: that Indonesians make puns on the name of Lorenzo Lamas? Veterans of soap operas and failed action/adventure series who once performed trapeze acts with Ricky Schroeder on "Battle of the Network Stars" live on in Indonesian slang, past stardom preserved in this linguistic amber. I wonder who else could be so excavated, their memories still luminous in the trash talk of far-flung countries? Herve Villechaize? Florence Henderson? They've been incorporated, without their consent, into foreign vocabularies. We'll have to send Ross Perot over with Christmas gifts, letters from loved ones and Meals-Ready-to-Eat for these cultural MIAS, demanding their whereabouts. Withholding normalized trade relations until all lounge singers have been accounted for.

Lovina, Nov. 18

I have discovered, to my horror, that a Christmas Reggae Disco album is climbing the Asian charts. It includes such standards as O Tanenbaum, I Saw Mommy Kissing Santa Claus, and We Three Kings of Orient Are set to a thumping backbeat and Gloria Gaynor samples. A tear comes to my eye as I think, there are some people who will never hear a Burl Ives extended remix. This is the ultimate koan, the question to which there is no answer. Do Zen masters include this album in their disciplines, a meditation on aging folksingers and their competing basslines? Burl, you are my one hand clapping. I can hear him now, the disco beat wafting gently through Japanese rock gardens. Images of John Travolta, selected Village People, Elvis in Hawaii flashed at random throughout the Zen compound. Like a Tennessee Williams play, words forming the backdrop, only this time it's Abba lyrics: "Dancing Queen, feel the heat of the tambourine." Matins with Donna Summer, early Michael Jackson; the sounds the first thing to rouse the senses in the morning. The disco equivalent of incense, a delicate mix of musical herbs: a touch of Andy Gibb, a tantalizing hint of "Play That Funky Music White Boy." Rows of shaved and dedicated ascetics chanting the lyrics to "Staying Alive," unlocking their profundity. The power of these words, working for universal peace. I see an image, a craggy, isolated mountain peak, surrounded by miles of pristine forest — undisturbed, save for the strains of "Disco Inferno," spilling out over the rosy-fingered dawn. "Burn, baby, burn." All time is geared towards that moment, on that Nietzschean mountain, when a dance mix will induce total enlightenment. Early Pointer Sisters under the Bodhi Tree. Deciding whether to engage oneself in the world, or to linger in disco nirvana. Oh, to be a cultural bodhisattva, not resting until everyone has moved to the canned rhythm, until every song has been bastardized into dancehall reggae with mispronounced lyrics. I will be the last one over the wall, willfully holding back until the last possible moment, when I will enter the land that flows with milk, honey, and Gloria Gaynor soundalikes.

Sengiggi Beach, Lombok, Nov. 20

I have just seen the end of the universe, when things will accelerate to such a speed that they will spontaneously break down, implode, restore the natural flow to entropy. The signs of humanity's achievement scattered and meaningless in a newly primitive world. I saw all this, naturally, on a t-shirt at Lombok's Sengiggi Beach. I will quote it in its entirety, to preserve the integrity of its chaos: "bigwavesareinsane idonf know if fhey are the ulfi in surfing i know fhey are fo so surfe." I like the idea of wearing this shirt, with its implicit declaration of the End Times. Perhaps it's linguistic terrorism: first the World Trade Centre or Oklahoma City federal buildings — next, proper syntax. The grammatical equivalent of a car bombing. Our language like smuggled nuclear material, its power no longer in our control. Pushing Linguistic Non-Proliferation Treaties on breakaway Soviet republics. At terminal velocity the engine of language shuts down, and this t-shirt is the result: words assembled randomly, the wonderful end of grammar, Javanese Jabberwocky. The Joycean brilliance of it, the reinvention of language, an affirmation of the capacities of words: Finnegan's Wake on 70% polyester. It is too nonsensical, it must be a deliberate project, a rethinking of the fundamentals of communication. A bulletin for the literary world: James Joyce lives, and he works for an Indonesian subsidiary of Hanes. It's the final deconstruction, on sale three for five dollars. The undermining of meaning, available in large or extra large. Armageddon — pre-shrunk.

PETER DARBYSHIRE is a Toronto writer. His work has appeared in forums across North America.

Still

PETER DARBYSHIRE

"CNN," MY MOTHER SAID when I answered the phone. "Quick."

"I'm a little busy," I said.

"I can't believe it," she said.

CNN was in mid-broadcast of a live car chase. Helicopter shot from above. A cluster of black-and-white cruisers slowly following a blue pickup through freeway traffic. The sound was off on my set but I could hear the commentator's distant voice coming from my parents' television. There was a bit of an echo.

"Hello?" my mother asked. "Still there?"

"Where else would I be?"

"It's California," my father said on the other extension, the one in my old bedroom. That explained the echo. I pictured him lying on my *Empire Strikes Back* bedspread, looking at the posters still on the walls. The white Ferrari, David Lee Roth, the Hawaiian Tropic girls. My mother alone on the living room couch, wrapped in her favorite pink afghan.

"He hijacked the truck," she said, "and went on a rampage, shooting at people and driving into them."

"I didn't see any of that," my father said.

"It happened earlier," she said. "The announcer told me while you were in the bathroom." She cleared her throat. "Anyway, I figure he's one of those people that are everywhere in California. You know the kind I mean."

"A vegetarian?" I asked. "An actor?"

"A druggie," she said, lowering her voice. "After he hijacked the truck — "

"Wait," I said. "Did he hijack the truck or steal it? Is there someone in it with him?"

"No," she said. "He forced them out at gunpoint."

"That's theft then," I said. "Not hijacking. Hijacking would be if he'd brought them along, if he had hostages."

"Really?"

"I'm pretty sure."

"I had no idea," my mother said.

"Where was I for all this?" my father muttered. I could hear the old springs of my bed squeak as he shifted around.

The pickup tried to pass on the shoulder and hit the guardrail, bouncing off and into a white van. Both vehicles stopped for a moment, and the police cruisers slowed. Then the pickup rolled forward again. It drove past one off-ramp after another, hesitating slightly at each one, as if looking for something.

"What I want to know," my mother said, "is where he's going." There was a long pause, then she added, "So, how are you?"

"Good," I said. "You?"

"Oh, you know. Fine." Another few seconds of dead air, during which the truck finally took an off-ramp into a run-down neighborhood. Then she asked, "How's work?"

"All right," I said. My last contract had run out two weeks earlier.

"That's good," she said. "Because these days . . . "

"Yes," I said.

She hummed a little while the truck drove through the parking lot of a boarded-up Kmart. My father belched softly and sighed. "Crazy from the heat," he said.

"Any new ladies in your life?" my mother suddenly asked.

"I had a wrong number the other day," I said. "We talked for a while."

"Oh, that's just like your father and me," she said, her voice rising a little.

"We met over the phone, isn't that right, hon?"

"Mm-hm."

Police cruisers blocked both ends of the narrow street now. The pickup turned at an intersection. Zoom out. An alley between old warehouses, no place to turn again. More cruisers approaching the opposite end.

"He called to talk to his cousin," my mother went on. "Only she was in the shower. We'd just been sunbathing in the backyard, you see, and we had lotion all over us. I showered later, when I got home. But first I answered the phone and your father thought I was his cousin. He started talking like he knew me, and he was just so nice and funny that I went along with it. Well, we all had a good laugh about it when he found out, but we'd gotten on so well that he asked me out for a date. I said yes, of course, and the next thing I knew I was walking down the aisle with him. And now here we are. Isn't that right?"

"Mm-hm."

Police cruisers blocked both ends of the narrow street now. The pickup stopped in the middle.

"Isn't that nice," my mother said. "I hope things work out."

"This isn't quite like that," I said.

"Still," she said.

Zoom in. A man in jeans and a white t-shirt jumped out of the pickup. He had a pistol in his hand. He started running for one of the warehouses and then a little pink cloud puffed from his head. He fell to the ground. Nothing moved but the camera.

"That's gotta hurt," my father said.

"I don't know what things are coming to when this can happen here," my mother sighed.

"It's happening in California," I pointed out.

"Still," she said.

"Well, I should probably go," I said. "Have to get up for work in the morning."

"Wait! Your father hasn't told you his news yet."

"News?" I asked.

Black-clad officers approached the fallen man slowly, guns levelled, like they expected him to rise at any moment.

My father cleared his throat. "You remember my back problems?" he asked. "My crushed verticals?"

"Vertebrae," I said. Three of them were fused together in his lower back, the result of twenty years driving a truck. He hadn't been able to walk straight in years, let alone work. The doctors had given up on him.

"Yeah," he said, "they're gone."

"What, the vertebrae?"

"No, the problems."

"What do you mean, gone?" I asked. "How could that happen?"

"You know that preacher on television, Jerry Falwell?" he asked.

"Yes," I said slowly. One of the cops nudged the man with a foot, flipping him over. He stared up at the helicopter, his face a blur from the distance.

"We were watching him the other day," my father said, "when he told everyone he'd been touched by God just before the show started."

"Well, not really God," my mother interrupted. "He said it was an angel whispering in his ear."

"They work for God," my father said. "That's the same thing in my book."

"Your back," I pleaded.

"Right. He said that God told him there'd be a trucker watching that day, one with back problems. He told me to touch the television set. Said he'd heal me if I confessed my sins and believed. So I went and kneeled in front of our television and put my arms around it. And I, ah, I talked about a few different things. But the most important thing was I was healed. I believed, son."

I had this vision, then, of thousands of unemployed truckers across North America — the world even — kneeling on their shaggy carpets, hugging their television sets, confessing their sins, while their wives looked on and wept.

"And my back problems are gone now," my father finished. "Not so much as an itch left."

"Healed by television," I said.

"Television and God," he said.

PETER DARBYSHIRE

"Well." I didn't know what else to say. "Well. I think I really have to go now."

"Isn't that something?" my mother asked.

"Yes, it certainly is."

One cop handcuffed the body and then another threw a blanket over it.

"I was there," my mother said. "I saw it all."

TODD BABIAK has appeared in *Blood and Aphorisms* and *Prism International*. He has recently completed his first novel, *Interception*, and is in the process of finding a publisher.

Bad Magic For Beginners

TODD BABIAK

IT TURNS OUT THE RUBBER PLANT Richard bought for his wife is infested with bugs. Tiny bugs who fly lazy circles around the big spatula arms. He slaps at an assembly of them and a few fall to the floor. Afraid they might spread to other living evidence of his love for Yvelaine, he stomps on the vanquished. If the phone were cordless, he tells himself, he'd wet some paper towel and wipe them up, the dead. But the phone isn't cordless.

"Hello?"

"Hi Martha. Is this Martha? It's Richard. Richard Kern."

"Yes Richard."

Slapping absently at a few more tiny bugs, Richard laughs a hopeful laugh. "So how the hell *are* you, Martha? Eh? Been taking care of yourself all right?"

"Fine."

"Okay. Great news. Just great." Richard laughs again, the same laugh. After a silence, listening to Martha's breathing, he coughs and nods his head and smiles and stops smiling. A car is honking outside, a blue Jeep Wrangler. Pulling the thin curtain aside, Richard squints at the driver. "Y'know Martha, there's a young guy in a Jeep outside the window here, honking away. Must be waiting for Carrie, the girl next door. Really honking."

"Can I help you with something, Richard?"

He twists the phone cord around his pointer finger. "Well I just thought I'd call to catch up. See if you wanted to grab a coffee some time if you're not too busy. We could talk."

"Why?"

Richard wishes he could see these bugs more closely. What is it they're doing, exactly? Eating the plant? Sticking a finger in the dirt, Richard realizes the rubber plant is dying. Lack of water. Yvelaine has not been watering her gift.

"I don't know."

Yvelaine picks at the raspberry seed in her teeth and sniffs at something.

"What *is* that?"

"It ain't me, if that's what you're thinking." Richard clips the next nail, sniffs too. Investigating the clipping, Richard smiles, pleased with its size and texture. Shiny, smooth, hard. A representative chunk. After giving her foot a celebratory rub with his supporting hand, Richard flicks the piece of her into the corner behind him, with the others.

"Smells like something's *rotting*, Rick."

What he's thinking is: does the candlelight flatter my chest and complexion? And my eyes and my cheekbones? Because it used to. He wonders about the top of his head.

"You almost done?" She lifts and stretches her leg, splashing him. "Because the water's getting cold. I'm cramping in here and pruning up. My hands are prunes. That's all I need, heading into my twilight years. More wrinkles."

"Done." Richard is more than pleased with his sample of Yvelaine. "Hey, sweets, you been watering your rubber plant? It's — "

"It's that awful temperature between hot and cold in here. It feels greasy and thick. Maybe it's the water that's smelly."

"It's the temperature of blood. Our temperature, body temperature. The water, sweets, has actually become an extension of our — "

"Why are you smiling like that, Rick? It's creepy. And I don't get why you're collecting my toenail clippings on the ledge. I told you they'd go down the drain with the rest of the water. You better not forget them there, that's what."

"I won't."

Greg comes tomorrow. Richard is collecting his wife's toenail clippings just in case.

There wasn't any kind of choice. Richard joined the Distinctive Book Club because Yvelaine said he was turning into a *regular dullard*. Seconds after he attempted to initiate a lively discussion about hockey at their last dinner party, Yvelaine kicked him under the table. And one afternoon when she caught him watching a *Full House* re-run, she blew a cloud of smoke in his direction and asked if she could bring him a six pack and a bag of chips. She told Richard's mom — his mom! — that his four years of university were leaking out his pores. His mom wrote a long letter. *We won't have dummies in this family.*

Dr. Kinneal, the expert panelist on the midnight DBC infomercial said, "A lethargic brain can transform your life into a sluggish and morose collection of episodes not worth remembering. One must read constantly," Dr. Kinneal stressed, his hands clasped hopefully, "to keep one's mind active and to amend one's popularity in the workplace and at social gatherings." Testimony from more than one DBC member supported Dr. Kinneal's findings. A woman in a yellow muumuu found the love of her life, an equally stout gentleman, after repeating a few lines from *Understanding Surrealism* at a retirement party; and a teenager overcame his acne-related shyness by absorbing the wisdom of *Secrets of the New Shamanism: from the mountains to the suburbs.*

Since the first three books were only one penny, plus shipping and handling and tax, Richard called the 800 number and joined DBC. The operator was pleasant, chewing something. Chewing. That reminded Richard: Sara Lee.

Greg is back from Germany, where he had been working in telecommunications. The divorce is final.

Greg is a cousin by marriage, a cousin of a cousin. Not blood, not officially. Richard has seen pictures: Greg and Yvelaine pre-teen slow-dancing at a family wedding, Greg and Yvelaine at the go-kart track, downhill skiing, in a canoe, on horseback, in Kung Fu class, the archer's club, high school graduation.

After hanging up the phone - a two hour conversation — Yvelaine had tears in her eyes, laughter tears. "Oh God, Rick, he is *so* funny, so intelligent. It'll be terrific to see him. You two'll get along so well."

So well. Swell. The way she looked out the window, smiling, grated on Richard's nerves. The way she uncorked a bottle of white wine and sat in the living-room, smiling, made his legs itch. Richard knew better than to show his distaste for the whole *idea* of Greg, so he sat with Yvelaine and they drank together, silent.

Then, after one glass each, Yvelaine laughed. "No wonder it didn't last. I can't see Greg in any *relationship*. Too impulsive, spontaneous."

Impulsive. Spontaneous. Richard fills his glass, just his, and walks into the kitchen. Opening the freezer door, he considers how Yvelaine had said the word relationship. The same way she might say *Hollywood*.

Oh, Richard can't sleep. The image of Greg's hair, black and shoulder-length like in the high school photos. Or worse, tied back into a pony tail. An Armani suit and a pony tail, that's it, and way over six feet.

Slapping his pillow, running his fingers over the three-inch bald spot on the back of his head, Richard imagines his baldness expanding, encroaching like a desert. Taking over the thin blonde hair she once loved. The elixirs and tonics giggle at him from the medicine cabinet. "Give it up," says the Minoxyldipropylene. Supergro III chuckles. "Might as well shave the whole head."

Yvelaine turns and mumbles in her sleep, hair still wet from their bath together. The apple-scented shampoo he bought her. Apples. Dreaming. Why can't he slip in there, into her dream, rip some shit up and let Greg know who's boss? She fell in love with me for a reason, Greg. And she can still see it. Can't you, Yvelaine? Can't you?

It was just one night. At the Black Dog, Martha sat with Richard and Jones because her friends had left early; she knew Jones from graduate school. As Richard sucked at the bottom of his eighth gin and tonic, he understood that Martha was beginning to *do things* to him in a particular way. His toes curled up in his shoes, he became uncomfortably erect and somehow electric — like an Earp before a gunfight. As Jones outlined Small Business Solutions, her smile brought him back to the Cocteau Twins, The Smiths, to cocaine in the car on the way to a party, his flat stomach. To a time when he participated in the game, when he was team captain. This should go on forever, he thought, this looking and looking away, the leaning forward, the brushes on the way to the bathroom.

At Martha's place — a small apartment in Old Strathcona - they drank some more, some cheap Chilean red, before engaging in two bouts of unadventurous and forgettable sex. First, Richard on top, then a rest and more wine, then Martha on top.

On the way home, Richard felt refuelled. Boom! He looked forward to slipping into bed with Yvelaine. He looked forward to being her man again. After a quick shower, he woke her with kisses.

They weren't kidding; DBC had a damn good selection. The absolutely free, no-obligation membership package he received after calling the toll-free number was full of social influence manuals and encyclopedias of dream interpretation, environmental doom warnings and secrets for tapping the spirit warrior within. Richard circled three books: *Tantric Sex for Busy Couples, Platinum Abs,* and, *Bad Magic For Beginners.* Something for the bedroom, something to counter the diabolical power of Sara Lee, and something to stimulate what Dr. Kinneal referred to as his intellectual and creative centers. Being inclined towards secrets and mysteries and buried treasures of various categories, Richard had a terrible time deciding between the bad magic and an exposé of Freemasonry; how they're ruthless and cruel and how they control the world and wreck Catholic things. Richard's dad was a Mason. He ultimately chose *Bad Magic For Beginners* because he didn't want to get on any lists.

As promised, they arrived in three weeks. The typeface in *Tantric Sex* was small, and the pictures were only mildly smutty; it made Richard sleepy. And even though he wanted platinum abs, even though the glistening washboard on the dust jacket was more *philosophically* desirable than Sara Lee, Richard decided the greater good would be served and guilt would be remedied by using *Platinum Abs* to even up a short chair leg in the kitchen.

TODD BABIAK

Yvelaine smokes at the kitchen table as Richard opens and closes a cupboard door, sitting on the counter.

"Nervous?" Richard takes a glass from the cupboard and fills it with water. Noticing his right hand is shaking, he bridges it with his left. The cuffs on these blue sleeves are longer than your standard man's dress shirt. Richard wears this shirt — his favorite one — and these flattering black Levi's for a reason. This outfit says, *Hi, Greg. I'm Richard.* It says, *You can traipse all over town with your pony tail and your fancy German divorce all you like, but no matter how much hair I've lost and no matter how much butter I've gained around the waistline, no matter how many of my brain cells are croaking with inactivity let me tell you this . . . I still got IT.*

"No. Of course not. We grew up together. I'm anxious, I suppose, because we haven't seen each other in a long time. And I want him to like you, and you to like him. But I'm not nervous. Why would I be?"

"Why *would* you be?"

Yvelaine butts her smoke and walks past Richard into the bathroom. Gargles. Because it's making his hands cold and he didn't really want it in the first place, Richard pours his water into the sink. Taking a deep breath, he decides not to be like this, not to let her know what he's thinking. It's weak. On her way back into the kitchen, Yvelaine brushes past him. "Rick, I — "

"I was just joking, Yves. You can stop storming around."

She closes her eyes and smiles then, and hugs Richard as the doorbell chimes. Feeling her bra strap, Richard wonders which one she's wearing. The black one? Slowly, she releases him. Tactfully, he thinks. As she walks around the corner, turning back for a wink, Richard hears her sloshing around in the purse, for fresh lipstick. The doorbell chimes again.

Should he go with her, stand beside his wife as the door opens, arm around her, smiling big, shameless, protecting his claim, letting the stranger get a good, long look at the way things go in these parts? No. He decides the shirt is enough. For the sake of presentation, he slides off the counter and plops into the now-solid chair. He sits back, sits forward with his elbows on the table, grabs the newspaper, folds it, opens it again, looks out into the courtyard. Checking the bald spot for any recent stress-induced hair loss, he listens. Faint laughter,

Yvelaine. Then he concentrates on the courtyard. Barbecue smells, the piano player doing his best with *Music Box Dancer*. The kids across and below playing the old Nintendo *Super Mario Brothers*. The university students straight across, walking past the window in their shorts and tight t-shirts, two young men and two young women walking and talking and drinking beer, singing along to something Richard can't hear. Techno from below, trance from the gay guy's place on the ground floor. Richard peeks his head out and the guy is sitting on the picnic table in the middle of the courtyard in a black shirt and silver pants, reading. Bleached hair. Silver pants! Richard feels old.

Deeper than he expected, Greg's voice. A fierce laugh. A heavy step.

Relax, Richard. Relax.

Enter Greg.

Three months before Greg's phone call, Richard bounced up the stairs with an extra-large vegetarian pizza and two liters of complimentary Diet Pepsi. Yvelaine stood at the door. It had been a long day at work, with all the Small Business Solutions he and Jones were offering. When Richard tried to kiss Yvelaine she backed away, and only after his fifth attempt at whipping up small talk did he give up and ask. "Who told you?"

"Martha has a sister. Her name is Heather. We used to do aerobics together in university, Heather and I. I met Martha once. Pretty."

"I'm sorry. It was — "

"Is it a regular thing, or?"

"Just the once."

"I'm in good shape, Rick. A lot of the men in the office say so. I'm a great dresser and I'm smart. Funny too, but I don't feel so funny right now."

Richard opened the box and took out a slice. Even though it wasn't hot, he blew on it.

Shaking her head, clearing her throat, Yvelaine dumped the pizza on the floor. "I'd say *I've* improved since our marriage. Intellectually, physically, sexually."

"Please, Yves."

"I'm entering my sexual peak. I'll be a junior partner in two years. You understand what I'm saying, Rick?"

He nodded. "Thought I needed it."

"Maybe you did."

Richard expected potions and a complimentary wand, mesmerism, curses. *Bad Magic for Beginners* was supposed to introduce him to that world where robust, glossy women writhe around drinking blood and conjuring dirty trouble for non-believers. History? Exposition? Inklings of Merlin and the witches from *Macbeth*? Richard wanted to grow his hair back, sculpt himself a beautiful body, force Yvelaine to desire him again, madly, force himself to desire her.

The night Greg called, Richard wanted to be skilled in the construction and application of voodoo dolls.

A good hard squeeze is what Greg gives Richard's hand. Gold watch. "Hiya Rick? Or Ricky is it?"

"Richard."

"Richard, then. I'm Greg."

Cologne fresh, icy with a hint of spice. Her cheeks flushed, head tipped to one side, Yvelaine stands beside Greg. Richard slips an *I love you* arm out towards Yvelaine, trying to stand up without adjusting the handicapped chair first. It falls backwards into the cupboard door and *Platinum Abs* is betrayed, at their feet. Ignoring Richard's arm, Yvelaine laughs.

An inch taller than Richard, Greg has a thin, black layer of stubble. A blue sweater with a white-collar shirt underneath. Richard likes the sweater and he likes Greg's shiny shoes, too. No matter what it says, Richard is aware that his shirt has been vanquished by the soft sweater. No pony-tail, thank God. Short hair, and the line is receding, but *not far enough.*

"So Greg and I were thinking we could all go out for Korean food."

Greg laughs. "Asian food is terrifyingly horrible in Germany."

"Terrifyingly horrible? That right?" Richard leans back to pick up the chair, trying to make it as smooth as possible. As Greg bends to help, Richard notices his hands. Beautiful hands. "No no. You two go ahead. You probably have so much to talk about. I don't want to be in the way. I have some work to do anyway."

"What do you do?"

"I'm a small business consultant."

"You're not *that* small," says Greg. "What? Five nine?"

Yvelaine laughs and slaps Greg's arm. She hits Richard's arm. "Come on, Rick. It'll be fun."

Certain she just wants to measure them up, to decide who is more terrifyingly horrible than the other, Richard shakes his head. "Nah."

"Come on, Rick." Greg adjusts his sweater. Flat stomach, of course.

"I prefer Richard, if you don't mind. Yvelaine calls me Rick against my will."

Yvelaine rolls her eyes at Greg and takes his arm. "If you're sure, *Rick*, we'll get going. I'll drive. We'll bring some wine home so we can drink and talk after dinner. That all right with you, Greg?"

"Perfecto."

Perfecto. Richard smiles. What a stupid thing to say. "I'll walk you to the door." As they break into a quick conversation about German beer, Richard pulls the little scissors out of his back pocket. When Greg laughs that big laugh, Richard tests them. Not too squeaky. Coughing violently to mask the sound, Richard cuts a small lock of Greg's hair as the European gentleman holds Yvelaine's jacket for her. Richard coughs some more. "Sorry. Dry air."

"In Germany some nights, on an otherwise lovely and enchanted evening along the Danube, the air becomes so, so moist, so . . . "

Yvelaine waves, and blows a kiss back at Richard. Richard smiles, twisting the hair in the hand behind his back.

Is it body parts or possessions? *Bad Magic for Beginners* isn't helping at all. Various TV shows featured voodoo episodes, but Richard can't remember how it works. Should he put Yvelaine's toe clippings and Greg's hair into a dough, and make a small bread doll? Should he use her locket and Greg's car keys? The hair, some chicken blood, cayenne pepper and spit and spiced rum? Can he just squeeze some boneless skinless breasts into a bowl, or is fresh blood necessary?

Does he *hate* Greg? Does he have to?

To help him think, Richard takes out the bottle of tequila — a gift from a client — and slices two lemons. He looks through the wedding

TODD BABIAK

photos. It rained that day. Poems, letters, cards. Something he wrote to her before they were married, something about getting a golden retriever. And maybe after that a kid. Candles at dinner and season tickets to the orchestra. A little cabin at an unpolluted lake. A four wheel drive.

Richard calls Martha back. Maybe he can use her to convince Yvelaine that he is still attractive and intense, and even impulsive and spontaneous. No answer, so he leaves a message. "Hi, it's me again. Richard. I wish you hadn't hung up on me yesterday. I really mean it. We should talk. Call me. No, I'll call you. I mean it."

Richard is drinking.

Maybe he isn't thinking right. Maybe he should give in. Maybe Greg is the key to his freedom. New women, new voices. New smells and skin, new baths and new fruit — why always raspberries? Rot away, raspberries.

On the front step he drinks more. Imagines Greg and Yvelaine together; his lips on hers, his chest on hers, his chest on her back. Her eyes closed, smiling. Greg points and squints. *I'm runnin you outta town, Ricky. Leave quiet-like or suck my lead.* Afterwards, over cigarettes, Yvelaine and Greg Earp laugh with the Minoxyldipropylene and the Sara Lee.

Richard throws the hair and the toenails into the shrub at the side of the step. He tries Martha again. More tequila. More.

"We bought white wine."

"The Bee Bim Barp was terrifically fantastic."

"Oh yeah? I'm pie-eyed." Richard lifts the bottle and displays it before them. "I've never gotten drunk on tequila before. Never just tequila."

"Why are you outside, Rick? It isn't so warm." Yvelaine has wrapped her jacket around herself.

"I'm not cold."

"Not after half a bottle of tequila, no. Did you eat anything?"

He holds up the vampired lemon wedges.

"Hearty," says Greg, and laughs that laugh like George Jefferson's laugh, with bass. Greg grabs the bottle and takes a swig before offering his other hand to Richard.

"I don't need any help, Greg. I'm twenty-nine-years-old you know."

"Just courtesy, Richard. Like football players. Respect is really what it is."

Football, eh? Richard allows the assistance and as they walk up the stairs together, he admires Greg's pants. Subtle pants, but flattering. They seem to give a guy a nice ass. Tan pants, or khaki. "So where'd you get the pants?"

"Germany. I can't seem to recall the name of the store." Greg returns the tequila to its master.

"Oh."

The phone rings as Yvelaine walks into the kitchen for glasses and a corkscrew. Richard jumps for it. "Kern residence."

"You listen to me, Richard."

Smiling, listening, Richard glances over at Greg, who returns the smile from where he sits in the comfortable chair, Richard's chair. The sweater is off and now it's just the white Polo shirt buttoned almost all the way to the top. Greg grabs *The New Yorker* off the coffee table. "How *are* you?"

"Don't take that tone with me. Are you messing with me? You think you can mess with me?"

Richard, swaying, thinks Martha may be drunk too. Why shouldn't she be? What else is there to do on a night like tonight? With the wind low and the air pleasantly cool. If you're drunk. "No, no."

"Are you calling because you and the lovely wife have split up? Are you looking for a booster?"

Since Greg looks up at him every few seconds, Richard smiles and says, "Well, you know, I feel the same way. The same way exactly. Let's move on that assumption."

"What the fuck are you talking about? Is your wife there? Is this *code*?"

"Tomorrow night, then? That sounds perfect, I'll call you then. Okay, till then. Bye."

Returning with the three glasses, the corkscrew, and a half-eaten Sara Lee, Yvelaine raises her eyebrows and tilts her head at the phone.

"Guy from work," says Richard, thinking *I know you*, about the cake.

"Who?"

TODD BABIAK

"You don't know him. Just a client, actually."

"All right. Could you grab three plates, a knife, and some forks?"

"Certainly."

"You all right, besides the tequila?" Yvelaine stands in front of him, the corkscrew still in hand, tapping it on her wrist. "You look pale."

Greg laughs and tosses the magazine behind the couch. Richard gives him a look. Spontaneous and impulsive enough to *destroy* a man's magazine?

"Nothing. I'm in a state of absolute rapture, to tell you the truth."

Greg has a couple of joints. But of course, thinks Richard, Greg has a couple of joints.

"From a friend who grows his own. An old high school buddy I met up with last week — you remember Keith Smolinsky, Yves? I guess he has a contract with the government to grow wheelchair weed for cancer patients, and they don't mind if he keeps some around for himself and his friends. Long as he isn't trafficking."

"I haven't in so long." Yvelaine's legs are draped over the side of her chair. Hair down, cheeks like squashed cranberries. "We haven't in so long, have we Rick?"

"Nope."

Yvelaine turns to Greg. "I guess after the bar exams I figured there was no turning back."

There it is again. Richard sees it. The glances they give one another, the way she can't help but smile as he says things. The warmth in the stories of their past together; the time they caught the magpie and threw it into Donny Slobodian's house; the bush parties where half the high school lost their cherries, present company included; Uncle Jerry's wake where a candle fell in the coffin; Yvelaine crying in Greg's arms on the backyard trampoline because that son of a bitch, Clint Buckler, dumped her at the grade ten dance. Richard can feel the magic in the room. Chaos. If the voodoo had only worked. If only it was a mean book, with hurtful potions and filthy incantations of dismemberment and sexual humiliation. Greg could use a boil on the forehead, and a nasty limp.

Richard reaches over the table to rest his hand on Yvelaine's lap.

She rests her hand on his. Her fingers are crossed.

Though they are completely still, Greg and Yvelaine are dancing. Richard watches them with eyes half-closed, pretending to be passed out. Clever is what he was. He didn't inhale.

Richard is pretty sure he has lost his wife. The couch he sits in, the TV and stereo and VCR in the corner, the plants and flowers and lamps and tables and framed photographs and the Edward Hopper print, everything they have together, their glue, has lost its strength. Their glue has lost its stick. No surprise, really. Richard has felt it, he has divined it, predicted it. The bad magic has backfired. Sometimes, when the music dictates it, Yvelaine puts her head into Greg's chest and looks off into the corner of the room, out the open window, as Greg stares into Richard. A studying stare.

On the stereo, Jeff Buckley sings all about love. None of this is hard for Greg, Richard thinks. He loses nothing and I lose everything. As Jeff says something about a cold night, Richard figures on standing up and challenging Greg to a shootout. A sandstorm should whip through the apartment, turning the vinyl couch and both chairs into whiskey-soaked saloon furnishings. The kitchen the bar. A cow skull above the fireplace, where the chief of the wedding pictures, a black and white one of them dancing to their dance, now hangs. None of these fancy clothes; they should be wearing chaps, hats, boots. Sunburns.

To gauge their reactions, Richard snorts a sleeping snort. Yvelaine looks over and smiles and says, "Sweet Rick."

Sweet Rick. Sweet, ineffectual, safe and boring Rick who fucked Martha. Rick the bald, the simple, the getting-old-getting-fat becoming predictable Rick. Sweet, sweet Rick.

Richard stands up. The blood rushes to his head and he wobbles, watches stars for a moment, but braces himself on the arm of the couch. The stars go out, one by one, as Greg and Yvelaine slowly separate. "How much of this you think I can take?"

Yvelaine steps forward with her hands out, to comfort him. "Rick. Were you dreaming or something? Are you okay?"

Backing away from her, he points at Yvelaine and then at Greg. "Practically having sex in front of your husband. Shame on you. Shame on both of you." He points, now, at the wedding picture.

TODD BABIAK

Where the cow's head could be. "Shame."

Greg smiles. "Settle down there, big buddy. We're just — "

"Big buddy? I'm not your buddy, mister. I should kick your ass right now."

Now Greg laughs. "Have another drink, buddy."

"One more buddy and we're taking this outside."

Yvelaine lights a cigarette. "We're practically brother and sister, Rick. Except for the lack of any official blood connection. And it isn't like that anyway. Not like you and *Martha*."

"So this is revenge is it? At least I didn't do it in front of you."

"Maybe you should have."

"I'm outta here. Goodnight, lovebirds. Thanks for the hospitality, Ricky." Greg takes his jacket and turns to the door. "Call me, Yves."

Richard runs up and blocks the door. Yes, he is drunk. Still drunk. The room seems huge, complex, he doesn't recognize it anymore. This is it. The magic is out of control. Payback, retribution. They're all in on it. Yvelaine, Greg, Martha, his mom, Dr. Kinneal that ingenuous bastard, the Masons. "No Greg. Don't go. I think the two of you . . . I think the happy couple should, you know, go right ahead. Do your thing if you want it so bad. Take a bath together. I'll run it for you. Then maybe fuck against the wall. Wouldn't that be nice and savage? Wouldn't that be impulsive? Spontaneous?"

Greg swallows, fumbling with his jacket. "Are you . . . is this . . . *what?*"

Yvelaine shrinks to the floor, and sits cross-legged. She tips her ashes into the rug.

If it wasn't over before, Richard knows it's over now. He is confused. He wonders, where did we meet? At a party? The library? At our own wedding? Where? What is my earliest memory of her? Where did all this *stuff* come from? Whose idea was this?

Who is to blame?

There is silence in the magic room. How long has it been? A song and a half. Richard swallows, and looks down at Yvelaine. Her head, now, is buried between her knees. Greg reads the liner in his jacket. Jeff Buckley is taking his time with a Leonard Cohen cover. There is mention of being inside someone, and Jeff Buckley mentions it well.

Richard remembers hearing that Jeff Buckley drowned somewhere in the Mississippi. Love song singer drowns.

Then, Yvelaine stands up. Clears the crease in her skirt and wipes her eyes. Snatches Greg's jacket out of his hands and throws it to Richard, who catches it.

Well, thinks Richard, folding the jacket. What next?

Yvelaine sticks her hand in between two buttons of Greg's shirt. Greg looks at Richard and shrugs.

They kiss.

JEAN SMITH is the singer/guitar player in Mecca Normal and 2 Foot Flame. She is the author of *The Ghost of Understanding* (Arsenal Pulp Press).

The Rearing of Likeable Bees

JEAN SMITH

"THE UNBEARABLE LIGHTNESS OF BEING?"

"No. The Rearing Of Likeable . . . I mean Likeable Bees."

From this hollow bed of water that I made and now lie on, propped against the wall, I'm reading Vanity Fair — an article on the strange math genius, John Nash. I look up at my black and white TV — a snowy grey screen. Oprah's on; her voice is clear, but I can't get a good picture since the antenna snapped off.

A woman in the studio audience is explaining how she's had botulism injected into the wrinkles on her forehead and between her eyebrows. "It has paralyzed my face so that it's impossible for me to frown. I look like Snow White all the time!"

Oprah says, "Go ahead and try to frown."

I put down the magazine and twiddle what's left of the antenna. A close-up of a woman's face with a strained expression comes in clearly, then returns to blurred streaks.

"Is it permanent?"

"No, it'll last about three months."

"And then what, Snow White?"

"Then have another injection."

I need rabbit ears. Jerry Springer barely comes in anyway; I wonder if I'll get him at all now. I wonder if kids today even know what rabbit ears are. I was once a kid today. Heather wore Levis; I'd gotten it into my head that Lees were cooler — back when 'cool' came around for the second time; after, I mean, post-jazz or post-beat. We bought our jeans at Bootlegger; in a mall that has been called the oldest mall, the first mall, in North America. If that were so, then Heather and I, at the age of nine or ten, would have been the first kids to go-hang-out-at-the-mall.

On a dark and rainy night I ran up and down our short street in my new, too-long Lees, getting the essential worn-off-at-the-heels look. It seemed strange: crisp denim scraping on wet pavement, but it was not for me to question cool; it was for me to imitate. Bee-like. A drone. In the suburbs the drone was so loud that parents wondered if their kids heard a word they said.

John Nash, a schizophrenic genius, believed he was slated to become the Emperor of Antarctica. His work reshaped the field of economics in the 50s. He believed aliens were recruiting him. He claimed that his ideas about supernatural beings came to him the same way his mathematical ideas did — so he took them seriously.

The news guy on TV says, "Playboy is in town this week looking for new talent, but does anyone really care? More after the break."

Through the fizzy veil on the screen there is a young woman with a stroller taking a photo of her mother in front of the Playboy logo on the audition trailer.

The top story is the news team returning to work after a five-week strike. The news is, again, the news.

As Sisyphean as the 649, I'm fine-tuning ideas for my latest invention. I'm going to combine pet rocks with plug-in air fresheners — the extra outlet built right in. Maybe it should be a multi-outlet-pet-rock-air-freshener. I don't know what regular people want. I know what pisses them off, though. D.C. and I were standing outside a theater waiting to go in to Tarkovsky's Stalker.

"You know what really pisses people off?" I ask. "That they can't have exactly what they want when they want it. They can't believe the injustice of not having exactly what they want."

This theme was more simply stated in the film. The character called Writer had a 'gobble, gobble, gobble' theory. D.C. told me this later — I was asleep for part of Stalker.

Things I do not have and do not want: car, beeper, VCR, pets, plants, RRSP, cell phone, mortgage, in-line skates, computer, electric typewriter, or swoosh. I have: an answering machine that fucks up when the fax machine is on. I have a clock with hands; it ticks too loudly. I keep it in the back of a kitchen cupboard. D.C. gave me a watch with hands. I have a recurring dream with all three hands floating above its face. My twenty-year-old blender broke — I'm thinking about buying a sieve. My brother loaned me a portable CD player. I bought a CD. Nick Drake. Guitar and voice. He was young and sensitive; he lived in England — that's hard to do. He killed himself.

I recently read a description of fiction. "It's fiction. You know — part truth, part not."

I met Shani Mootoo at a writers' festival last weekend. She told me that she usually starts a book in the middle and only reads about a quarter of it. I ran upstairs to get my book, very excited to give it to her. Dave and I had the room at the end of the hall, the room with the bunk bed. It was small. We had to walk past beautiful big rooms with antiques and fine linen.

After an authors' reception at Mill Bay we returned to the manor, picked up foil-covered dinners and moved through the French doors to the wraparound porch to find places at plastic tables with matching chairs. I ended up at an agitated table of ego and accusation. I went up to my room, lay on my stomach and ate off the floor.

When I arrived at the festival I was taken to the manor. I was greeted by a nervous young woman, invited in, told to take my shoes off and asked if I'd like my case of beer put in the fridge. I agreed to all, handed her the beer and bent down to undo my sandals. I was looking down when she dropped my beer.

Dave and I monitored the comings and goings on our floor. It seemed like the big room had been vacated. We went and sat in there, at a gateleg table, sipping coffee, waiting for bissett and Purdy to finish breakfast so we could go down for ours. Eventually Dave said, "Come on. If want breakfast, we've got to go down there."

"OK," I said.

We walked in, sat down, and gathered cutlery that had been arranged in geometric patterns on the tablecloth. I dismantled a teepee of knives. A children's author named Walters was asking Purdy, "How much money would it take for you to kiss Mulroney on the lips?"

Purdy said something about his tongue turning to worms, instant disintegration and the extinguishing of his soul. I was examining a spinach-filled pastry with my fork. Walters called out increasing figures in the tens of millions. There was a pause, in which I said,

"I'd do it for $250, but that probably just reflects my gender and my economic situation."

bissett said, "Carla Holmolka (sp) [ed.: please leave in (sp) and note to ed. Re: (sp) ect. (sic)] studied philosophy and cosmetology in prison. A neighbor of mine knows a relative of hers or something. Someone."

Purdy said, "Cosmetology? Is that like the study of the universe?"

"No," said bissett. "It's the study of cosmetics. Imagine her with a nail file working on you."

Walters said he knew some guy who had accidentally gone out with her; he'd met her in a bar and didn't recognize her from the news.

I turned to bissett and revised the plan to get Mulroney's money away from him. "The objective is to get as much of Mulroney's money as possible, right? There's where Purdy and Walters are going wrong. Purdy's supposed to get some number of millions for kissing him on the lips, but what does Mulroney get out of it? We'll kidnap Mila and make her believe she's at a spa. We'll use the bathtub in front of the windows upstairs. She'll be having a bubble bath and we'll have a tiny camera mounted in the corner of the room — we'll replace the bubbles automatically, as necessary. We'll take over the CBC and put a camera on a giant clock, giant hands flicking forward, ticking loudly. Periodically we'll cut to Mila — live in the tub. If Mulroney doesn't pay we'll threaten to broadcast Mila getting a manicure from Carla Holmolka. I'll go run the bath."

I'd been planning a bath anyway. I left the breakfast table and started the bath water. The windows should have looked out over the sea, or at least the lake — not the neighbor's yard.

By the early 90s John Nash had spontaneously recovered from

JEAN SMITH

schizophrenia. After more than twenty years of life lived in dreamlike obscurity, he received the Nobel Prize for economics in 1994.

The orange-orchid tender moves through the humid air, chanting his crystal wishes, rubbing the stiffness around his glass eye. All worlds collide in Flower House 5. To be polite, the night before, I'd turned down the last piece of chicken. To be polite, at least he'd asked before he slid it off the plate for the ginger cat. The gift, the trade, the debt he was trying to barter, left me cold. It wasn't to his discredit to try to even up the score, but no one else was counting. The wishing-well in Flower House 5 held the answer. Submerged. His counted change was heavy in his pocket. He couldn't say if his love could be trusted, like a flower could be trusted, to grow, to bloom, and then to fold.

My mother was forty when I was born. Every obstetrician in the hospital gathered around her. She loves, and expects, to be the center of attention. She said yes to any drugs to stop the pain, even though she'd been meticulous about what she'd ingested through the pregnancy. "Not a drop of alcohol, not even an aspirin." She must have said it a hundred times.

She was not expected to push me out; they got hold of my soft little skull and pulled me out with forceps. I was brought to their first architecturally designed home. It was in the country. Next to their lot, massive towers supported high-tension wires. At forty, the chances of having a child with Down's syndrome and the chances of having a genius are both higher. I wonder how many geniuses with Down's syndrome there are.

I live on the top floor of a small apartment building. The penthouse. The huge front deck was totally private until my landlord recently leased space on the roof to Cantel. They put their ladders up the side of the building and appear whenever they like. No notice. I've told them, "The next time I see a ladder I'm calling the cops!" They've put their towers up on my roof — I guess it's their roof now. I rented a totally private penthouse, and my landlord rents out the roof. The two towers are right above the bed — virtual bedposts — twisting my mind with their forces, spawning electro-flutter dream waves, cells collide under their influence, massing in tumors. Maybe I'll rent out my deck.

My mother told me her name when I was on ecstasy. When I took it — for the first time — I had no idea it would last until lunch with my parents the next day. We had an amazing conversation. I was assuring her that I'd never been in a porn film. She turned to my father and asked, "Should I tell her?"

"Yes, I think you should."

"Tell me what?"

"You might be upset by this," she said emotionally. "My real name is Georgia April Johnson."

I hid my face in my hands and cried. My eyes were open; I looked through my fingers — a watery blur of yes/no, good/bad, true/false.

"I spent the first month with my mother before I was adopted. I checked the records; they can't tell me anything more. The file is sealed, but they sent me a photograph of the building I was born in."

"They sent you a photograph of a building?" I sobbed.

"Yes, it's an old building near the hospital. It isn't there any more. Doctors came over on their lunch breaks to deliver the babies of unwed mothers."

My mother has all my school photos — kindergarten through grade seven. She keeps them in a chocolate box in her dresser drawer. I asked for them when I was moving out.

"They're mine," she said. "Who do you think gave you the dollar every year?"

I think of them as mine; my friends, my class, my teachers. What could the little faces of strangers mean to her?

Jill was the dog my mother liked more than me. I was jealous of a black lab. Freddie was the turtle from Woolworth's that my grandmother killed while my parents were out of town. She wouldn't clean the slime off Freddie's shell with the toothbrush. Mom brushed the slime off every day. Freddie lived in a plastic dish with a ramp in it. A plastic palm tree at the top of the ramp gave him shade from his heat lamp.

My brother had Pepper, an obnoxious, nippy budgie. Cuttle bone had to be replaced regularly so Pepper could keep his little beak sharp, honing it relentlessly. His nub of a tongue was a rigid device he rarely used to imitate human sounds, but we all kept waiting — sweeping up millet husks, sliding stained newspaper out of the bottom of his cage.

JEAN SMITH

The guinea pigs lived outside, under my brother's window. He fed them because their hungry bleating drifted into his room. The guinea pigs lived in an architecturally designed hutch. Our house had been designed by a student of Frank Lloyd Wright. It was a beautiful flat-roofed house with a Japanese influence, floor-to-ceiling windows, tongue-and-groove cedar paneling and a seven-foot fence. My brother had a toy box that, when empty, was big enough to sit in — a ship at sea. The architect of the guinea pig hutch built them. My brother and I, sitting in our toy boxes, were guinea pigs of another kind.

Where I learned some good lessons: 1.) the bank manager's office 2.) a school dance 3.) my bed

1.) I'd just graduated from high school with a cash scholarship. I put the money in the bank. When it struck my mother that I had about $800, she started to think I might take off. She took me to the bank; we went into the manager's office. My mother explained to him that she wanted control over my money. I was crying. I'd taken Law 11; I knew this was duress. The bank manager spun my file around and pointed to the line for her to sign on.

2.) In grade ten, Cathy and I were behind the school drinking and smoking pot before a school dance. J.T. joined us. We finished his nickel bag, emptied our jar of rum and Coke, and smoked a final cig-arette amongst us. Cathy and I sprayed ourselves with Love's Baby Soft, squirted Visine in each other's eyes and ate frozen-concentrated orange juice from a Tupperware fruit cup. I offered J.T. the Visine. "Gets the red out," I quipped, mimicking the TV ad.

"I'm not going in," said J.T.

"What do you mean?" I asked. "You've already got your ticket."

"I don't want to go. What's the point in going just because I have a ticket? I'm going home."

About three years later J.T. blew his head off with a shotgun. Eventually it struck me — J.T. wasn't enjoying living. He had his ticket, but he really didn't want to be there. He'd acted on the philosophy he'd stated behind the school that night.

3.) My first apartment was in an attic on the side of the mountain. I'd rented it without telling my parents I was moving out. I knew they'd be furious. I told them the night before the move. I'd done my laundry, showered and washed my waist-length hair, and changed the sheets on my bed thinking: tomorrow I'll be sleeping in my own place! I was sitting up in bed reading. My father opened the door. He stood there in his striped pyjamas holding a huge glass of chocolate milk. He was too angry to speak. With a flick of his wrist, perfect aim and projection, he doused me.

I take D.C. his morning coffee. He's still in bed. We usually get up together, but he's trying to stay out of my way. Last night ended with me saying, "I need to start writing first thing in the morning or I don't get around to it all day." I told him, "I can't write when other people are around." Which is true, but not very fair — he's hardly around as it is.

"Good morning, Salvadore," I say, handing him his coffee. "Don't spill this on your tea towel. I want to see a little pool of coffee in your belly button."

D.C. read a book on Salvadore Dali and learned that Dali routinely had coffee in bed, and enjoyed dribbling it down his chest. I started calling D.C.'s undersized blanket his tea towel. I had a quilt on my bed when he first started staying the night — a cheap, fiber-filled quilt from Zellers. When he rolled onto his side, his broad shoulders held the quilt up like a tent, leaving me without covers. I took the quilt and he came over with his tea towel.

"Would you prefer to be called Salvadore or D.C. today?"

"D.C."

"So, you like being D.C.?"

"Well, sometimes I do and sometimes I don't. But, the thing is, I've never met another person I'd rather be."

"What about me?" I shriek. "You wouldn't want to be me?"

"I wouldn't want to be you."

"Well thanks a lot! Why? Because then you'd be stuck with a guy like you?" I say, almost surprising myself.

"Anyway. Did these guinea pigs of yours run on one of those wheels?"

"Those are hamsters," I say. "No, they didn't run on a wheel."

"Hey," he says, pointing at the ceiling. "Can you explain to me why there's a Nike swoosh on the ceiling?"

"Yes, I can," I say, without looking up at the Nike swoosh that appears on the ceiling on sunny mornings. "They're pissed off that we're the only two people on the planet who won't wear a swoosh, so they're projecting it onto our ceiling, into our home, whether we like it or not; we have a swoosh. They beam it in via satellite from the compound in Oregon."

D.C. gets up during Wheel Of Fortune. He's putting his shoes on, getting ready to go down to the liquor store: nine hours/six days a week/no breaks. He's a busker.

"Thanks for putting my water bottle in the freezer," he says.

In this record-breaking heat he's been freezing it for work.

"I have to keep an eye on it down there. If I turn away for a second someone tries to grab it."

"But there isn't a refund on them," I say.

"I know. You know that guy who pretends he's blind but sees a pop can three blocks away?"

"No."

"He's constantly trying to steal it."

From the bedroom I hear, "I assume you want to spin the wheel."

The contestant spins, it clicks along, she is clapping.

"Vacation!" says Pat, when it stops clicking.

"R!" she yells, sounding like a deranged pirate.

No 'r'. Click, click, click.

"I can't accept that I'm going to die," I said to A.S. in a noisy bar. "I can't believe that I have to die. I would live forever if I could."

"I want you to read William Golding's *Pincher Martin*. I'll lend it to you. Let me know what you make of it. I wonder if you'll get the point," he said.

"Right. I wonder," I said, noting his condescending tone.

A.S. is a biologist and a student of Zen. His scientific mind is a problem to his spirit. He stares at walls for eight hours at a time, priming himself for a satori-like experience. I think it bugs him when I tell him I've had the experience at least twice — without staring at walls. I think he's jealous.

I took the book home, and left it on the table, where D.C. found it. He and I were having a minor argument; we were trying to steer clear of each other. He thought I'd left the book out for him, that there was some message in it from me. He started reading about this totally tortured guy, shipwrecked, clinging to a barren rock in the middle of the ocean; D.C. wondering all along what I was getting at.

I was reading Milan Kundera's *Identity*. A man is lying in the hospital; he's just come out of a coma. He describes the coma as dreamlike. He says he was aware, conscious, of what was going on, but in a distorted way. Then the dream would turn into a nightmare — he couldn't yell out, as he would in his sleep, to wake himself. He had come to believe that to be dead would be living an endless nightmare.

In *Pincher Martin* there is a question: how long does the agony between life and death last? Milan Kundera's character tells us: if you return to life from that place, you will know to fear death.

In *Pincher Martin* the body floats up on shore to be retrieved and buried. The soul stays at sea to watch the lightning sear the horizon with every ghastly color in the anti-rainbow of the dead.

I am curious about the conspiracy of synchronicity. Books borrowed, books taken to find messages in, books picked up randomly. Sometimes it's easier that others collect up information, which assists you to figure out something you are supposed to know. Sometimes the path is clearer.

ROBERT STRANDQUIST is a Vancouver writer.

The Inanimate World

ROBERT STRANDQUIST

TO GET AN IDEA of this room's maturity, examine the mouldings and trim. The edges are blunt from untold coats of paint, various layers of white, gray, yellow, and blue, exposed where I rammed it with the speaker cabinet I carried in yesterday. Until then it was pristine, egg shell white, freshly laid. The living room is L-shaped with a large window at each end. Part of the ceiling slopes charmingly where a curiously small door divulges leftover space. This is where we keep boxes of unfashionable books, the Herman Hesse, the Kahlil Gibran, the romance novels Lucille secretly gorges on. There is a fireplace with a lovely mantle where we display first editions and obscure antiquarian works. There is a tastefully small Christmas tree in the corner. The house was designed by Francis Rattenbury, of grand schemes, the Legislature, and Empress Hotel fame. That he ran off with a mistress and was murdered in a love triangle lends an extra air of quality to these parities. Lucille and I feel lucky to have the top floor. It's on a leafy street with other heritage houses, in a wealthy, peaceful neighborhood. We feel fortunate indeed to live in Victoria. We have t-shirts that say I LIVE HERE. It's a dig to the pushy operators of tourist attractions, the horse drawn sight-seeing tours, to the clown passing out brochures on Miniature World, to Queen Elizabeth, who has pamphlets for the Royal Victoria Wax Museum. Lucille is disdainful of tourists yet is employed in the industry. A nice contradiction that is not lost on her. Genius is the ability to hold two contradictory ideas at once. Who said that? I don't know who said it first. But Lucille says it often enough. She has a Master of Library Sciences degree and works as a part-time receptionist at the wax museum. When tourists come through the glass doors she likes to sit perfectly still, with a waxy stare. They approach her desk wearily, in a trance, unsure of what is or what is not real. Then she smiles and her quarry laughs nervously, captured and swallowed whole. She gets a kick out of this. It allows her to feel superior. We all do it, we citizens of the capital, work at feeling superior to the lowly tourist in his gaudy grin and appalling camera. I'm drinking my tenth beer and smoking my twentieth cigarette of the evening. Most of the people here are Lucille's friends, writers, editors, curators, professors. My two friends, Elmer and Elvis, are students like myself, poorly dressed, expert only on themselves. They are guzzling beer and comparing Johnny Rotten's lyrics to Ionesco's Rhinoceros. Present as well, is the most gorgeous woman I have ever seen. She fits into the world like it was designed around her. Her hair has gold and red highlights, is loosely held in a single braid that hangs down her back. Her hand is a nurturing place. It holds a wine glass. Susan Henry. I nearly swoon at the musicality of her name when I learn it. She is not pretty in any ordinary sense. She would have been a homely child. Becoming an adult, she would have been startled by what radiates from deep within her, as men are startled by it. I raise my bottle and suck on air. Before I can make a move to get another, one of Lucille's friends is standing in front of me. He is a young socialist, a non-drinker. He is the one who brought the Perrier. From off the carpet he picks up a lit cigarette, hands it to me. I look for the cigarette that was supposed to be in my hand. *Did I drop that?* I ask him. *Yes*, he says. *Thank you*, I say with too much sincerity, trying to cover my drunkenness. I can see that he pities me, and I decide to hate his guts. Lucille places a loving hand on my arm and tells me to pick some music. Lucille's and my records are intermingled. There are two copies of many, John Lennon in particular. Of his first solo work there are three copies. I don't know where the third came from — delicate initials in the upper right corner, *TK*, point to it belonging to a woman. Lennon's solo stuff was never uplifting, and now that he is murdered it positively impoverishes. Lucille's best friend Gillian kneels beside me. She smells gorgeous even if she's not. Leaning over me I could suck her hair. Referring to the record, she says *I love this one, too, but maybe we better not play it. I might cry.* What she really means is that Lucille might cry, or worse. Lennon was shot two weeks ago. It was a night similar to this one. Friends were hosting a party, everyone was having a good time. News of the murder arrived like a drunken adult at a children's party. Everyone was confused at first, awkward. The air grew cold and smelled of wet pavement. Someone put on the TV looking for news of it. A strange excitement began to grow, a funereal celebration. Loss can be so invigorating. Lucille was in shock and disgusted with her friends. I had to take her home. Gillian chooses a Joni Mitchell album. I carefully place it on the platter, clean the brush on my shirt sleeve, drag it over the record, twice. The tone arm slips from my fingers and the needle zippers halfway through the first song. The volume of conversation increases to compete with my new speakers. I go into the kitchen to get a beer. Susan Henry is leaning on the fridge. She is talking with some intellectual geek. Her voice is music, resonant crystal, wet finger. I'm hoping they let me into the conversation. The geek is resentful of my presence. He won't look at me. He is in love with her, too. I am quite drunk. I watch her from a distance even though I'm two feet away.

Waves thrash against the massive blocks of the breakwater. When they withdraw, look into the trough before the next one, see with a painter's pentimento eye the descending pyramid of rough hewn stones, the jade forest of kelp and glass weed, fluid and sentient. The breakwater extends a quarter mile, a crooked finger protecting a calm bay, a lighthouse on the end. Lucille shows me a small white stick in her fingers. This is a question. I nod. Our hair buffeted by wind, we huddle around an unlikely flame. Inner expansiveness comes in with the smoke. We continue walking in silence. Soon the expansiveness collapses and I wish I hadn't smoked it. The gray clouds and dull blue Olympic range and hard whitecaps march towards us, a campaign of endless patience, they will outlast us, when we have gone full circle, are forgotten, have become prehistory.

What about John? she asks.

Perfect, I say, *after Lennon,* trying to wrench myself out of the anodyne gloom. Grin at the wind. We are not alone out here. I adjust my face. People make me nervous, particularly when I'm stoned. I study them, wonder if I will greet them or pretend to ignore them. A lot depends on what they do. I like to be caught off guard, then I don't have time to think about it, just react in a normal way. It's becoming more and more difficult to act normally. I used to know how. Now I'm not so sure. We pass them and they smile at Lucille, but don't even look at me. I feel insulted. The waves clash here at the end, like two armies, the wind, the current, fighting over something, the privilege of being first, last.

And if it's a girl, Joni. Lucille says.

Sure. I say, losing courage. I cram my hands into pockets, push my shoulders closer to my neck. I feel mixed up. The idea of having a child with Lucille was easy before I started thinking. Would we really be good parents? The kid would be nice looking and smart, really? I am baffled by my indecision. Could we still afford to buy dope and beer. Would I be able to sit for hours working out poetical problems, looking for the perfect verb? Though legally separated, how would it sit with my wife and first child? Would it be a betrayal? Would I have to wear one of those packs with the baby and spare diapers stuffed into it? I picture myself in the supermarket, on the bus. My face burns anticipating embarrassment. I barely have enough self-esteem to get myself through a day, let alone enough for two of us. Changing diapers in public rest rooms. Talking googoo language. I haven't spoken for a while. Lucille is getting uneasy. She should be. I left my wife when she was pregnant.

John or Joni it is, I say.

If we decide to keep it, she says.

I thought it was decided.

I want you to decide.

Me? You want me to decide?

I want to make sure this is what you want.

Sometimes what I want isn't what I want.

You'd better figure it out.

Twist and turn through neighborhoods ablaze with children, race along like a couple of mice on a greeting card. Quiet mice, sad mice. It's early December. I pick up Lucille from work and we drive the twelve miles to our new place at Glen Lake. The abortion sits between us like an extortionist. It laughs at our attempts to get past it. My car is a Volkswagen Beetle, faded cartoon blue, noisy. Exhaust fumes seep in through rusted heating ducts. We leave the windows partially down in all weather to prevent asphyxiation. We stop at the IGA on the outskirts of Victoria, the Liquor store in Brentwood. At the edge of civilization, before the forest takes over, is the last corner store. We get cigarettes for me, and ice, lots of ice. We glide down the road past our few neighbor's houses and pull up on our half of the driveway at the end of the cul-de-sac. Lucille fills bowls with snacks. I put the beer in the fridge. She runs the vacuum over the rug. I make a fire. She dresses like a vamp. I put on my lumberjack shirt. Among the regulars, the party is attended by the great grand niece of Alexander Romanoff, the personal friend of a Nobel laureate, a CBC news personality, the niece of Canada's most note-worthy novelist, the illegitimate daughter of a former prime minister. It's my job to keep the fire going and to not drink too much. When Susan Henry arrives she flows into the party like hot sugar over cake. Arms are extended for her, wine glass proffered. I tend the fire, work a nice dry piece of cherry into the flames. I watch it catch, slowly draw the screen closed. She stands nearby, sleeves rolled loosely below her elbows, tentative braid dangling to her bum. She is careful our eyes should not meet. I grab four beer from the fridge, one each for Elmer and Elvis and two for me. One I down, the other I drink quickly. On the porch we smoke up and stare in at the party. I am tongue-tied except when flirting with homely women. With my hand on the small of Gillian's back I show her around the suite, the yard, the deck over-looking the lake. I prattle on like an English actor on speed, like the attending prigs I resent so much. In the furnace room I take her in my arms. She reaches into my pants for my kite string. I back her against the wall. She stands on a wooden crate and a pipe coming out the furnace. She guides me to her moisture and I float free of the world. It's all over in a few minutes and we laugh nervously at our gall. In the living room an anecdote about the Nobel laureate has everyone tittering irreverently. I have never cheated on a girlfriend before. A wife is one thing, but you should never cheat on a girlfriend. I go outside and smoke, splash down a beer trying to loosen the guilt so I can peel it off. Lucille comes out to find me. I am nervous she might smell fear, and woman. She doesn't believe that I am having a good time, says I shouldn't drink so much, and goes back to her party. Susan Henry wanders down the path in the back yard, down the steps to the little dock in the little lake. I would follow her, be maybe boyishly charming, but I feel like dirt at the moment, drunk dirt. I lean on the Linden tree and watch her. She stares across the water thinking beautiful thoughts. She is motionless as the planets. I want to die because I know I'll never have her. Her figure is an hourglass. I see my time flowing away.

I am in town meeting Lucille for lunch. She is late again. We count the days, mark them on the calendar. I look at the clock on the wall above the bar. Quarter after. At two weeks she made an appointment with her doctor. Yesterday she went for the test. Today she would have gotten the news. Why do beer parlors smell so bad? I wait on the street, growing impatient. I check my mood. Cranky is not the face I want her to encounter. Finally she appears. I can't read her body language. She emanates quixotic self-confidence, same as usual. We turn down a back lane and I light up a joint.

Have you heard? I ask, speaking and holding the smoke down simultaneously.

No, she says, cool as steel.

I thought . . .

My doctor's receptionist is going to call me this aft.

Oh.

There's something you should know, she says, as though pressing a knife against my skin. *The abortion, it wasn't the first. Spontaneous and otherwise. I have no intention of having another. I want a baby badly.*

It was your idea to give me the choice last time, I say foolishly.

I just want you to know where I stand.

It was stupid to name it first.

We walk in silence for a while. I do love this woman, regardless of my moods. I feel good. It is so much easier accepting a thing than trying to deal with it. We get a sandwich from a take-out place and eat walking back to the museum.

137   ROBERT STRANDQUIST

Of course we will keep it, I tell her.

There is a message waiting for her to call the doctor. She sits at her desk and dials. Tourists gather round her counter like tadpoles around an egg. They clutch pamphlets, have important questions at the ready, jingle radio-active coins over their gene pool. She finishes her call, hangs up, catches her breath, then says to them all *I'm pregnant.* They are stunned, unable to move or speak. Maybe she wants witnesses, that they might help to fix the fetus in her, so that nature can't dislodge it, so that I can't dislodge it. The moment passes. Back in gear they proceed to express to her their fear of death and to explain what they hope to find so far away from home.

I'll pick you up at five, I tell her.

She smiles at me without seeing me, in love with who is inside her. I go into the gallery of figures. Queen Victoria looks me over with a sexless frown. Looks can be deceiving. Ugly women make the best lovers. Einstein greets me with a conspiratorial stare. I feel light as air, redeemed. All past sins will be forgiven. The Beatles are sly young fellows, blushing, sharing with me an in-joke, that we are all wax figures, but that in knowing it we can have a laugh. In the dungeon are figures in chains, some with gaping wounds, others being tortured. Here it is, the other side of the bright coin, inextricably bound to our comfortable lives. Comedy and horror, side by side, like strands of DNA, essential parts of the whole. To work for peace is frivolous to the point of being imprudent. War is ultimately a good thing. I'm offended by my thoughts. I sensor them. Give peace a chance. I stand for freedom and tolerance. So where do these other ideas come from?

I am face down on an operating table. The doctor stands over me. On the tray beside him is a lance, gauze, a small aerosol spray. A couple weeks ago the cyst on my neck became infected. The doctor treated it unsuccessfully with oral antibiotics. He says to me now *it will be a little uncomfortable.* The tone of his voice makes me uneasy. There is a quality of fear in it, pity. He sprays the cyst, which freezes the surface. He cuts. I don't feel anything so far. Then he starts pushing the puss out of my neck. I can't believe the pain. I writhe under his primitive thumbs. They push me down, to the edge of the earth's mantel, through it and beyond. I let out an inhuman moan. When it's over he hurries away as though ashamed. My thoughts run in circles. My breathing is shallow and my heart is erratic. I get off the slab and sit in a chair. I think my mantra a few times and the chaos in my mind begins to order itself. Lucille's doctor enters the room and introduces himself even though I know him from one of our parties. He is walking bedside manner, humorless and friendly. He has news, bad news. Lucille has sent him to find me here in ambulatory care. She has miscarried, was just brought in, a room down the hall. I slowly put on my shirt, wander in a daze to find her. I left her in bed an hour ago. She was fine. The coincidence of us both being here vibrates in me. I find her, pale and aloof. I am saddened and relieved, anesthetized by the lose. Redemption would have been too much of a burden. Lucille has the gaze of a wax figure, a lack of spark, personality void, the flat depression of the inanimate world.

Elvis has used most of his student loan disbursement to pay for a new stereo system. He is very proud of it, and I am impressed, until he puts on a Sid Vicious record. It sounds like noise. I shiver. His room has the smell of an abandoned building. There are empty beer cans stacked in cardboard trays beside the fridge. The sofa is covered with text books and comics. There are two piles of laundry on the floor. One is clean and the other dirty, I presume. I ask him the point of playing that kind of music on such a good system. I suggest it would sound as good or better on a cheap mono record player. The cheaper the better, in fact. He gives me a blank stare, and then smiles. He thinks I'm kidding.

We drink quickly for the warmth and stand in the center of the room, debating the extinction of the dinosaurs. I maintain they died out from bad dental hygiene, there being no fluoride in the water.

Have you ever heard of a dinosaur going to the dentist? I ask impertinently.

I see your point, he says, humbled, *though I think it more likely that it was a mass suicide on the planetary scale.*

For what possible reason?

Something pseudo-religious undoubtedly.

Elmer says, being more earnest than I think the situation calls for, *Actually I heard it's because they didn't get enough roughage in their diet and died of severe diarrhea.*

Lucille is having a party tonight, one that I was not invited to. She is showing off her new husband. He is a famous naturalist, apparently, credited with discovering a lost tribe in the Amazon jungle. He has promised to introduce her to Jane Goodall. He just hiked into the wax museum one afternoon and there was Lucille. Now she is good and pregnant.

I am bent over Elvis's turntable, with a large pair of pliers, trying to remove the cartridge. My intention is to replace it with one Elvis claims will increase the midrange. He was going to have the dealer do it, but I've done it a few times, and I insisted I give it a try. He is nervous watching me. The light is bad.

Don't they ever heat this fucking place, I complain. After I have disconnected the wires I stop. *I can't change that fucking thing with cold hands.*

You just going to leave it like that? He is incredulous.

What can I do, I shrug him off.

I can't live without my music.

You can't seriously call that music, I drawl.

What do I call it then?

I consider his question. *Graffiti,* I say, expecting him to congratulate me on the clever choice word.

But he hisses *Jerk.*

Moron, I snarl back.

From the unlit back lane I watch the windows of Lucille's top floor suite. Laughter and music emanate from one that is open. I need a beer. The house is owned by a famous travel writer. Lucille has made friends with him and his elegant wife, and earned a standing invitation to use their condo on the *big island.* Ducking in with the conversationalists I hear those words, with irritating regularity, bob to the surface of the hubbub. The *big* island. To make it even more impressive, Lucille never says the other word. It sounds better when the person she speaks with says it for her. *You mean the big island of* Hawaii? That word also floats up there like an empty bleach bottle. We talked about staying together after she found this place. There is so much room compared with the Rattenbury, or the Glen Lake basement suite. I could do my thing and she could do hers. We would have separate rooms, studies, as it were. The one facing the street is merely large, but the smaller one at the back is charm itself, two steps down into an airy space with a hardwood floor and large windows on three sides, over-looking a lush back yard. The discussion about my moving in centered around who would get the good study. She found that offensive, but would not relent and let me have it. So the idea petered out and I took a small room down the street where I live with my records and boxes of books. Lucille is holding court and looks radiant. I expect her newly minted husband to be flamboyant, in command of the room. But the man my eyes fall on is standing a little to the side, aloof and sad, at a loss for words, horribly sober. He reminds me of someone, myself before drink. I make my way to the kitchen through the crush of Lucille's friends. She hasn't seen me yet, or isn't letting on she has. Someone passes me a joint. I take a hit and try to pass it on but no one is paying attention. I extinguish it between thumb and finger, put it in my shirt pocket. In the kitchen I am surprised to find no beer in the fridge. On the table and counters are many wine bottles. What's with these people? I take an unopened liter of Kressman. On the stairs I meet Susan Henry coming up. Alone, she seems vulnerable, open. Her eyes sparkle, her lips are moist. We smile. Then I hear from the kitchen that I'm going to be pursued by the owner of the wine. I nod and disappear.

It's a Friday night and the church basement is full. I take a seat near the back, in case I decide to leave early, before they form the sweaty-handed circle and do the serenity prayer. I am here half an hour early. I forgot this meeting starts at eight-thirty rather than eight, like most of them. There is an excited air. It's a reunion. They mill around, talking, hugging. Toughs in leather. Slut in leopard. Bums. Jocks. Little old man. Fine-boned rich girl. Somebody's mother. Everyone is in conversation, well almost everyone. A timid man stands up at the front and says a few words of welcome. He asks one of the women to read How it Works. *AA is a fellowship of men and women who share a common goal . . .* A man reads the twelve steps, someone else the twelve promises. I am comforted by the familiar words, the unskilled drone, the assurance of freedom. The first speaker is called up. I want to hear the horrific details of ruined life that will ease this urgent need of mine to find companionship in a bottle. But the speaker is an old hand. He speaks in generalities. He is not helping. The second speaker is another regular, an eccentric woman who tells a convoluted story in a patronizing tone. I want it to end. I look back at the door to make sure nothing blocks my escape. The speaker asks if anyone else would like to share. I know I should get up. But my story involves too many empty rooms, too many inanimate dreams. I have tried, but I lose their attention, eyes glaze over, skin yellows and softens under the lights. During the break, a man approaches me and introduces himself. We shake hands. He is working the program. I grin uncomfortably, not knowing what to say. They tell me I should go to meetings regularly, to get involved, stack chairs, chair a few meetings, get a sponsor, be a sponsor. But I get by, attend when there's need. I was walking at Jerico Beach this morning when I saw Susan Henry. It has been ten years, and she has changed, but I recognized her instantly. And I think she knew me, regardless of the weight I've put on. This morning was cool and windy. The tide was in and waves ran at me, held back by their singing chains. She and her female companion walked slowly, leaning into each other, choosing words carefully, like bits of glass, worn soft from centuries of rolling on the tongue. It gave me a lift to see her. And then it brought me down hard and I wanted to get drunk. The meeting ends, chairs are scraped out of the way. We all join hands and form a circle. It expands nearly to the walls. I hate this part. I reach for the hand of the woman in the leopard skin pants, and on my right a big man who hates me as much as I do him. I bow my head, surrender. *God, grant me the serenity,* one hundred voices in unison, *to accept the things I cannot change, courage to change the things I can, and the wisdom to know the difference.*

Concentrate on the food, the California rolls, and egg rolls, chicken wingettes and teriyaki salmon. There is a bean salad, potato salad, Caesar salad and a delicious cole slaw. Four different kinds of breads, as well as the cheap French loaf I brought and the quarter pound of garlic butter. There are crackers with exotic dips, oysters on the half shell and pickled herring. Rice Crispy squares, Nanaimo bars, brownies and a box of chocolates. Entree's, hors d'oeuvres and desserts all laid out at once, so democratic, so tasty. I make my way around the table. I want to sample everything. When my plate is full I make for an empty chair. I intend to concentrate on eating. Hopefully I won't have to stutter through any tedious discourse. When I've eaten, I make my way through a clutch of women gathered around the kitchen door and find my bottle of non-alcoholic beverage and a clean glass. I pour some and take a sip. I realize I'm not having the terrible time I expected. Parties can be torture. Then Susan Henry walks in.

She says, *We've been running into each at parties for years, haven't we.* I say, *Yes we have.*

She says, *You know Lucille,* by way of clarifying our connection.

Yes, I tell her.

Isn't that great about her having twins again?

Yes . . . indeed, I sputter, pretending I know all about it.

She goes into the other room before I can think up something to say. I pour another drink of my expensive fruit juice, find a chair near the food where I can keep an eye on the room. Susan Henry has gained a little weight, and gone is the long hair. She is dressed more to hide her body than show it off, though she is still attractive. I am determined to talk to her. I ready some topics: Lucille's children, that they're still coming, the charm of Victoria compared with the substance of Vancouver, or the substance of Victoria and the rain of Vancouver. But then a rumor darts about the room like a trapped bird, bruising its wings, that Princess Diana has been killed. Everyone becomes agitated. Someone turns on the TV, looking for confirmation. So much for small talk.

Later, when the TV is off, and conversation is drifting back to original sin, I am scavenging at the table. Susan Henry comes by looking for a bite. She gives me the briefest smile. I say to her, *You know, in all these years we've never really had a chance to talk.* The hostess of the party suddenly appears and offers to show Susan Henry her paintings. She immediately agrees and I'm left holding a gooey chocolate thing, looking for a napkin.

LAURA LUSH is a Toronto poet. Her fiction has appeared in such journals as *dig* and *The Brobdingnagian Times*.

Women Who Run With Buffalo

LAURA LUSH

"TINA! TINA!"

That's the name on my name tag, the one that was given to me when I started here. My real name is Katherine, but my boss, Karl, won't give me a new name tag until my probation period is over. So, Tina it is, and I wince every time I hear one of the drunks from table ten yelling my name.

"More wine, Tina!"

"The soup's cold, Tina."

"What's this called again, Tina?"

"Tina? That's a pretty name. How do you spell it?"

Six dollars an hour. That's how much the thief Karl is paying me. Six dollars an hour to cater. But it is 1998 and I am lucky to have a job. I got the job through my friend, Winnie. She is a caterer as well, and since Karl's not the interviewing type, he just takes referrals from his staff. The staff is always willing to come up with names. They never refer close friends, only acquaintances or sometimes even enemies. Having your enemies work for Karl is sweet revenge. Winnie and I are an exception. We are friends and classmates. We are both taking a Holistic Health Practitioner's course when we're not working for Karl. We are learning about anger management and meridian points and how to open our chakras.

I work the weekend shifts. I do weddings and company parties. I start at 3:00 in the afternoon and work straight until 4:00 in the morning. There are no official breaks. I just take them on the occasional down-times between 3:00 and 4:00 a.m. I steal all the left over desserts and share my slave treats with my two cats when I get back home. I despair over the deteriorating state of my feet, the toes blunt and bleeding, the arches fallen. This is what my life has come to at twenty-six years of age. Six dollars and hour and feet that look like hooves.

We get tips, of course, but Karl has a special system whereby he divides them according to seniority. Although Winnie and I lug the same tables and chairs back and forth every shift, hoist the same twenty-pound trays over our heads, clear and clean plates, mop up spilled soup, turn the other way when we feel those hands on our bot-toms, we still make less tips than the others. All because of seniority.

Karl is an expert on seniority. He has climbed the food services slave ladder. He has worked his way up from dishwasher to catering manager. There's not a thing Karl doesn't know about lifting and place settings and napkin rings.

I was a manager once myself. But that was long ago in the eighties when jobs were plentiful and employers actually appreciated you.

"We're just going through a bit of a rough patch," Winnie says to me. "Wait till we become fully certified Holistic Health Practitioners. Wait till we get to open our chakras."

"Ti-naaaaa!"

"Ti-naaaaa!"

And then, "Ti-naaa Baa-by!"

It is the Head Table. I take a deep breath and walk over to the father of the bride. He is smashed and wants another bottle of wine. He also wants me to sit on his lap. "Just kidding there, Tina," he says, as his hands hover dangerously low around my hips. "Tell me some-thing," he slurs. "How come somebody hasn't snatched you up yet? A fine filly like you."

I lean close into the father of the bride's big red boozy face. "Do you really want to know?"

He smiles as one of his eyebrows crawls up his forehead. "Yeah Tina," he says. "I really wanna know."

But the chef saves me. "Tina," he yells. "Soup's up."

I do a mock curtsy, then walk back into the kitchen.

"Hey," the chef says, leaning into me. "You're not from around here, are you?"

"No," I say wearily. "I'm not from around here."

"I bet you're from," he says wagging a soup spoon at me. "I bet you're from The West. Edmonton, right? No — *Calgary*. Yeah. That's it. You look like you're from *Cal-gar-y*."

"How's that?" I say.

"I dunno, Tina. You just got that look."

"What look?" I say.

"Like you don't put up with any crap."

"I'm working here, aren't I?" I say. The rest of the night is one big Tina fest.

"Tina! You're too slow!" Karl yells.

"Tina! Lift that!" the assistant manager bellows.

"Tina! More wine!" the father of the bride shouts.

"Tina," the chef says. "You're not from around here, are you?"

Marco, one of the veteran waiters, gives me a lift home. He's been here for six years. He has hooves as well. Whenever Marco drives me home, he likes to talk about his life in Spain before he became a professional caterer. He looks over at me and speaks in a low, conspiratorial voice.

"I wuz Spain's greatest matador."

"Is that so?"

"Uh huh," he says smiling.

I smile back at Marco smiling. I smile back at his out-and-out lie, at his unwavering certitude. And I smile at my own willingness to play along with such a charade. But I figure that anybody who can shake a table cloth night after night like Marco can deserves to be indulged from time to time.

He slides across the seat, gives me one of those intense Marco stares. "Catering is *garbage*, Tina."

"Katherine."

"A nice girl like you shouldn't have to put up with *garbage.*" I feel the cold tickling of his fingers on my neck as I open the door.

"Thanks, Marco," I say, getting out. Then I draw a little happy face on his window, blow him a kiss. Marco smiles up at me through the frosty window, then screeches away down the street. A car pulls out in front of him and I see his big Spanish fist shoot into the air, hear the long rant of Marco's *Garrr-baaa-gee* as I quickly retreat into my basement apartment.

The slowest server has to carry the buffalo. The buffalo is the banquet hall's show piece, Karl's pride and joy, seventy pounds of hairy buffalo head and white handlebar horns. According to Karl's calculations, Winnie and I are the slowest servers, and we have the honor of carrying the buffalo from the banquet hall back up to the smoking parlor where it will sit until the next function. Normally, the buffalo is only brought out for guy functions, sales meetings and stag parties, but once a women's group requested the buffalo. According to the chef, they were a bunch of broomball players from Thunder Bay and they did unspeakable things with the buffalo. After that, the buffalo was only brought out for male functions. Only men, according to Karl, have an innate respect for the buffalo.

I could carry the buffalo easily by myself. I am that angry. In fact, I could probably run with it. I could probably hold it above my head and charge through the banquet hall yelling Marco's famous battle cry, but Winnie is also that angry and she would like to own a little piece of this fantasy as well. Instead, we walk the stairs from the banquet hall to the smoking parlor cursing and swearing as the buffalo teeters precariously above us. When we finally get the buffalo to its proper resting place, our shirts are ringed with big manly circles of sweat. Little buffalo hairs are plastered to our foreheads.

"That was one *f'in* heavy buffalo," Winnie says.

"You can say that again."

The chef is beaming. "Tina," he says.

"What?"

"Guess who's coming to dinner?"

"Who?" I say suspiciously. It's not like the chef to be cheery.

He leans over so his mouth is almost on my ear. "The buffalo's

LAURA LUSH

scheduled to come out again," he says in a sinister sing-song voice.

"Oh no, not the Brothers of Boyhood again?"

"Uh uh," he says, shaking his head.

"Who then?" I say as I wind a napkin tighter and tighter around my hand.

"Women Who Run With Buffalo."

"Get real."

"I'm serious," he says smiling.

"You mean Karl's going to let a bunch of women have the buffalo? I don't believe it."

"He checked them out," he says. "They're OK. They're just some wacko nature group, that's all."

I run over and tell Winnie, who is unscrewing lids off sugar canisters and wiping them with a cloth. She's so excited she waves the cloth above her head, sending a spray of sugar through our hair. Then we look at each other and smile. We are hoping that the Women Who Run With Buffalo like to rant and stomp. We are hoping they like a little thunder, a little drama, a little fun. We are hoping that they have chosen the buffalo because it is strong, unyielding, and highly unpredictable. Winnie and I are counting on it.

All day, Karl has been watching us. He made me pay for two teacups I broke in the back kitchen. He told me I was *slow*, so I went faster and broke things. Probability is not one of Karl's stronger points. He can't seem to see that if twenty servers rush around each other in a cramped, messy kitchen while he yells at us, then we drop things. Winnie was luckier. She didn't drop anything. But she was a little sloppy when it came to her dessert spoon positioning. Karl brought this to her attention after she had set places for 300 guests. Lately, Karl has been putting Winnie and I on clean-up, where there's less chance of breaking things or messing up. There's also less tips and more tables, and you-name-it to move, drag, lift. My shoulder is starting to act up again. Not to mention my hernia and that little disc of mine. Thank God, I have a holistic health trainee at my side. Winnie administers a quick shiatsu massage to the various meridian points and I'm back in business.

"Break time," Winnie says, taking out her cigarettes. Although we're holistic health trainees, we still have our little vices. Cigarettes and slave labor go hand in hand. It's a working girl thing.

We are lying head to head on the table and smoking. Karl is nowhere to be seen, although part of us wishes he'd walk right in this very second and fire us for a break on his table. We pull our legs over us so the blood rushes down from our toes. We wrap our feet now. Bind them like the women in China used to do. Then we stuff them into Doc Martens for good measure. Then Winnie and I do a little meditation. We invoke the white light of the universe, ask it to wrap its loving, healing energy around us. We ask for wealth and abundance and for Karl to die a long, slow, cruel death.

Then we finish moving the table. It is after four in the morning and we have been working just over twelve hours. The last two hours have been solid U-Haul stuff. There is no need for our little black bowties or vests. There's no need for our insipid little serving smiles either. At least, we can be ourselves. Marco helps us with the last table. The other servers, the ones with seniority, which is everyone but Winnie and me, aren't required to move anything. Their job is to go over tomorrow's schedule while they sit in the back kitchen playing poker with our tips.

The next day Winnie and I conduct a secret holistic health assessment on Karl. We figure his energy fields are way out of whack. So are his lymph nodes and his penial gland. In fact, he is one big holistic health nightmare.

"I bet his problems go way back to when he was a dishwasher," I tell Winnie.

"Jesus," Winnie says. "That's real deep shit. It would take years of undoing. I dunno."

Karl doesn't know this other side of Winnie and me, that we have a life outside of catering. He is surprised when we ask him what time we'll be getting off tonight. He just looks at us and grunts. No, we'll never be professional caterers, nor will we ever climb the food services slave ladder. He knows all this, but he doesn't say anything. He doesn't say anything because tonight is the last night of my probation period and Karl knows that I know he is going to give me the axe after the last shift. He knows I know this because when I ask him if he's going to give me a new name tag, he just turns away. That's OK with me. I've come to terms with the fact that no matter how hard I try, I cannot really lift,

serve, sweep, and clear tables as well as the rest of them. But, I now have
another career to add to my interesting CV:

Mental Health Worker

Caterer

Buffalo Head Lifter

Murderer

Tonight also happens to be the Women Who Run With Buffalo
banquet. Karl has asked everyone, including the chef, to come in a few
hours early. He wants everything to be perfect. He wants Winnie and
I to clean the buffalo. We buff and polish the buffalo's nose, comb its
ear hair, rub a cloth with musk oil up and down its beautiful smooth
ten-inch horns. When we finish, the buffalo is sparkling, shiny, happy
as a hood ornament. Even Karl comments on what a fine job we've
done and flicks his nails against the horns so he can hear that little *ting*
of perfection.

The plan is like this. Karl will send Marco out first. Then the rest of us
will follow with our big silver trays. The Women Who Run With Buffalo
have put in a special request. They want meat. In everything. Right
from the little dainty finger food to the dessert. They want steak, and
the rich blood-brown gravy of roast beef swimming around on their
plates. They want pork ions in the air. They want intestines, and cow
tongue and chicken's feet. They want bull's balls.

At least six buses bring the Women Who Run With Buffalo to the
banquet hall. Karl has us all lined up with our little trays above our
shoulders. We are waiting for his command. Then The Women Who
Run With Buffalo enter. We look at each other, then at the steady
procession of larger than life women who are donned in moccasins and
hide leggings and tunics, women with brightly-colored head dresses and
massive incisor-tooth necklaces, then we look at Karl.

"Oh God," he finally says. "Not them."

The chef confirms it "Fraid so, boss," he says matter-of-factly.
"They're back."

Yes. The broom ball players from Thunder Bay are back with a new
name and a new look. I turn to Winnie and smile.

Then Karl turns to us. "Listen up," he says. "If there's any — *any* —

rumbling out there — anything — they're out the door. Out. Understand?"

"Rumbling?" Winnie says.

"Yeah," Karl says. "Rumbling. Fighting. Hair pulling. Y'know?"

I look at the chef and suppress a giggle.

"OK," Karl seethes. "Hit the floor."

The Women Who Run With Buffalo huddle in small herds of threes and fours. They throw back their heads when they swig down their beer. They pat each other on the back. They lift each other up when they hug. They take turns holding our trays.

Karl hasn't moved from the back of the banquet hall since they came in. He stands, arms crossed, feet tapping, waiting, waiting. Winnie and I turn to the buffalo. It is sitting at the head table, guttering and gloating.

Then we serve dinner. There are no need for forks or knives or the dainty little dessert spoons. The Women Who Run With Buffalo just clear their cutlery to one side of the table and proceed to eat with their hands. Gravy drips off their faces as their tongues, thick and pink, lick and curl around the bones until they are clean and white. Every once in a while, two of them stand up and pull at the same piece of meat until the winner totters back holding the tattered morsel victoriously in her hands.

"This is great," Winnie says. "So savage! So primal!"

"Yeah," I say, staring at the head table. I can't keep my eyes off her. The Animal Mistress. She is the leader, a bonafide buffalo aficionado, lover of all creatures big and small. She is also a mass of jingly jangly bones that adorn every part of her body: nose, ears, wrists, belly button. I walk over and smile.

"That can't be your real name," the Animal Mistress says. And she gives me a gentle reproachful look.

"No," I say. "It's not my real name."

"Thank Christ," she says. "You look more like a *Raven Hawk* or a *Spirit Wolf.*"

I smile. "Thank you."

"Why don't you have your real name tag?"

"Because I'm on probation."

"Probation?" she says. "Probation?"

"Uh huh."

"Says who?"

I point to the back of the banquet hall where Karl is standing, a still, lone figure in white.

"Not him. Jesus, is he still here?"

"Uh huh."

"So what's your real name?"

"Katherine."

She lays her jingly hand on my shoulder. "Don't worry, Katherine. We'll see to it that you get a name tag by the end of the night."

I walk away a changed woman. The trays have never been so light. The serving never so smooth. The night never so easy. Tonight, I am the Karen Kain of catering. I glide, I jump, I twirl. Even the chef notices something. "Tina, you're not yourself tonight. You seem so — so — *happy.*"

"I am," I say, smiling. Then I glide back onto the banquet hall floor to finish serving The Women Who Run With Buffalo. They are kind. They are considerate. They are perfect ladies. I tell all of this to Karl, who is slowly biting a hole through his lip. He refuses to go into the kitchen. He's watching The Women Who Run with Buffalo's every move. He's waiting for things to get out of hand. He's waiting for a rumble. And when he calls my name, I feel a little laugh, gurgling victoriously in my throat.

There are lots of speeches and toasts. 1997 has been an especially good year for the Women Who Run With Buffalo. The Animal Mistress makes the final speech. She turns to the buffalo as Karl's fists tighten into little baby fists.

"Ladies," the Animal Mistress says as she holds up a huge silver wine goblet. "Here's to the buffalo."

There is a thunderous applause. Even the chef starts to clap.

"As you know, all living things have souls. Give and take is the essence of everything. And as we feast on nature's gifts, ponder for a moment, if you will, the link between the hunter and the hunted. As you chew on every morsel of tender meat, acknowledge the timelessness and indestructibility of the great spirit that is within all of these creatures. Think not of the hunter who takes life, but of the animal who *gives* you its life. So, as we look upon this great symbol of eternal life, look at it through the eyes of those fearless sisters — and brothers — who had the courage to run with the buffalo."

The Women Who Run With Buffalo go crazy. They thump their bones on the tables and whistle through their gravy-stained fingers.

"Finally, I'd like to make a toast to our wonderful servers tonight. And to one in particular." Then all eyes fall on me. "To Katherine, who, despite what her name tag says, is most definitely *not a Tina*."

There is more applause. Winnie pats my back. Karl just glares. Then the Animal Mistress turns to me. "And bring your lovely friend as well." Winnie and I walk over. We watch intently as the Animal Mistress motions to her two assistants to lift the buffalo.

"No," Karl mutters, stepping forward. "Over my dead — "

But the Animal Mistress just smiles. "Ladies," she says. "This buffalo is for you."

That's when we take the buffalo and run with it. It's the same fantasy. Nothing changes. We charge down the entire floor of the banquet hall, knocking glasses and plates off the tables. We charge to the clapping and the stomping. We charge to Marco's famous battlecry as he snaps the table cloth off the table with one hand and swirls it around our legs. We charge with the buffalo high in the air and keep going until Karl is exactly where we want him.

SKY GILBERT is a renowned thespian and author of *Guilty* (Insomniac Press). "St. Stephen's" is an excerpt from his novel of the same name, forthcoming from Insomniac Press in 1999.

St. Stephen's

SKY GILBERT

LET ME TELL YOU about my favorite teachers. And it seems to me that they were my favorite teachers because they revealed something personal — something about their feelings, or their bodies, or both.

The first best teacher I remember was Mr. Lavey. He taught me history in grades seven to nine. At the time this was called Junior High School. On some level I was as in love with Mr. Lavey, as I was with Miss O'Brian. I don't know if he knew it. He did encourage me to hang out with him though.

In his history class Mr. Lavey encouraged controversy and argument; boy did I used to like to argue. I was very opinionated, about — well, I can't remember what. I think my views were pretty right-wing (I didn't get lefty until I became a homosexual and realized how oppressive life could be) but the point is, the whole class would just sit there like dumb thugs until I began to argue. I really could stir things up (still can!). I think that's why Mr. Lavey liked me so much; it made his job easier. And I wrote these papers for him that were incredibly cheery and funny. They were supposed to be essays about The War of 1812 and stuff, but I'd give them great titles like "How to have a Stupid War and Alienate a Whole Bunch of People and Spend Lots of Money and Solve Nothing." And the essay would be organized like a conversation between two soldiers. And each of them would have empty pockets, say, complaining about how little money they had when the war was over and why. Looking back on it, these essays were incredibly creative. And Mr. Lavey loved them. And I would hang out with him after class and well . . . and I fell for him. He wasn't attractive in a traditional way. He was short and he looked something like a monkey, with a pug nose. He had acne scars. But it didn't matter to me. And I'd tell Mr. Lavey that I was too unpopular and I wanted to quit being a brainer (browner) and try and get lower marks. We actually made that a project. For me to get lower marks. So he was sort of a friend, too, and psychotherapist. He came over to my house once. And he had dinner with my mom. And I wanted like anything for them to get married (my parents were divorced). I mean it made perfect sense to me! I thought of myself as Hayley Mills in The Parent Trap. Of course, I didn't realize that the only thing these two people had in common was that I loved them more than anything in the world.

Another great teacher I had was Mr. Manley. This was earlier, grade five. Mr. Manley was incredibly handsome and I had him for a whole year. It was hard for me to study because he was so cute and I was (even in grade five) always imagining what he was like under his clothes. Well, I remember one day he said we were going to have a "special" class. He closed all the doors and windows and pulled the curtains and rolled up his sleeves. It was so exciting. He told us this was a very important day for all of us. I couldn't believe it. He said he was going to show us something very important. I was sure he was going to show us his dick. I was sure of it. I remember thinking, at the time, how educational that would be. He didn't, though. Instead, he took out a pack of cigarettes and smoked one, in front of us, in the classroom. (He looked so sexy when he smoked, it was unbearable, just like James Dean, and he was our teacher!) And then he took a paper napkin and he breathed into the napkin after taking a smoke and showed us the mess of nicotine on the paper. And then he said "This is what happens when you smoke. This is why you must never smoke." He was so serious. I almost came in my pants. And I remember thinking, at the time, how privileged we were to see this side of Mr. Manley. The sincere, smoking side of him. It really was like seeing him naked. When it was over Mr. Manley opened the door again, and rolled down his sleeves. I spent six years in elementary school. The only day I remember clearly in that whole time was when Mr. Manley rolled up his sleeves and smoked. He showed me something of himself. I wish he showed me more. (By the way, I didn't start smoking until I was almost thirty-years-old. Which means my skin is very clear and unwrinkled for an older guy. Was this due to Mr. Manley? You be the judge.)

And then there was Mr. Quelch. He's still alive. That's what I have to say about Mr. Quelch. He's still alive and I still see him now and then in the gay ghetto.

Mr. Quelch was my music teacher. When I was about seventeen-years-old I used to play in a quartet at music school. I almost went into music before I started acting. I played the cello (it's where I met Marco, the handsome and romantic trumpet player). And Mr. Quelch used to teach us how to play the Schubert "Trout" quintet every Saturday morning. I remember it was a bright, sunny room with windows all around, and empty music stands, and all the charming musical paraphernalia littering the room. I loved getting up early and dragging my cello over there to practice. I don't know why, considering Mr. Quelch was a horrible man, a sadist. He was about sixty-years-old at the time (this was thirty years ago, and he's still alive) and he was all bent over and bald. He was your nightmare music teacher. You'd play like one note and he'd go "No, no no!" And he'd make you do it again. And again, and again and again until you never wanted to hear that note again. He made me hate the "Trout" quintet. (Even today, I can't listen to it without getting tense, and I'm a Schubert lover). He treated you like you were totally stupid, and he was very easily exasperated. I hated him. But I also felt sorry for him, because he just seemed so terribly unhappy. You couldn't make old Quelch smile, ever. And his whole life was music. Everything. And it seemed like he knew about another world, that was somewhere in his brain, where every note was played perfectly, by someone, but not you. Because every note had to be right.

So that would have been the whole story, but I inadvertently learned other stuff about Quelch. I asked some people at the school about him, and they said that Quelch had been a child prodigy, and that something had happened (an unexplained tragedy) and he had never realized his potential. I always wondered what happened, but it explained his bitterness.

And later, when I became a total faggot, I was lying in a room in the most depraved bathhouse in The Big City. And, it was many years after this, I was an adult, and who should come cruising by my room but a very very old Mr. Quelch. You have to realize that this bathhouse was where people would pee on people, and tie each other up, and do various other indignities. And there was old Quelch, he must have been eighty-five, hobbling around, all bent over. It all made sense now. He was a sadist, in art, and in life. I'm sure he tied people up and made them beg for things. And when they begged wrong he'd make them do it again and again until they got it right.

Those are the three teacher teachers, that is, real teachers, who showed me part off their life, and helped me to learn.

Then there were two people in my life I want to tell you about who taught me stuff, but they weren't hired to teach me. They just did. Kate and Michael.

Kate was this s/m dyke that I met because I moved into this group house once and she lived there part time. I remember being afraid of her. The guys in the house said "Oh a dyke lives here part of the time and her name is Kate. And you'll really like her, she makes porn movies." At the time I didn't know any dykes and I was basically scared of them. Kate changed all that. She was probably the funniest person I ever met. She was a professor of political philosophy and she made porn movies. When I first met her she asked me if I was a "top" or a "bottom." I said I didn't know. She said:

"When you have sex, do you like to do all the work, or do you like to have someone do all the work?" I said, "They can do all the work, that's fine with me." Then she said, "Do you like to come up with the fantasies and the ideas for great sex, or do you want your partner to do that?" And I said, "Someone else can do that, thank you." Then she said, "Well you're a 'bottom' then."

It was very interesting to find that out. Then she gave me some advice. She said, "Since you're a masochist, just don't tell a lot of people, except the ones you want to fuck. First of all, there are too many masochists in the world anyway. Secondly, you'll get treated badly when you wait in line (she meant any old line, like at the grocery store). People find out you're a bottom and they'll make you go to the end of the line. If I were you, don't tell anybody but the ones you want to go to bed with that you're a 'bottom'." It was good advice (nowadays I don't know what I am. I think maybe I'm an active bottom or a submissive top). She also told me I was a "pervert." "What's that?" I said. She said it just meant that I was a sexual person. And that sex was of prime importance to me. She said she was a pervert, too. She hung out mainly with street hookers who were usually quite beautiful and sometimes a little tragic and dangerous. She taught me a lot.

And then years later I was over at her house in London and we were having a party and she was trying to get me to fuck her friend (male — very cute). And we were staggering around and all stoned, and this guy and I peed together, and she watched, and the next morning she told me that my dick was really great.

I don't know why, but it seemed like a special kind of bond to have with a lesbian, and it made me feel really good about myself that she liked my dick.

Then finally, Michael, can't talk about him really, except he makes me think of Theodore, in a way. I think maybe Theodore was the incarnation of Michael for me. Just to say Michael was a boy I loved. He was a crazy punk ex-hooker brat. He did too many drugs and got AIDS. And we used to fuck occasionally, in strange places (toilets in restaurants for instance). One day we were looking for pot so desperately and we couldn't find any. So we just used some tea from the cupboard and smoked it. And suddenly everything got so slow. Very slow. I remember crossing a very small field and just never getting to the other side. Afterwards, when Michael was gone (he died of AIDS) I tried to figure out what fucking tea that was, a tea that you can find in any cupboard that makes you completely stoned out of your mind. Of course I couldn't find the damn tea. Maybe it didn't exist. What did we get high on? Only Michael knows, and he's not around.

And when he was dying in San Francisco he phoned me and I didn't know what to say. I literally didn't know what to say. I could hear he was all drugged up. Michael was always completely stoned and wounded and I always wanted to help him. But there isn't much you can do sometimes. Michael completely accepted me. We loved each other in a completely relaxed way, whenever we felt like it, sometimes sexual, sometimes non-sexual. I remember Michael once wanted to fuck me without a condom. He just wanted to shove his big hard dick up my ass so badly. He was going to use spit. "Spit and push," he said. "Remember the old spit and push? I like the old spit and push . . . " I didn't let him and so I didn't get AIDS then, at least. (I never got tested so I don't know whether I have it now.)

So those are the major teachers of my life besides Miss O'Brian and Mr. Lowenstien and Steve.

I just had to tell you about all my best teachers and how they showed me a part of their lives.

DAVID HENDERSON is an Ottawa writer. He has published extensively through-out North America and is a two-time finalist in the Robert Penn Warren Poetry Competition.

Spider in his Head

DAVID HENDERSON

HE AWAKES IN THE MORNING LIGHT with a killer headache, skull an overripe watermelon about to burst. He is aware that this is something he experiences most mornings, but for the life of him, he can't remember who or where he is. He doesn't panic, though. Panic will make the block worse. He simply lies there in bed, waiting, his mind blank, his eyes on the ceiling — on the corner around which the light globe is hiding, a spatial deformation he knows isn't there.

Finally, the block lessens. "Miles," he says with relief. He has some difficulty with enunciation. "My name's Miles." And it comes to him that he's at his parent's house in Ottawa, in the guest bedroom.

He gets out of bed and goes into the bathroom, gulps down steroids to reduce the pressure, to placate the spider in his head with its restless legs and bloating abdomen. The sink and toilet have melted together, so it takes him a moment to figure out which is where and relieve himself. After, he finds his razor and plugs it in, but as he raises it to his face, he looks in the mirror, and stops cold.

There's a great crease, like a chasm, down the middle of his face. His shaved skull, scarred from the operation and bald in patches from treatments, is still visible, but his mouth and nose are lost at the dark bottom of the chasm, and his eyes are spilling, Daliesque, over the edge. The crease is something new. He touches his face, but of course the crease isn't really there. It's in his head, not on it. The spider again, playing games. He tries to conjure up his face from memory, for reassurance, but it bears the same crease. Shaken, he tries to recall Marge's face, his sister Carole's face, his parents' faces, but they all have the same disfiguring crease down the middle. In fact, he can't think of anyone who doesn't have the same damned crease. They are all alien.

He takes a couple of deep breaths to steady himself, and shaves his face and head by feel.

After a shower, he decides he better go and get something to eat, headache or no. The steroids are agitating for it, and he'll start feeling worse before long if he doesn't comply. As soon as he leaves the bedroom, however, he comes to a confused standstill in the hallway. This is the house his parents moved to after his father retired from government two years before. It's a simple layout, and of course he knows where the kitchen is, but he's inexplicably uncertain for the moment how to get there. He's still standing in the hallway, trying to sort this out, when his mother comes upstairs. Her face is disguised by the crease, but he knows it's her. She's wearing her new flowered summer dress.

"Geography problems?" she asks, lightly.

He manages a grin. Lately, he's been having more and more difficulties like this, to the point that he can't take the bus any more because he can't figure where to get off even when he knows the route. Shortcomings like this embarrass him, make him feel the fool.

"I was going to get some breakfast," he says, the words coming hesitantly.

"It's all ready," she says. "Pancakes and bacon. Come on. I'll keep you company. I've got something to tell you." And she turns and heads downstairs, Miles following.

"Where's Dad?" he asks as he pours syrup on his pancakes. "He's supposed to drive me to the doctor's for an appointment this morning." The pressure in his head is lessening. His mother's nose and mouth surface as the crease fades, as if air is being pumped into her head.

"I'll take you," she says. "Your father's playing an early round of golf before it gets too hot and muggy."

"Oh." He half-expected something like this. "What did you want to tell me?"

His mother hesitates, appears abashed as she fiddles with her coffee spoon. "You've got another appointment," she says, "tomorrow, at 2:30. I'd really like you to go. I'll drive you, of course."

Miles delays the progress of a forkful of pancake towards his mouth, and asks, "Appointment? What appointment?"

She sighs, and the response comes flooding out. "Miles, this may sound a little strange and I hope you understand, but I met a woman named Nancy Broadhurst when I went to Laura Petersen's for cake and coffee after choral practice last night. Laura brought us together on purpose. She knows how distressed I am about you, about your — oh, you know what I mean. Anyway, Nancy has a fifteen-year-old daughter who's been cured of a malignant brain tumor. Her name's Gillian, and she was there, too. Her voice quavers and her walk is unsteady, but she's definitely very much alive and well. We talked for a long time, and then this morning Nancy called and made an appointment for you at the clinic because I asked her if she would . . . "

"Whoa, Mom," Miles says. "Whoa." He sets the fork down on his plate. "What do you mean, cured? What did she have? What sort of tumor?"

"She had a medulla-something . . . "

"Medulloblastoma?" There are few tumors he hasn't heard of.

"That's it," his mother says. "That's the one. The doctors operated, but couldn't get it all, just like you. They gave her first-line radiation and chemotherapy, but the tumor grew back, again just like you. Gillian was in bad shape, dying, and the doctors were about to operate a second time, but she didn't want another operation and Nancy heard about the clinic from a friend, so she checked Gillian out of the hospital and carried her into the clinic for her first treatment. After that, it was twice a day for seven months. By the end of the treatment, Gillian was fine. She went back to the doctors for a CT scan and tests, and the tumor was gone. Gone! It had done a little damage, but there was no longer any trace of it. The doctors were amazed. That was nearly a year ago."

"All right, Mom, all right. So I'm curious. What's this clinic all about? Imaging? Laetrile? Wheatgrass? Psychic healing? There are enough quacks out there to fill a duck pond. I know because I've looked."

"It's an acupuncture clinic."

"Acupuncture!" Miles can't help smiling.

"At least go for the appointment. Just to see what it's all about. For my sake."

Miles picks up his fork again. "Tomorrow at 2:30?" he says, and shrugs. "Alright. If you like."

Miles and his mother return from his medical appointment around noon. As they walk in the back door of the house, Miles's father is pouring himself a beer.

"Have a good game?" Miles asks him.

His father looks in his direction, but past him, as he often does now. Is it the nakedness of the scalp that troubles him? "I forgot I'd arranged to play a round with André Thérien," his father says.

"That's alright. Mom took me to the doctor's."

"I didn't like the doctor at all," his mother puts in. "An inconsiderate know-it-all."

"Oh? What did he have to say?"

"Nothing new, really," Miles says.

His father takes his beer out onto the back patio and buries himself in the newspaper. He is a tall, silver-haired man who folds himself awkwardly into chairs, and is more serious than severe. Miles goes out and sits near him, taking in the warmth of the sun and listening to the cardinal in the apple tree. For the moment, his head isn't too bad. A short while later, his mother brings out sandwiches, iced tea and pastries, and they have a silent lunch.

As he eats, Miles looks around the garden — the beds of begonias his mother has planted, the lilies, the yellow-flowering potentilla, the great maple heavy with leaves in the corner opposite the apple tree. He admires all the lushness of the brief but intense Ottawa summer. And it comes to him suddenly and ineffably that he isn't ready to die, that somehow he can evade the end the doctors have charted for him. A temporary euphoria grips him. "It's going to be alright," he says, as he looks up at the top of the two-hundred-year-old maple. "I'm going to be fine." The thought comforts him for a few moments before its evanescence, even though he's aware it's probably one of the spider's tricks. His father grunts and continues reading the paper. His mother's lips tremble briefly.

It is late that afternoon. Miles is lying on his bed with his eyes closed. He's resting after a *petit mal* episode that came on shortly after lunch. In addition, he's experiencing a hallucination in which surfaces like table tops or floors seem dangerously tilted. His private horror flick is the way he thinks of hallucinations like this. They don't frighten him that much anymore, but they can be disorienting.

His mother walks in. "The mail's just come," she says. "There's a letter for you from Marge. Here." She puts the letter in his hand.

"Great," he says, his eyes still closed. "I'll get to it in a moment."

"Want me to read it to you?"

"No," he says. "I'll manage."

His mother leaves. Miles waits a while until the hallucination lessens, then looks at the envelope with its familiar return address. Marge Hilliard-Norton on Kitchener in Vancouver. His wife finds it hard to talk with him on the phone these days. It's upsetting. She prefers the emotional distance correspondence provides. This is understandable, he supposes. It hasn't been easy for her.

He sits up on the bed, pillows behind him, and opens the letter. He can see only half of each word, but he brings out the missing halves by underlining them with a finger, word by word. Marge is fine. She got the promotion she wanted in the accounting firm she works for. She's been out sailing a couple of times with Morgan and Jack, Miles's partners in their Port Moody boatyard. The boatyard's doing fine, turning a nice profit on three up-scale commissions. Morgan and Jack send their best. She misses him and hopes things will take a turn for the better. Love, Marge.

It's the part about sailing that sends unexpected and uncontrollable tears coursing down his cheeks (the spider likes to exaggerate). Marge and good health aside, it's what he misses most. Being out on the Strait of Georgia on the *Coriander*, their twenty-six foot sloop, just the two of them. Sometimes, when he's feeling low, he replays one of the trips they made on the boat before his illness overtook him, catching him up in its wash. Today it's the Sechelt trip.

It was three summers ago. Miles and Marge sailed the *Coriander* up the coast to Sechelt and stayed there overnight. On the return leg, they anchored off Gower Point and strip-cast for salmon. Miles caught a five-pound coho, and was razzing Marge because all she could come up with was an ugly rock cod, when a sudden storm came down the Strait and caught them, waves growing in size by the minute.

Miles reeled in his line, and went forward to raise anchor while Marge started the motor. When the motor was running smoothly, she took her rod out of the bracket to reel it in only to find she couldn't.

"I've got something!" she yelled to Miles above the wind and rain, and the rumble of the motor. "It's *huge!* I can hardly move it."

Miles secured the anchor to the deck and went aft. "You've probably got bottom," he said. "Cut your line and let's get out of here."

"No way!" she cried. "It's a fish, maybe a great spring. I can feel it move. I'm going to land it, damn you, shut you up about your silly coho!"

It took her an hour. Miles kept the boat pointed into the ten-foot waves while she struggled to bring the fish to the surface without breaking the line. She was soaked to the skin by the rain, her short dark hair plastered to her scalp.

"Jesus!" Miles exclaimed when the fish first surfaced, all gray and white and monstrous in the water beside the boat. "It's a skate. Must be six or seven feet across." And he laughed. They both laughed. "Some spring salmon!" he said.

"Help me get it on board," Marge said.

"Too big. And dangerous. Better cut it free."

"No! We're bringing it home. I want a picture of it, or no one will believe me. Besides, the meat in the wings is supposed to be as good as crab meat."

So Miles gaffed the skate and severed its life to stop it thrashing about. Then he carved a hole through the snout and secured the fish to the boat with a cord, and they towed it through the storm, past Salmon Rock, past Point Atkinson, under the Lions Gate Bridge and up

DAVID HENDERSON

Burrard Inlet. It was the dead of night by the time they reached their berth at the boatyard on the Port Moody shore. They were cold, exhausted, but unquestionably happy.

As Miles reads through Marge's letter again, he can sense in it some of the sadness of the last two years. No, it hasn't been easy for her, all that time and energy spent nursing him through radiation treatments and chemotherapy. Especially the chemo — days of vomiting everything up and continuing to retch even when his stomach was empty, days of guzzling protein supplement in a race to get some strength and nourishment from it before heaving it up as well. Miles became terribly familiar with toilet bowls. Simply the sight of one could bring on nausea.

Sometimes he asked himself whether it was worth going through so much pain and unpleasantness. Maybe it would be better to choose a shortcut and end the misery. But then he would see the hope that still lit Marge's eyes, and he'd persist for a while longer, and then a little longer again.

Still, it was hard for her to be continually optimistic, and he knew there were times when a smile cost her dearly, when the strain became almost too much.

Yet, for all that, she was the one who hadn't wanted him to go back east.

He remembers the evening he told her the neurosurgeon's prognosis after the tumor had started to grow again. Three or four months, the doctor had said, and nothing more they could do about it. The tumor was too spread out to be operable, and too virulent to be treated by chemo or radiation. There were tears in her eyes as he told her he'd decided to go back to Ottawa to stay with his parents until the end, but she forced a smile, and said, "What? You don't like the quality of the care you get around here?" And she wouldn't hear of it.

But after he pointed out that it wasn't fair to expect her to work and look after him as well, that the last two years since the operation had been tough enough for her and things were going to get a lot worse, and that, most of all, he didn't want to stick around and die falling apart bit-by-bit in front of her, she eventually and reluctantly agreed that his going east might be a good idea, and he remembers sensing in her a relief caught up inside the sadness of giving way and letting him go.

The day after the arrival of Marge's letter, Miles's mother drives him to his acupuncture appointment.

Dr Phuong's clinic is an old three-story house in a commercial area to the west of downtown Ottawa, and is only a short drive from where Miles's parents live.

The first thing that strikes Miles, as he and his mother come through the front door, is the heavy, pervasive odor of rubbing alcohol. The second is the number and variety of shoes (loafers, sandals, brogues, pumps, Reeboks) lining the long, narrow reception area. To Miles's left, in what used to be a living room, are some nine or ten beds with barely enough space between them for passage, while in front of him, at the end of the reception area in which several patients await their turn, is a small sunroom with four beds. His mother has been told there are some twenty-five beds in the clinic. The rest, Miles concludes, must be upstairs or down. All of the beds he can see are occupied by half-dressed men, women or children lying either on their backs or their sides. Some are talking, others are silent. One snores.

In the sunroom, a man in a sports shirt and grey flannels stands over the body of a female patient, sticking needles in her legs with quick, deft movements. This must be Dr Phuong. He looks to be in his forties or fifties.

A Vietnamese woman stands beside a small, high reception desk. Dr Phuong's wife. "You have appointment?" she asks Miles and his mother. There is an air of easy authority about her.

Miles's mother says, "Nancy Broadhurst made an appointment for my son. We've come for a consultation."

"Ah, Nancy. Yes, yes. What your name?" she asks Miles. Miles tells her. She checks a list, nods. "Yes. Good. Please sit." She calls out a couple of sentences of Vietnamese to her husband. He replies briefly, places two needles between the patient's eyebrows.

Miles and his mother take neighboring chairs. "Where's Dr Phuong's office?" she asks Mrs Phuong. "For the consultation."

Mrs Phuong laughs. "Consultation now," she says.

Dr Phuong moves to another patient in the sunroom. He looks

DAVID HENDERSON

over at Miles, squints at his head. "How many operation?" he asks. His accent is heavy.

"One," Miles said. "Two years ago."

"What kind of tumor?"

"An astrocytoma in the right parietal lobe, the size of an egg." Miles holds out his hand, fingers dangling down limply, a gesture borrowed from his neurosurgeon in Vancouver. "It looks like this, like a spider."

The doctor doesn't react to the information, but he's studying Miles. At the same time, he's placing needles by feel, glancing only occasionally at what he's doing. Once, he takes a needle out and places it again. The patient, a man, doesn't stir. "Bad headache?" Dr Phuong asks Miles. "Convulsion?"

"Sometimes," says Miles.

"Problem with memory?"

"Yeah."

"How your stomach?" He pronounced the 'ch' soft.

"Okay, I guess."

"Thirty-five?"

"Thirty-three."

"How your eyes?"

"They see funny things sometimes."

Dr Phuong finishes with the male patient, then walks into the living room and starts on another patient, an elderly woman. As he places the needles, his line of questioning changes. "You like chicken, cheese?"

"Yeah."

Someone murmurs, "Wrong answer." Laughter.

"Too bad," Dr Phuong says. "You smoke?"

"No."

"Good. How many girlfriends?" Chuckles from the patients. Obviously a popular question. Miles says he's married. More chuckles. "Where your wife?" Dr Phuong continues. Miles tells him. No one chuckles this time.

Dr Phuong finishes with the old woman and comes and stands in the doorway. "Eight month and you good as new. Start Monday. Twice a day. I make your teeth white, too. No extra charge."

Chuckles again from the patients. "You always say that, Dr Phuong," a woman says.

"Because it true," Dr Phuong says, and breaks into a grin. He looks at Miles again. "You have picture?"

"They did a CT scan a couple of weeks ago."

"Bring it," Dr Phuong says.

Miles's mother's face is a mixture of hope and incredulity. "You really think you can help him doctor?" she asks.

"Sure, no problem. Eight month. You speak to my boss." He indicates his wife. "She tell you what to do." He turns away and goes back into the living room.

Mrs Phuong instructs Miles to wear shorts, and bring a towel to put on the bed. He's to come every weekday at eight in the morning, and again at two, and he's to pay the fee for the week every Friday. She says he'll have his own needles and he'll have to change them every couple of months. He's to take vitamin C and B-1, and follow a special diet. She gives him a list of what he can and cannot eat. Most cooked fruits and vegetables are all right. Pork. Lamb. But no cheese, no chicken, no beef, no seafood, no butter, no eggs, no . . . it's a long list.

"How essential is this?" he asks Mrs Phuong.

"Very important," Mrs Phuong says, "for needle."

"I see," says Miles, although he doesn't.

"Now isn't that one for the books," his mother says when they're in the car.

"Yeah. Wall-to-wall bodies. I wonder what they all have."

"Nancy Broadhurst says he handles just about everything. Back problems. Migraines. Colitis. You name it."

"And he cures them all?"

"I rather doubt it," his mother says. "But he must help some or people wouldn't come to him. How do you feel about it? You don't have to show up on Monday, you know."

"Well, I'm kind of skeptical. But what the hell, I'll give it a try. It'll keep me busy."

By 8:10 Monday morning, Miles is lying on his back with needles in the soles of his feet, needles up and down his legs, needles in his elbows, needles in the soft flesh between thumb and forefinger, needles in his temples, needles between his eyebrows, and a needle just below his

DAVID HENDERSON

throat. To his surprise, they don't hurt. The ends sticking out of him have little grips on them. The pattern of placement, a fellow patient informs him, varies subtly over time.

After a half hour, Mrs Phuong removes the needles in his legs and elbows, and the one in the right temple. She staunches any bleeding with cotton wool and rubbing alcohol, and tells Miles to turn onto his right side, facing the wall. A few minutes later, Dr Phuong sticks needles into his neck, and up and down his back. Another half hour and all the needles are removed, and that's it till two o'clock.

This is the way it goes, morning and afternoon, five days a week. Sometimes Miles is on the main floor of the clinic, sometimes upstairs, or in the basement. Sometimes he talks with the patients around him, other times he just listens. People are always changing their appointments around, so he gets to see a broad cross-section of his fellow patients. They come in all shapes and sizes, and about the only thing they have in common is that medical science can't seem to help them. What draws them is hope, and word of any improvement spreads like wildfire. Miles hears of a woman cured of leukemia, two teenage girls whose MS has gone into remission, a man with bladder cancer whose CT scan is now clean, and more. These stories are repeated over and over. They become legend.

After three weeks, Miles starts to feel better. He has more energy. While he still has bad headaches and visual problems, he experiences fewer seizures, and the hallucinations are gone. He finds he can reduce his steroid intake, which is great. "Something's happening up here," he tells his mother, touching his head with a forefinger. He's out on the patio with his parents. "The needles are helping."

"Oh, good, Miles," she says. "I'm happy to hear it." She turns to her husband. "Isn't that wonderful, dear?"

But his father makes no comment. He looks up briefly at her, then goes on reading his newspaper.

Throughout the colorful autumn in Ottawa, Miles senses small ameliorations. His speech is clearer, and his sense of orientation improves to the point he can often take the bus to the clinic. There are setbacks, to be sure, but Dr Phuong says these are to be expected. The acupuncturist's confidence in the ultimate outcome is unshakable. It's infectious.

One day in late October, Miles finds himself sharing a small room in the basement of the clinic with a teenage girl. She is slim, with an oval face and a hesitant walk. Her brown hair is waved so that it nearly hides the scars on her head. As Dr Phuong places her needles, he talks to her, and Miles discovers that it's Gillian Broadhurst, the daughter of the woman who got him his first appointment at the clinic. When the doctor goes on to another room, leaving the two of them lying there on their backs, full of needles, Miles introduces himself, and asks, "Why have you come back? I thought you were fine."

"I am," she replies. "But the tumor messed things up a bit while it was there. Dr Phuong thinks he can reverse that, so I'm back for a while." The tremor in her voice is obvious.

"Is it helping?"

"I've just started. How's it going with you?"

"Making progress, I think."

"Great."

"What I can't figure out," Miles says, after a moment's silence, "is the difference around here between those who get better and those who don't. I mean, we all get roughly the same treatment, but not everyone walks out healthy. What makes the difference?"

Gillian ponders the question. "Have you met Kristin?" she asks.

"The dark-haired woman with bone cancer and two mastectomies?"

"And all those sores. The pain must be *incredible*, but she never complains. The doctors can't believe she's still alive. And you know something? I'll bet she makes it. She's convinced she will, and she has this special quality, like the pain has burned up everything bad in her."

"Is that what happened to you?"

Gillian laughs. "Not likely! I'm not at all like Kristin. When it comes to pain, I'm a big coward and whiner. But, deep down inside, I really wanted to live, and I think that helped a lot. Some people have already given up by the time they get here. Like, they're just going through the motions to please their families, or whatever."

"It's hard sometimes not to let go," Miles remarks. He recalls a patient who has stopped showing up, an old Dutchman with cancer of the pancreas. A gaunt, dour man, he came only because his daughter insisted. "You not eat," Dr Phuong once exclaimed to him in exasperation. "You give me no help." "Eating hurts," the old man said. "Life hurt more than death," was Dr Phuong's reply. "All Vietnam people know that."

Gillian shifts gingerly on her bed. "Sure it's hard. I mean, there were days when I thought I'd couldn't take any more, specially when the tumor did strange things with my mind . . . "

"Tell me about it," Miles says, softly.

"I guess you know what it's like," she says, "but I got through those days, one way or another. Yet now . . . well . . . I sometimes wonder if it was worth the struggle."

Miles is startled. "Why do you say that?"

She says nothing.

"Gillian?"

"It's kind of embarrassing . . . "

"Hey, what can be more embarrassing than throwing up all the time and having your hair fall out in clumps?"

She breaks out laughing. She has a nice laugh. More adult than child. "It's just that, you know, who would want to go out with me, like on a date? I mean, maybe I drool."

"There'll be lots of guys," Miles says. "Wait and see. I would myself if I were your age." And he means it. He likes her spunk.

"You serious? Even with my funny voice and walk?"

"I'm serious. They're not important." He pauses. "Now, drooling's another thing . . . " And she cracks up.

But he understands her worry. He remembers being surprised at first that Marge would stay with someone whose head was scarred and whose prospects were limited. One of life's miracles, her constancy. And he wonders, if, in her shoes, he would've been capable of staying the course. He hopes so.

Christmas arrives, and the clinic is closed until January 2. Marge couldn't come east for the holidays like they'd planned. Pressures of work, and a Scrooge-like boss.

Miles gets a history of wooden boat building from his parents, and a Sony Walkman from his sister Carole in Toronto, which is nice because he broke his in November. He gives his mother a silk scarf, his father a wool sweater, and Carole (who's spending Christmas with her in-laws in Hamilton) a cotton shirt. He's sent Marge a pair of eighteen carat gold earrings crafted by an artisan in Quebec, and receives from her an antique brass sextant, lying polished in its blue velvet-lined wooden case. The sextant, Marge writes in a note, is 'to chart a happier course in the new year.' He sights the lamp across the room. The sextant has a nice feel to it. On impulse, he calls Marge to thank her.

"So, how are you doing?" she asks after an awkward pause in the conversation.

"Not bad," he says. "I'm having a CT scan in mid-January. That'll give us some idea of where we are. I think the tumor's shrunk." He goes on to tell her that the neurosurgeon and oncologist he's been seeing in Ottawa both seem put out he's still alive. He says this to amuse her, although there's an element of truth to it.

But all she says is, "Are they, now?"

"Marge, I think I'm making real progress." He tries to put enough conviction in this for both of them.

"That's great," she replies, "but don't let me get my hopes up till you're sure, Miles. All right? Hope's a fragile thing. Now let me speak to your folks so I can wish them a Merry Christmas."

For Christmas dinner, his mother serves a baked ham. Turkey is one of the foods banned by Dr Phuong.

As the three of them eat, Miles's father reflects on how many of their retired friends will be packing up and heading for Florida, the Caribbean or Portugal after the holidays.

"Why don't you go, then?" Miles says sharply. "Don't stick around for my sake." Then, shifting direction and tone before his father can react, he adds, "Wait till next year, Dad. Marge and I'll come with you. We can hire a boat and sail around the Caribbean. How's that sound?"

His father cuts another slice from the ham for himself, and changes the subject.

Later, when Miles is alone with his mother, he says, "I think Dad's written me off."

"No, he hasn't," she says. "He's just heartsick to see you going through all this, and doesn't know how to react."

"He could try being more positive."

"I know. I'll speak to him."

"Don't. It isn't worth anything if it's forced."

Toward the end of January, Miles goes to see the neurosurgeon for the results of the CT scan. The doctor's name is Schwartz, and he's a pompous man.

"The tumor has paused in its growth," Dr Schwartz says. "It's the same size as in the last scan. But that's a temporary thing. It will start up again soon, and the disease will take its unfortunate course. There's no doubt about that. I'd be remiss in my duty if I pretended otherwise."

Depressed, Miles takes the CT scan and shows it to Dr Phuong. "Tumor not grow," Dr Phuong says, looking pleased. "Five month and it not grow. Look, much less dense. Pretty soon — poof! — it go. Four month more and no more tumor."

"You're sure?" Miles asks, uncertainly.

"No problem. Four month. Don't worry, be happy, and I take care of it. You much better. Remember when you first come? You much better now. Don't worry."

Miles thinks it over, and decides there's nothing to be gained in believing Dr Schwartz. He isn't ready to give in to the spider.

He calls Marge. "The tumor's stopped growing," he says. "I'm going to beat the rap."

"Oh Miles, I hope you're right."

"Can you take your holidays in June?"

"I suppose. Why?"

"I thought we'd sail the *Coriander* down and around Puget Sound."

Pause. "Are you sure about this? I mean, isn't it a bit soon to make plans?"

"I need something to aim for. It's important."

Another pause; then she says, "All right, Miles. If you think so. I'll stock the boat and make the arrangements."

"Great!" he says, his heart as full as a spinnaker straining at the rigging in a brisk following wind. "We'll have a fantastic trip. Best ever."

"Just be sure you show up."

"I'll be there," Miles says, closing his eyes and trying to imagine it all. "I'll be there."

SHELLEY LEEDAHL is a Saskatoon writer. She is the author of *Sky Kickers* and *A Few Words For January*, both published by Thistledown Press.

Wintering

SHELLEY LEEDAHL

"DID YOU CARVE THE PUMPKIN YET?" Dominique asks, in the kitchen, unloading groceries. Groceries that *she* bought with *her* money, which she'll no doubt remind me about before this Halloween day is done.

"Just getting to it," I call from my office. "I've been working." I flick on my computer and pull an old story onto the screen. Anything will do. My wife wouldn't know new from old; she wouldn't look that closely.

In the kitchen she slams cupboard drawers, loads the fridge, then pounds across the dining room floor to my office on the other side. "Jesus, Pete. I've been asking you to get on that for two days already. It's tonight, you know. Where's Tina?" She stamps out and calls our daughter, who won't call back because she's playing at the neighbors'.

I let her search for a moment, then yell: "She's at the neighbors'!" I turn off the computer and head for the kitchen, where the pumpkin awaits its face. I dig in the cutlery drawer for a suitable knife. "They're having a party. I told you about it last night." Dominique's gone upstairs and I'm not sure if she hears me. I make the first slice.

When she returns she's shed her short plaid skirt, blazer and silk blouse — her office attire — for jeans and a Toronto Blue Jays sweatshirt, but she's forgotten to take off the oversized earrings that match the suit. "What were you yelling?"

"I said she's at the party next door. We talked about it last night." I've spread newspapers across the kitchen table, gutted the pumpkin, and am working on one mangled eye when I feel her, glaring over my shoulder.

"You should be doing this with Tina," she says. "I'm going to call her."

I finish the first eye and proceed to the second. They are not parallel, which I hope will add to the effect. One will look down, the other up. A lazy eye pumpkin.

Dominique's on the phone to the neighbor. I tune in and out. "Yes . . . a long day . . . the Quebec referendum."

My wife is the news director at a rock and roll radio station. Until yesterday, when the future of a united Canada was dangling from a thin high wire, her world had been dominated by the referendum, but now that the votes have been counted and the "Non" side's won by a sliver, it will revert back to civic squabbles and police chases.

The kids who listen to her station do not listen for the news, presented in tiny capsules at thirty minute intervals, and the station owners are reacting in kind. There's been talk of cutbacks; Dominique may lose two of her prodigies. That revelation, plus the uncertainty that's rocked the country over the past several months, plus the sad fact that her husband hasn't earned a check since February, have all shown themselves in a new crease across her forehead. She's taken to wearing her bangs down now, rather than combing them off to the side and spraying them in place. I wonder if her lover has noticed the change, or if this is something only a husband of nine years would pick up on.

"She'll be home in ten minutes," Dominique says, hanging up. "But you better carry on. I know how long these things take you."

"Of course *you'd* have it carved in five minutes," I say. I have pumpkin pulp on my hand, and I wing it onto the newspaper.

"Four," she says, hands braced on the hips which continue to appeal to me. I know this stance. I know this tilt of her head, this tone of voice.

"And it would look like shit."

She fills the big pot with water. "You could have at least started supper. It's not enough that I buy the groceries, but I work all day then have to come home and cook, too."

"I told you, I was working." I'm having trouble with the left eye. I've cut out far too much.

I hear the crack as Dominique breaks a handful of spaghetti in half, then the plop as she drops it into the pot. It'll only be a matter of minutes before she remarks on the power bill I stuck to the fridge.

"Ninety-four dollars! Thank God someone in this house has a job."

There. She's said it. A half turn of the knife already deeply imbedded back there. I slash through the pumpkin to create a mouth, a perfect oval to let the scream out.

Every afternoon at 3:15, a little man skirts past my window, scratching his chin and looking pensive. Although it's late November and Saskatchewan, his light jacket's unzipped and he doesn't protect his head. His hands, when not scratching his stubbly chin, are stuffed into the jacket pockets. I see that his wrists are small, even frail, like a sparrow's wing. A harmless eccentric; there used to be several in this neighborhood, an old area, near City Hospital and the river.

He walks like a Geisha Girl. I'll give him a dog and a ramshackle basement suite, littered with empty chip bags and bottles. And a friend named Dave who has to pound on his door eight times before he answers, because he's busy with his dog, Pogey. The Geisha Girl man is training Pogey to play the harmonica. He's fastened the dented instrument to a length of wire which he's looped over the small dog's head. So far, it's not going well.

I push the button that turns my screen off. I am beginning to loathe November, for no one reason in particular. It should be a good month to "buckle down," as Dominique says, to "get focused."

Today I am focused on three facts: I am a husband, a father and a writer of unsuccessful stories, not necessarily in that order. My wife is having an affair with a stock broker named Les and my daughter is being brought up by someone else. Tina spends mornings in kindergarten and afternoons in daycare. At times the guilt of having her in

177   SHELLEY LEEDAHL

daycare while I'm supposedly creating *successful* stories is too much, and I contemplate giving it all up in favor of what Dominique refers to as a real job. But not yet.

Besides, I am not without meagre success. Three years ago a reviewer at Canada's national newspaper gushed about my second collection of stories, stating that I possessed "a chameleon talent for creating colorful characters in ever-changing environs." Others critics predicted that my work-in-progress would secure me a coveted place in the ranks of Canadian literature. That much-awaited collection is still more locked inside me than in the manila folder on my desk. The chameleon, it seems, has crept on. In its absence I've enjoyed several long, lazy afternoons of tiddling away at the piano. I've attended many a "meeting" with my cohorts at the Senator Hotel. I've hidden under whatever rock's available.

Dominique says I don't live, I *subsist*. She says I have an uncanny knack for it, for subsisting. It's true. Thus far I've survived on small honorariums, the royalties from the two mildly successful books, and the occasional godsend grant from the Canada Council. She never used to mind. She used to tell the story herself of how on the night of March 15th, 1989, I cashed a two-hundred-dollar advance and succeeded to squander the entire amount on several rounds with strangers at the pub. She used to laugh about it.

The computer, blind without its flashing cursor, hums contentedly. Sometimes this soft sound puts me to sleep, right here at my desk. My office is adequate, with room enough for a six foot fig tree, my wraparound desk and chair, a lamp, small table and a reading chair, where Tina curls up on my knee with her books.

The room is surrounded on three sides by tall windows that do not open. The twisted vines of a derelict Virginia Creeper obscure my view on one side. Through the south windows I look out onto the street, and beyond that, the parking lot of the corner store and two newspaper recycling bins. The west windows, which I face, frame the avenue and my neighbors' tidy houses.

In the daytime this is a quiet block. Most are at work, and the children, of which there are several more each year as retired neighbors reluctantly move to seniors' highrises and a new generation moves in, are either infants or school-aged.

I miss the old man across the street who used to get up at six o'clock to cut his grass. His wife trimmed the edges of the lawn with scissors. Now professionals are taking over the neighborhood and it scares me. Professors, engineers, a theologian, a podiatrist. There are no more two-and-a-half storey houses that advertise "Suites for rent." Just seven years before, when Dominique and I bought our corner house, I blended in. Painters and writers occupied the top floors of these rental houses, but one by one, the houses were sold, renovated and resold; my friends displaced.

I stare at my computer screen, where I have typed an opening sentence: "I suppose this would be a good time to tell you I don't love you anymore." These are the words I expect to hear every day, the words whispered through my dreams. Dominique has made no apology for her affair, and, what's worse, it's not just sex.

If Tina has noticed her mother's preoccupation of late she's keeping it inside. Inside is where she and I stay while Dominique is off cavorting most week nights and Saturday evenings. I don't wait up.

"I suppose this would be a good time to tell you I don't love you anymore." I want to build a story around this line, but I'm blocked. I've been blocked for many months, never getting beyond the first few paragraphs of a new idea. The batch of stories I sent out in the spring have been coming back rejected, like hate mail. "You deliberately wrote a non-story." "We suggest you take a writing course." One nasty editor, a man whose own book I reviewed for a literary journal years ago and who has apparently not yet lived it down, wrote: "This has all the symptoms of AIDS."

In particular, editors have been stressing the lack of physical description in my work, the tendency to wash over characters and story lines like a child's primitive drawing. My characters are all neuroses. There are no fingers. No ear lobes.

There have been other times during my writing life when I've felt I've lost it, but those times it always came back. This time I fear it's gone for good. I no longer have the patience, the desire to dig deep into my psyche or wherever else it is one goes to retrieve the past, pontificate on the present, speculate on the future, disguise it and slap it all down so someone can tear it apart.

Perhaps it's my age. At forty-three, I've stopped playing the game.

I've had it with the pretentious literary crowd I was once so enamored with. Book store readings, university lectures, the library circuit . . . ultimately tedious, and there's no place for a fat, forty-three-year-old among all those controversial and articulate young writers who have their first books published before they've had their first knock-down-drag-out hangover.

Forty-three is fat, lying low and balding. It's never picking up the ringing phone in the fear that it'll be someone wanting something from me. It's being supported by a wife in full-blown love with a stock broker; the mother of our child dragging my name through the gutter any chance she gets; a bright, coiffured, upwardly mobile woman who's just waiting for the right moment to bolt.

I delete the sentence I've been mesmerized by for several minutes. Maybe the little man will become my saving grace. Maybe Pogey will learn a few notes on the harmonica, and the pair will busk downtown in front of the Midtown Plaza. I sit and wait for the words, fingers ready, but nothing happens. It's just not there.

Dominique, in bra and leggings, is packing sweaters into our burgundy luggage set, a wedding gift from my sister. "Pete, it's work."

"Work? A four day ski trip to Whitefish?"

She zips the suitcase shut and buckles it up. "It's a client appreciation thing. The station does something every year for its best clients." She heaves the crammed suitcase off the bed and sets it near the door.

"I suppose Les is going."

She slides her arms into the sleeves of a black turtleneck, then ducks her head through. "There's four of us from the station and four clients, and yes, Les is one of them."

I swirl the ice cubes in my five o'clock drink. Tina's playing dolls in her room across the hall, so I'm careful to keep my voice down. "What about Tina? How long's it been since you gave that kid sixty consecutive minutes of your time?"

"Tina's fine." Dominique brushes out her auburn hair, then pulls it back in a ponytail which makes her look younger, perky. "She's a bright, well-adjusted — "

"You missed her Christmas concert for fuck's sake!"

Dominique doesn't say anything, but there's a sharp intake of breath. It was unforgivable that she wasn't there and she knows it. "I'm sorry about that. You know I was held up. There'll be other concerts."

"There'll never be another *first* concert!" I finish the last of my drink, and push the suitcase out of the doorway into the hall so I can close the door. "Don't even pretend you've ever been her mother. She's an inconvenience. That's all either of us have ever been to you. Baggage."

Dominique reaches for the doorknob but I block her.

"You son of a bitch. Don't you dare tell me what kind of a mother I am." She screws her face up against mine. "I work forty, even fifty hours a week so there'll be food on the table, gas in the car, a mortgage payment made at the end of the month." She jabs me in the chest. "I work so you can sit at home and pretend to be writing the great Canadian novel."

She pushes me aside, opens the door and goes to Tina. I hear her tell our daughter that she's going away for a few days, and that Daddy's going to take her to McDonald's for supper. Tomorrow maybe he'll take her tobogganing. Won't that be fun?

A car honks twice and I walk to the window. My wife's cab awaits.

The talk show host is introducing two men who've been raped by women. I didn't know this was physically possible and have to watch. Earlier, on the news at noon, I watched a segment on a Vancouver artist who's been accused of promoting pornography through her nude paintings. At least three of the fastest rising stars in Canadian literature were once prostitutes.

Well, it's one way. I could, for example, exploit the casual friendship I have with the podiatrist's wife next door. It's not even a friendship, really. We say hello. We've batted the weather, that favorite Saskatchewan topic, back and forth across the snowy hedge that separates our two yards. She is quite beautiful. I could exploit her long, smooth neck, that noble head held high like a race horse. Blue eyes that could slice your heart in two.

She's taking a class in art history, carries a green campus knapsack slung across her shoulder on the days she walks to the university. Her golden hair is always free, flying, as she propels those shapely legs past my house.

I could take ten years off her thirty, erase the fact that she has a six-year-old son whom Tina plays with. Give her a lover, the university professor, much younger than her doctor husband, who, because he doesn't get any at home, places ads in dirty magazines. *Hi, I'm a professional and my name is John. I'm looking for women heavily into masturbation, phone sex, toys. I like to take Polaroids and videos. Write me. Box #11938*

In my mind I block and delete the whole thing, then take a sip of my beer, gone warm in the glass. Tina will be home from daycare soon. I've only got a few more minutes alone before Mrs. Murphy drops her off. I'll enjoy them at my window perch. I could sit like this all day. I often do. Who needs television, with so much going on outside every window? People just don't look. Too busy, or maybe they're afraid. Maybe they think all the action will make them dizzy, like one of those merry-go-rounds in the park where I take Tina. Maybe they think they'll fall off.

The Geisha Girl man is fifteen minutes late today. He shuffles past just as the school bus drops off the students by the recycling bins. A band of loud boys, exaggerating his walk, pursue him down the street. I stand up and crane my neck for a better look. The little man continues down the street looking very much like a donkey, the ragtag group behind like those donkey boy's in *Pinocchio*. One boy is having a real go at him. A large hunk of a kid who will lose his baby fat in a few months and take to breaking windshields with baseball bats. Give him a few years and even his own mother won't trust him.

They are almost out of my sight now. Something inside me wants to chase after them, to bring the feeble man into my home and protect him from this adolescent wrath, but Mrs. Murphy from the daycare pulls up with Tina. I see her reach across the backseat to unlock my daughter's door. Someone at the daycare, maybe Mrs. Murphy, maybe her helper, has gathered Tina's long hair in a ponytail high on her head. It flaps as she runs toward the house.

I hoist myself out of the chair to greet her at the side door.

"Papa!" she says, and throws her snow-dusted arms around my neck. I don't know why she calls me that. I'm much more a "Dad," or "Daddy." Too much *Hansel and Gretel*, I guess. We've collected a rather large number of children's books since Tina was born. She loves the classic fairy tales, and I don't mind reading them over and over again.

"How was your day, sweetheart?" I undo the scarf, pull off the parka.

"Great! We made snowflakes. See?" She opens her knapsack and pulls out a handful of paper snowflakes.

I admire her handiwork and together we tape the flimsy snowflakes to the window. "There," I say, "doesn't that look pretty?"

"Uh huh," she says, brushing her hair from her face and looking up as if to ask *what's next*. "Is Mom coming home for supper?"

"Not tonight, honey. She's working late."

"Oh." She flicks on the television.

"You know what I'm going to do? I'm going to make a big fire in the fireplace and order a pizza for supper."

"Okay."

I build the fire and order the pizza. We spread a blanket on the living room rug. Our pizza arrives and we have a picnic. After supper we throw our paper plates in the fireplace. They burn, we read. *Sleeping Beauty, Peter Pan, The Emperor's New Clothes.*

Tina falls asleep on the couch.

Dominique is in Mexico. Indefinitely. Her note said that she'd left the radio station and the marriage, and our divorce is on the horizon.

I am making breakfast for Tina, who's hunched over in her chair at the table, her chin propped on her fist. She could be asleep but her slippered feet, swinging below the chair, prove otherwise. "Where's Mexico, Papa?"

"I'll show you," I say, taking her hand and leading her into my office. Years ago, when I first I embarked on my dubious journey as a writer, I surrounded myself with accoutrements, thinking, falsely, that their presence might somehow inspire me. An expensive letter opener with a carved mallard at one end; a good pen set; bookends to keep my reference books in place, as if there were any fear they would get up on their own and walk away. I also purchased a globe that lights up when it's plugged in. I give it a spin. "Mexico is here," I say, pointing.

"Is it far away?" She runs her finger over the topographical surface of the country, feeling all the ridges.

"Very far away. We live here," I point out our dot in the middle of the prairies, "and Mommy's all the way down here, where there's no snow at all."

"Does it look like the postcard?" Tina asks, referring to the beach scene that arrived from Cancun two weeks ago.

"Yes. It looks just like that." The toaster buzzes and I pop up two slices. "Just peanut butter, right?"

"Uh huh."

We've settled into quite a comfortable routine, Tina and I. Up at 8:00 and at the table by 8:15, where we eat toast and slurp hot chocolate together. By 8:30 Tina's bundled up and ready for Mrs. Murphy's helper, who picks her up and takes her to daycare. I don't write for the next seven-and-a-half hours and we meet again at four o'clock. Weekends are walks in the park. Chopsticks on the piano. McDonald's and Saturday morning cartoons. On a scale of one to ten, I'd say I'm operating at about an eight.

The doctor's wife says I'm adjusting well, but the truth is it's so much easier now. I don't wonder when Dominique will be home. I don't have to listen to her daily diatribes.

Tina is a neat kid, a surprise package. On our weekend excursion to the art gallery, she asked to throw a coin in the wishing well. I had a nickel and a dime in my pocket. We closed our eyes and threw them. As we walked home through the snow, too thin to be called beautiful, I asked her what she wished for. "World peace," she said, fitting her gloved hand into mine. "What about you?"

On February 1, my estranged wife calls. I refuse to wake Tina, who's fallen asleep in my bed. The connection is bad. "I'll be home in three days," she says. "I'm putting the house up. I'm willing to split with you on it even though I paid for most of it myself. I think that's being overly generous but I don't want to haggle over anything with lawyers. Oh, and Pete, are you still there? Have Tina's stuff ready."

I've known this was coming, did not expect it so soon. I carry Tina to her own bed and stumble on an errant picturebook. *Pinocchio.* Tina loves the timeless characters: the benevolent shoemaker and the giant fish that swallowed the poor puppet. I tuck her under the covers and kiss her warm cheek. I pick the book off the floor on my way out.

Downstairs, in my office, I settle into my reading chair and light a cigarette, a habit I've taken up again in the month that Dominique's been away. *Pinocchio* rests in my lap. I open and read about the poor puppet who makes a career out of screwing up.

It's so simple. I don't know why I've never thought of it before. I could do this. I could write children's books. The market's guaranteed, and I could make children happy. What could be more important than that? I close the book, light another cigarette and look up to the doorway, expecting to see Dominique. "I'll start in the morning," I say, as if she is right there, leaning against the door frame, arms crossed below her breasts, watching and judging as she so often has. "I promise."

EMMY-RAE WILDFIELD is from Owen Sound, Ontario. "Doing Lunch" is one in a series of *Cheatin' Man* stories.

Doing Lunch

EMMY-RAE WILDFIELD

"WINE?" THE WAITER ASKS.

"Although I deserve to," answers a man dressed in a three-piece suit, "I'll have a scotch and soda . . . while I'm waiting." He consults his *Rolex* before he settles back to watch the business brokers and ladies who lunch at Tattlers.

An attractive brunette arrives on-the-run, her vulnerability causing a ripple to undulate through the crowd. Breathless, she stops and leans against the reservation desk, scans the room, then, spotting someone, waves. A mass of curls tumbles helter-skelter to her shoulders as she rushes to join a precise-looking blonde in beige. "Sorry I'm late, Steph," she says when they exchange air kisses, neither smudging make-up.

"What is going on?" Stephanie asks. Despite the drape of her pantsuit, she could be described as all angles.

"Tom is having an affair."

"Oh Juliette, are you sure?"

"Of course I'm sure. I've been married long enough to know the signs: Tom is never home; when I call his office after hours I get the answering service; and . . . " Juliette gropes for her handbag, pulls out a tissue, takes a breath, and says, " . . . he's jogging."

The waiter plunks a whiskey in front of the man wearing the three-piece suit. "Men can be bastards."

"How long has this been going on?" Stephanie asks.

"Since December. I think it started at the staff Christmas party. The doctors were looking for a way to say *thank you* to the nurses."

"It sounds like one of the nurses found a way to say *thank you* to the Doctor." The waiter, turning away from the man wearing the three-piece suit, walks in the direction of his work-station.

"Who is she?" Stephanie asks.

"She's an Intensive Care nurse, her name's Patricia, but . . . Tom calls her Patsy."

"What do you want to do about it?"

The waiter approaches their table and, without interrupting, places menus between Stephanie and Juliette. He stands and waits, as motionlessly as a statue.

"I just want *the Patsy* to leave Tom alone," Juliette answers.

The waiter pulls a list from his pocket, glances at it and, balancing on the balls of his feet, appears poised to launch details of daily specials.

"You have to be realistic," Stephanie says. "What are you going to do about Tom's adultery?"

Juliette exhales. "What can I do?"

"You might like to start with a Screwdriver."

Juliette blanches.

"Today's cocktail," the waiter says. "Do you need a moment?"

Stephanie orders two glasses of dry white wine, then faces Juliette. "Have you talked to Tom about this?"

"I can't do that. You know what Tom's like. First he'd deny everything, then he'd use his logic to turn things around. By the end of the conversation I'd be convinced I was the one having the affair."

"Either you can forgive and forget, or you can get rid of him and move on. There are no other options."

"May I suggest our battered pork." The waiter places a basket of fresh rolls between Stephanie and Juliette. "We can chop and skewer the swine right here at your table."

Stephanie flares her nostrils as if tempted by the smell of sizzling hide, but orders a vegetarian quiche with a small, green salad on the side. Juliette asks for the same.

"The *tart of the day*." The waiter reclaims their menus, and turns away. "Cheap and flaky. "

"You would feel better if you knew where you stood," Stephanie says. "You should discuss things with my lawyer — she has the papers to make ball-busting legal, you know."

The waiter winces as he sets glasses of wine on their table.

"Well . . . I guess I don't have anything to lose." Juliette fingers her glass.

"In that case, you should consider a third option." The waiter plucks Juliette's napkin from the table. "You can get rid of the bitch." He snaps her napkin. "You can get revenge. And . . . " He drapes the napkin across Juliette's lap, with a flourish. " . . . you can get your husband back."

"What did you say?" Juliette asks.

"Don't pay any attention to him," Stephanie says. "He's a waiter — probably an unemployed actor."

"But he seems to know what I want," Juliette says. "I want to get rid of the sow, get revenge and get Tom back."

Stephanie asks the waiter what *exactly* he is suggesting.

The waiter leans over the table. "It's a simple strategy: wage the war against your real opponent — set your sights on the bitch. Step one is to convince her that your husband considers her to be nothing more than another meaningless affair. Then, you must force her to be the one that confronts your husband about his unfaithfulness with other women."

"You mean . . . make the bimbo believe that, in Tom's eyes, she's just a brief and meaningless sexual encounter . . . " Stephanie smiles.

"One of a string," the waiter says, his chest expanding. "Like the ponies."

"But . . . how can I do that?" Juliette asks.

"Smother your husband with messages of affection."

"I'd rather smother Miss Patsy."

"Forget that," Stephanie says. "You'll find entrapment much more rewarding."

The waiter looks directly into Juliette's pale blue eyes. "The key to your success is to plant signs of active romance where the little fox will find them. Overwhelm your husband with the onslaught. And remember: don't let your husband know who is leaving them."

"When is your next business trip?" Stephanie asks.

"I'm supposed to be away on assignment next week, but I can't stand the thought of giving Tom the opportunity to have his wench over and . . . in our bed."

"You must go," Stephanie says. "Be sure to leave love notes that say, *'Can't wait until I'm wrapped around you again'*, folded inside your bath towels."

"But . . . won't it annoy Tom if Miss Patsy discovers them?"

"You're his wife. You have every right to annoy him." The waiter refills their water glasses.

"I believe he's onto something." Stephanie explains that Tom can't say anything to Juliette without revealing his little fling, and he can't question the minx without exposing that his wife (or someone else) is alive and well and still in the picture. "No matter which way he turns, Tom will be trapped by his cheating character."

"Sign those notes with a kiss," the waiter says.

However, when the waiter suggests pink lipstick, Stephanie cautions against making silly mistakes and asks Juliette if she ever wears pink lipstick. Although Juliette doesn't, she reveals that Patsy does. So, to keep things exciting, they decide to use orange. Then Stephanie demands that Juliette tell everything she knows about Patsy.

"Well . . . you know she's a nurse, she's in her early twenties, she's blonde . . . kind of plump . . . has big breasts. I don't think she's very interesting."

"Tom obviously does," Stephanie says, flatly.

"It doesn't matter how hard we work to stay attractive, our men are lured away by the first blonde bombshell wearing a polyester uniform that comes along," the waiter says.

Stephanie's stern stare sends him scurrying towards the kitchen.

"Oh Steph, if this scheme backfires, I'm going to end up alone." Juliette smooths her tiny hand across her stomach and down her right hip.

"That's not possible; there's something about you that men find irresistible. It's like flies being attracted to honey."

"Well, I wish my man would stick to me." Juliette bites her lower lip, then proposes that the reason some women find other people's husbands so appealing is . . . "They've proved they're the marrying kind."

"Before you leave next week," Stephanie says, "Drench your pillow case with perfume, but not *Seduction*."

"No risk of me leaving traces of my scent," Juliette answers. "I'll lace it with *Poison*."

"*Obsession* would be more to the point," the waiter says, as he serves lunch.

"I'll find an excuse to drop in on Tom at his office," Stephanie says, "And slip a tube of orange lipstick into his lab-coat pocket."

"Perfect. If Patsy feels something there, she's bound to pull it out." Then, responding to the expression on Stephanie's face, Juliette says, "I was talking about the lipstick."

"If the vixen wants to find out if there are other woman in Tom's life," Stephanie says, "She'll have to hang around his office — and he won't like that."

Juliette wonders whether Tom's been feeding the nymph all the standard lines in order to make her think she has a chance of luring him away.

"*We have grown apart*." The waiter grimaces as he twists the neck of a pepper grinder. "*The romance has left our relationship. She doesn't understand me*."

Stephanie holds up her hand to stop his gyrations, and the increasing levy of spice . . . Then, the three of them fall silent, as if suddenly aware of the gravity of the situation. They vow to make their plan work, and agree that it will as long as they plant enough evidence to expose Tom's active love life. Juliette suggests stashing a pair of red stiletto heels behind Doctor Tom's examination table, but Stephanie thinks their efforts would be better served if they hid them under his desk. However, despite the enthusiasm of their plotting, the waiter's offer of "a black, lace, 36-D teddy to hang behind the Doctor's examination-room door," startles Stephanie and Juliette.

The first to recover, Stephanie says, "At least the bimbo will know it isn't yours, Julie."

"You really are ruthless, Steph, but what if it's Tom that finds all this stuff?"

"If Tom doesn't know who is responsible he won't know how to respond and, as long as you stay away from the hospital, you can't be accused of anything," Stephanie says. "In fact, in Tom's calculating mind, it will raise the possibility that his young temptress is leaving these things behind — in hopes of exposing their affair and trapping him. No matter how much fun Tom thinks he's having, you can be sure he's feeling guilty."

"Before you two are through," the waiter says, "He'll be feeling desperate. And we haven't talked about condoms. They come in a variety of flavors: cherry, banana, licorice . . . "

Rather than respond, Stephanie asks Juliette to lend her a set of Tom's car keys.

"I thought this was about condoms," Juliette says.

"I'll tuck a condom into Tom's passenger-side vanity mirror. And, next time the little tramp turns down the visor to check her lipstick, the condom will fall right into her lap."

Juliette frets that Patsy might think Tom's leaving sex toys for her, and Juliette doesn't want to encourage Patsy to think that way.

"He won't — not if the condom is edible and you attach a card that reads, *'Hungry for you!'* Or if it's a glow-in-the-dark, and the note says, *'Can't wait to see you again!'*. Naturally the note should be signed with an orange kiss." The waiter puckers as if offering a full pair of lips to perform the service.

Juliette looks directly at the waiter. "Didn't you promise me revenge?"

"Valentine's Day is just around the corner. That's the perfect time to go in for the kill. Why not send a strip-o-gram to your husband at his office? Have the stripper carry a bunch of orange, lip-shaped helium-filled balloons and, of course, wear a nurse's uniform."

"The hospital gossips will be vicious," Stephanie says.

"I'm counting on it." Juliette reaches for her purse, pulls out a credit card, and, handing it to the waiter, says, "Tom will pay for this."

The waiter takes her card, thanks Juliette, and wishes them both good luck before he excuses himself

Juliette and Stephanie settle back in their chairs. As they sip their wine, they watch the waiter lead a well-dressed man across the room to join the man wearing the three-piece suit.

And, when the waiter places a basket of fresh rolls on the table between the two men, Juliette comments, "That's what I call great-looking buns."

"He works in my lawyer's office — corporate law. I always see him with financial types," Stephanie says. "Do you want to meet him?"

"I want my husband back."

"I know I'd be tempted to give the good Doctor a taste of his own medicine," Stephanie replies.

Their giggles are drowned out by the voices of the lawyer and the man wearing the three-piece suit.

"Sorry I kept you waiting, Donald," says the lawyer.

"What's going on?" Donald asks.

"The *Mathews-Appelby* takeover bid has stalled."

"The word on the street is that you're still not offering enough. I hear they're trolling for a bigger catch."

"Bottom feeders." The waiter approaches their table, deals out menus, picks up the lawyer's napkin, and lays it across his pin-striped lap. "Why don't you let me help you with that?"

The lawyer thanks the waiter, then turns back to Donald. "You don't think they'd walk from a deal at this stage, do you?"

"If they burn their bridges on this one," Donald replies, "they better be able to swim."

The waiter drops a napkin into the lap of Donald's three-piece suit. "Gentlemen, before we sink our teeth into corporate resuscitation today, I recommend we start with the shark steaks . . . "

IAN COLFORD lives in Halifax. He has appeared in *The Journey Prize Anthology* and is the editor of *Water Studies: New Voices in Maritime Fiction* (Pottersfield Press).

Stone Temple

IAN COLFORD

AS DAY BREAKS A MAN APPEARS holding the hand of a small boy, leading him across the frozen waste of an empty field. The two figures are backlit by the rising sun. The horizon is streaked pink and mauve. Behind the stand of pine they've just passed through is an old house. It's the house where, until a few minutes ago, the boy lived with his mother.

The boy's name is Luke and the man, his father, is Bobby Flint. He's tall and gaunt and unsure what he's doing is right, but he's doing it anyway because what else can a man do when he's denied his son through a perversion of justice? Mary Beth lied to the judge. When she said that he'd beaten her and threatened Luke, Bobby could hardly believe he'd heard correctly. He understood at once that her mother had put her up to it. On her own Mary Beth would never dream of lying. But it was too late for him to invent a story of his own. Everyone was staring at him. Nothing he said was going to convince them Mary Beth's story wasn't true. So he didn't say anything.

Excited at first, Luke is tired now and when he stumbles Bobby lifts him gently into his arms. Luke is still wearing his pyjamas and has only running shoes on his feet and nothing on his head because Bobby had to move quickly and quietly to get him out of the house. It's February. They breathe thick fog into the air. Bobby has a blanket and some food in the truck, which once they get across the field and over the fence will be visible just where the Old Mill Road veers into the Hatcher property. The truck will be warm, too, because Bobby left the engine running. Nobody will be out there to notice a truck with its engine running, not at this hour.

The moon sits placid behind slivers of drifting cloud. It grazes the top branches of the tallest trees.

"Daddy, look!"

Luke, who is three going on four, has spotted a huge bird gliding in silhouette against the brightening sky. He points, his small hand bare, and Bobby realizes he's forgotten mittens as well as boots and a cap.

For a moment he stops walking and lifts Luke higher, seating him on his shoulder. He adjusts the wool cap that covers his own head. It turned cold this morning, very cold.

The bird could be a hawk, or an owl, or maybe it's only a crow. He can't see well enough in this dusky light to be sure. But there are eagles in these woods, too. Bobby's seen them at Colby's, fifteen of them perched in a willow tree, waiting to be fed chicken entrails.

"It's beautiful," Bobby murmurs and glances around at Luke. Luke watches as the bird lowers itself into the trees, which shudder for just a second. Then he turns and smiles at his father.

"Neat, huh?"

"Neat, huh?" Luke echoes. His breath stirs the air.

Bobby starts walking again. When they reach the fence he lifts Luke from his shoulder and places him on the ground on the other side. As he's climbing over the fence he realizes his mistake. The snow will hold his footprints. He should have worn rubber boots and taken a wider route, crossed the stream behind Hatcher's and approached the house through the forest. Then he could have gone back and waded upstream, away from the truck, before retracing his steps.

"Daddy, I'm cold!"

Luke is about to wail.

"Sorry, Bud."

Bobby's over the fence. His heart thudding, he hoists Luke high into the air and sets off at a trot, his son's delighted squeals echoing like the tolling of bells off the trees and across the snow-smooth field back toward the house.

"You like that?"

Luke is examining a plastic package containing a small foamy chocolate cake. He can't open it himself so Bobby takes it and, one hand on the wheel, splits the plastic with his teeth.

"There you go," he says, and, returning it to his son's hands, forces a smile.

Luke seems happy now. The truck bounces over ruts and through potholes. This is a game for the boy. But Bobby has realized that his plan ended the second he opened the door and put Luke into the cab of the truck.

He wanted to get on the highway and just keep driving. Once they were safely out of the province they'd stop for gas and something to eat; a real breakfast with coffee, not the sweets he's brought for Luke. Then he'd put his foot to the floor and keep driving — New Brunswick, Quebec, Ontario.

But two RCMP cruisers silently passing the truck at high speed was enough to convince him that Mary Beth had already been on the phone to her mother, who had called the police. Bobby has been turning over in his mind the idea of being hunted. He does not want to go to jail. He does not want to lose his son.

So he left the highway at Windsor Junction and found the trail out to Barrel Lake. He remembers that the trail follows the edge of the lake and that if you stay on this trail it will take you all the way to Highway 6. He's driven the route before, but only in summer, only in daylight, and only on an all-terrain vehicle. Taking the truck through there will be a new experience. But then, as Mary Beth used to say, if we don't keep up the search for new experiences we might as well be dead.

When he looks over he sees that Luke has chocolate icing all over his face and fingers. But at least he's smiling.

With a grunt, Bobby raises the log to a standing position and lets it topple over backward. It's no problem. He feels good, like he could do this

195   IAN COLFORD

forever. But this is already the third time he's had to stop the truck in order to clear debris and fallen branches from the path he's been following. He's pushing himself through snow up to his knees. His feet are wet inside his work boots, and he knows that's not a good thing. He had hoped to be long gone from here by now — it's nearly noon — but a while ago the trail fooled him by swerving away from the lake and has narrowed to the point that he doubts he can drive much further. Luke grins at him from behind the windshield and Bobby stops what he's doing to wave.

He's going to have to leave and scout ahead to find out where they are. It's too cold to take Luke. The panic that stilled his blood the first time he struck rock and spun the tires has subsided to a languid, almost contented state of anxiety. He's confident he can find a way through, but until he catches sight of the highway he won't be able to conceal his doubts, at least not from himself.

He returns to the truck and climbs inside. It's warm. The droning engine and the whirring fan mask the forest's silence. He removes his wet gloves, folds his hands together over his mouth and blows. He deliberately does not look at the gas gauge.

Luke is eating a jam-filled pastry. The sweet sticky smell of raspberries nearly turns Bobby's empty stomach. New problems arise by the minute. He'd brought food but nothing to drink. A few miles back when he realized this he retrieved a crushed Tim Horton's cup from under the seat, blew it up like a balloon, and went outside to fill it with snow. He takes a sip from the cup now.

"Luke, Daddy's going to go on ahead for a bit to see if the road's over there." He gestures expansively as if indicating distance, vastness. But they are surrounded by trees. He can see no more than ten meters in any direction. "When I come back we'll hit the road and make good time."

Luke raises his fist.

"Hit the road!" he shrieks. "Hit the road!"

Pastry crumbs fall from his mouth to his lap. One of the reasons Bobby lost his temper was because Luke screamed and screamed for no reason. He just let loose, hitting those high notes and shattering the quiet that Bobby wanted preserved after working another ten-hour shift at Colby's meat-packing plant. The cushioned rasp of saws ripping through flesh and bone still rang in his ears hours after he got home.

Luke whoops and hollers, but Bobby doesn't say anything, just sips water and stares through the windshield at these trees that have him utterly confounded. They *couldn't* be that far from the highway, not after going all this distance. He knows these woods. He grew up here. But the forest in winter . . . His father had told him once when they were out rabbit hunting, *the forest is a wild animal with a bloody leg. Make one mistake and it turns on you.*

He was only going to be gone fifteen minutes. He rolled Luke up in the red blanket and told him to go to sleep. Then he turned off the engine and slammed the door quickly to preserve the warmth inside. He knew it would get cold in the cab very fast. But he wanted to save gas in case he was able to get the truck out of here.

But now it's more than twenty minutes since he left. There's nothing but trees in every direction. He came upon a clearing where the remains of a collapsed hunting shack were visible: a mound of twisted slats and boards, like bones beneath the snow. He found the lake and stood at its edge gazing out over its undisturbed surface. He shielded his eyes against the glare and, after urinating against a tree, turned to go back to the truck. His heart is throbbing now with the effort of dragging himself through snow that's two feet deep in places. He knows the highway is close, but he'll never get the truck through. He'll have to back out, or else just leave it there and walk to the highway with Luke in his arms.

As he nears the truck he hears crying. He runs.

The window on Luke's side is down three inches and the inside of the cab is freezing; Luke is sobbing. Bobby jumps in and rolls the window up and inserts the key into the ignition. To his relief the engine immediately turns over.

"What in the . . ."

"I opened the window to say hi."

Hardly comprehending the words, Bobby looks at his son. It's at least minus twenty outside, probably colder. He hadn't said anything about not rolling the window down. It hadn't occurred to him that he'd have to.

IAN COLFORD

"There was a deer . . ."

He rubs his hands together and then takes the trembling boy into his lap and holds him. He doesn't want to get angry. Anger is pointless. He'll get them out of here first. The lecture can come later.

He closes his eyes.

"I'm sorry Daddy . . ."

"Shhhh," Bobby whispers, rocking his son in his arms. "It's all right now. I'm here."

In a few minutes Luke has calmed down and their shivering limbs are warmed and Bobby is able to think. It's one o'clock. They have four hours of daylight left and++ a quarter of a tank of gas. He switches on the radio. He doesn't remember any snowstorms in the forecast, but then he wasn't listening closely because he assumed that by now he'd be in another province.

They sit quietly listening to Garth Brooks on the country music station. Bobby tries to concentrate on the music, tries to ignore the tensing of muscles in his abdomen. When he looks down he notices that Luke has fallen asleep, his thumb in his mouth. No wonder. Poor kid's been up since five a.m.

Finally there's a weather forecast. Clear today, flurries overnight and clear again tomorrow. Very cold. He switches the radio off and carefully moves Luke from his lap to the other seat. He grips the steering wheel. The sun has descended to a point just below the tops of the trees and it blinks at him through the branches. The truck flinches as he shifts into reverse. He twists around to get a view through the rear window and presses the accelerator. A grinding noise comes from below, but the truck doesn't move. He tries not to swear as he opens the door and gets out. The back tires are wedged against a fallen tree that was buried by snow and not visible earlier. He tries shifting into neutral and pushing from the front. But it's no good. He can't budge it.

Now he swears.

They have to abandon the truck.

Luke is wrapped tightly inside the red blanket. Bobby cradles the bundle in his arms as he strides quickly over the uneven forest floor. The only sounds are his steps and his laboured breathing.

Luke asked once where Mommy is. Bobby could not prevent his lips from curling into a sneer. Luke has not asked again.

Bobby's ears throb with the cold. His toes are numb, as are his fingers. He cannot feel his face and his eyes are as dry as cinders. Overall, however, he's in good shape and proud of it. He never abuses his body, doesn't smoke, seldom drinks. He knows he can walk for a long time. But with each lungful of air he feels more like a slab of meat than a living creature, a carcass stripped of skin and hanging from a hook in a freezer. He's beginning to hate what he's done. But he can't see how he could have done anything else. His son is still his son. Nothing will change that no matter how many lies Mary Beth tells.

Suddenly he sinks into snow to his hips, and as he struggles to pull himself free he realizes that he's wondering *if* he can get them out of here. The thought of failure empties his mind of everything else. All he can see are the trees that surround them on all sides. He doesn't have any idea where they are. He's been following the sun, but now he's confused. If he was heading in the right direction he would have reached the highway long ago. Every few minutes he stops to listen for the swish of car tires on asphalt, the moaning whine of trucks gearing down.

It occurs to him, as he kicks free of the snow and starts walking again, that it's all Mary Beth's fault. If she hadn't stood there and lied he would have been allowed to see Luke every week. He wouldn't have had to take him from her. He didn't want to do this, but she left him no choice. Their life together was over, he could understand that. But it didn't mean she had to lie about him. All he'd ever done was frighten her. He'd frightened himself too. Whenever he got angry it was like a fire in his head, lights flashing in his eyes. He yelled and threw things. He broke furniture. But he never hit anyone. He'd seen enough of that growing up. Anger was his father's only legacy. He didn't want to complete the circle.

He got himself into therapy and talked about it. But it was already too late. Even though he controlled his outbursts from that day forward, Mary Beth was afraid of him. He could see the fear in her eyes and it reminded him of being small and in bed huddling under the covers listening to his parents fight. He moved into his own place and visited whenever he found the time. But one Saturday he went over and

Mary Beth's mother was there and she wouldn't let him in. She called him names and said he was dirt — said that his whole family was dirt — and told him he'd get inside over her dead body. So he went and grabbed the rifle from the truck and emptied a couple of rounds into the front door. And he knew, even before the explosions faded, that he'd done exactly what she wanted him to.

So before forcing the window this morning and creeping upstairs to Luke's room, he hadn't seen his son in more than two months. He knows he's lucky they didn't send him to jail. But he also knows it isn't fair what they did to him. He isn't a criminal. He didn't do anything wrong.

A branch strikes his face. He stumbles but keeps his balance. There is desperation in his actions. He feels it, a tightness in his bowels. He's never been this cold or this alone in his life. Nothing has gone right and he senses the futility of each step he takes. When he slows his pace for a moment and listens, all he hears is the sighing of the trees as a breeze passes through their limbs. He wonders how many miles he's strayed from the path he wanted, and at this thought his burden seems to lighten because maybe the house he shared with Mary Beth for almost four years is just over the next rise. Preposterous. But to his exhausted mind even this appears as a possibility.

As he enters a clearing a sob emerges from within the blanket and when he separates the folds a biting stench follows. Reeking steam. He flinches, averts his head. Luke howls, kicks against the restraint of the blanket. His pyjamas are a mess of piss and shit.

"God dammit! God dammit!" Bobby growls, but he can't even hear himself above Luke's wild bellowing.

He drops the blanket on the snow and sets Luke on it. He pulls the wet running shoes from Luke's feet and uses the pyjamas to wipe the boy off as best he can. Everything stinks. He feels tears in his eyes when he sees Luke's bare skin redden as the freezing air assaults it. The tiny genitals shrink from the cold.

"Hold still!" he shouts and grips Luke tightly by the arm.

But there's no need to yell. Luke is suddenly quiet. Bobby can almost see the heat being drained like blood from the boy's slumping body. He tosses the pyjamas away and hoists Luke into his arms. It's happened faster than he would have thought possible. Luke's eyes are glazed; he seems to be sleeping. Bobby lowers the zipper of his coat and squeezes Luke inside. But the coat is too small; Bobby can't get the zipper up again, even with Luke pressed firmly against his ribs. Cold air pours in and grips him in a painful embrace.

He takes Luke out and pulls the zipper up. Luke, nearly naked, flops limply in his arms like a freshly cut side of ribs. Bobby seizes the blanket and pulls, but it rips where frozen urine has cemented it to the ground. He drops it and searches the clearing with his eyes, as if the forest is hiding a secret fountain of warmth. But there are only trees, snow, bare domes of exposed stone. He rests Luke on the blanket and starts removing his coat. But the cold air singes his throat and for a moment he struggles to breathe. He stops what he's doing as a sound of muffled whimpering reaches him — the kind of mewling groan a trapped animal might make as it chews off its captured limb. He holds himself motionless to listen, hoping that it's Luke making the noise. But it isn't. Tears burn his eyes. He's so tired — he sways, almost falling.

Slowly he pulls the coat back on. Gently, solemnly, he folds the corners of the blanket over the small body until it's hidden. He wipes his eyes and watches the blanket for signs of movement.

He stands before the shrouded remains of his son and scours his mind for words that will excuse, or explain, what has happened. His breath steams the air.

"I'm sorry, Bud," he says and focuses his eyes on the blanket, still watching for movement.

Behind the trees the sun is almost level with the horizon. It's rays peek through and catch Bobby's eyes, making him squint. The blue of the sky has deepened and taken on hints of green, yellow, red. He feels he should stay but a clenching in his stomach tells him to get moving. He adjusts his wool cap and backs off, his eyes on the blanket. At the edge of the clearing he steadies himself against a tree, then lowers his head and turns away.

IAN COLFORD

So Like Candy

ROB PAYNE

1

GLASS OF COKE, cheez doodles, Sex Pistols causing anarchy in the background . . . I'm set for the 10:00 show.

She's undressing slowly tonight. She's a heavy girl, so much to see, so much to touch and rub and love. That's it. She's touching those nasty panties, hand slipping between her legs, caressing the silky wet white cotton.

I can't eat chocolate or sweet stuff when the show is on. You'd think I would. Because it fits. Chocolate, sex, masturbation, rock and roll. But I get gassy. Last week she used a bottle. Tonight it's back to her vibrator. Less impulsive, but the show must go on.

God save the Queen, we mean it man. Johnny's got the idea. Just as she's about to climax I pick up the phone and hit speed dial.

Seconds pass. Ten rings. I want to hear that voice at its pitch.

"Hello?" Slightly impatient, slightly flustered, slightly lost.

"Hello, is this Cynthia Harris, apartment 1041, Sparrow Lane North?"

"Um, yeah."

"I hope I'm not disturbing you."

"Oh, no, no." Slight paranoia.

"This is Gavin, Mr. Chutley's assistant."

Chutley is the owner of all of these shitty highrises.

"Oh yes."

She's never heard of me.

"I'm scheduled to come look at your kitchen pipes. Routine inspection. Is there a good time for you."

Blood draining back into her brain.

"Um, evenings would be best."

"How's tomorrow at seven?"

Pause. Colors returning.

"Fine. I'm sorry, what was your name again?"

The tone is almost condescending now. I'm not impressed.

"Gavin."

"Ok, Gavin. Tomorrow at seven. Please don't be late."

Don't be late. Don't be late. She never leaves the apartment on weeknights, but we mustn't upset the Queen's routine.

2

The telescope was a gift. Never had much use for it until I got bored one night and went snooping. Her shades aren't thick — Walmart cheap — and most nights she doesn't bother to close them. That's why the world is in the shape it is: an ugly, lazy apathy. And everyone's fat. But it's all related. Too soft, too slow, too stupid. I blame television.

Tonight is The Cure. I'm feeling giddy. She's really agitated, and the frustration is plain to see. Last night ended in a bust and tonight she's been waiting for the Super's kid to show up and look at the pipes. But it's 10:00. The little bastard never showed up . . .

The full length mirror is garnered in satin cloth, a strap-on-penis attached to a board hangs on the bed post. She's turned the red light in the closet on to flood the room in a devilishly-delicious glow.

Now she's out of the shower and the towel is dropped. The flesh is pink and wet, jiggly. She likes the way it hangs and folds, admires the smooth contours. I can tell she enjoys her body, can tell by the way her fingers start slowly, buckling her knees as she leans back on the bed, that firm, high mattress — can tell by the way she draws out the strokes in long, slow licks. Now she takes her fingers and puts them in her mouth. Back to her vagina. Back to her mouth. I suddenly realize that she isn't going to make it to the strap-on.

As Robert Smith chants "Hot hot hot," I'm bolting out the door, attempting to zipper my pants back up. My erection burns as I skip the elevator and pound down five long flights and headlong across the parking lot. Fingers fumbling, I key in 1041 and wait. No response and I'm cursing myself for getting caught up in act one, unprepared, unprofessional. A useless old man is hobbling through the security door, so I wait and do the last minute grab-and-go. Five minutes. It's been five minutes. Unless she's eased off to tease herself, I've failed.

1037, 1039, 1041 . . . pounding — not knocking — pounding. Breathless.

"Hi, sorry I'm late."

Her face is beat red, her neck is tense. She's in a houserobe and her hands are shaking slightly. Sweet success.

"Who are you? You can't come pounding at my goddamn door in the middle of the night, I don't care who you are. WHO ARE YOU?"

"I am so, so sincerely sorry. I really am. I don't know what I was thinking. I just . . . "

Pilgrims at Mecca aren't this reverent.

"I'm Gregory, the Super's assistant."

"Gregory? I spoke to someone named Gavin, yesterday . . . "

My fuckup. I can barely breath. Sweating profusely.

"Gavin Gregory. My name is Gavin Gregory. Yeah, most people just call me Gregory. My last name."

I wish I could stop panting. My shirt is streaked with sweat.

"Mmmm. I was expecting you a bit earlier than this, Mr. Gregory. I don't expect you to show up now. I was getting ready for bed."

I'd laugh, but there's that fucking pretentious attitude again.

"I apologize. I was on the eighth floor and found some problems. Just between me and you, these inspections are way overdue."

Silent, irritated nod.

"I dropped by to apologize and say I'd be back tomorrow. Seven sharp, and . . . "

Yada yada yada. Placated, she closes the door and forgets me, waves me away like a tick. Maybe she finishes her session, but it's a letdown. I know it won't ease the pressure building up day after day.

3

I'm breaking my self-imposed rule and having wine and chocolate tonight. Call me crazy. It's a dry wine. German. A two. I don't profess to be a connoisseur, but I know what I like. I'm feeling lazy this evening, and I can tell by the way Cynthia's stroking her flabby body, slowly licking her breasts, that she can't get into it tonight either. I want passion, but she's just going through the motions. I walk over to the stereo, put on Leonard Cohen, grab a *Penthouse* from the stack. Maybe I'll let her come, because I know it won't be explosive or satisfying. But I'm so unimpressed by this performance that I decide she doesn't deserve it. Why doesn't she get a man, whipped cream, maybe a movie?

10:14 and she still hasn't come. Her colour appears to be darker, a bit of a flush, but it's difficult to tell from this distance. I sigh. Close enough. I hit speed dial.

Five rings.

"Hello?" Annoyance bordering on anger. Obviously she's frustrated with the way things are going tonight, too.

"Yes, this is Stuart Granger from United Liberty Health and Mutual. Is this a good time?"

Straight hangup. Not even a "no," or an "I'm not interested." The straight hangup.

I redial.

"Yes?"

"You should use the bottle."

"What?"

I hang up the phone.

4

The shades are down the next night and for the first time the show is cancelled. Well, unless she's secretly touching herself under the sheets. But I doubt it. It's not her style. She's a performer, that special kind of dreamer who knows the beauty of her own body. I admire that spirit, that determination to make herself happy when no one else will.

I want to call and encourage her, root for the home team, but I know it won't do any good. She's got to work herself out of this slump without my help. And when she does, I'll be ready, penis in hand.

5

Iggy Pop, nachos with extra-hot salsa, twelve Bud, three days and no action. That's the current story. She's just not a pro. I am so disappointed.

Last night the shades were down. She was moving around a bit. I dialled, waited for a ring and then hung up — just in case she got any ideas.

Now the gifts. Call me a big softy, but I bought her a nifty polyurethane fist dildo. I also sent her some literature on weight-watchers — in case that was on her mind — and a polaroid of my penis lathered in whipped cream. I figure my goodies arrived, cause she's been pacing around for the last hour and now a friend has arrived. But what can she say? "My masturbation routine has been upset by some interloper . . . "

At 11:00 I take her off my speed dial. The game is up. They're putting up new, thicker blinds.

6

A week later and, not surprisingly, her apartment is up for rent. I feel like we've reached the end of things, like autumn in the countryside, or Christmas after all the presents have been ripped open and pawed like ugly kittens. Elvis Costello is crooning to "Alison" and I'm packing up the telescope, sliding it under the bed in case the police happen to knock on my door and ask questions, or want to take a look around. They were in her apartment yesterday, and I have to say I'm upset. It's so hypocritical.

By now she's come hard and fast — a blow-your-head-off come . . . a perpetual-motion-niagara-falls-supersonic orgasm that most people only dream of. You know, waves of eternal bliss and the whole deal. And

I'm responsible for that. I engineered the teasing, the waiting, the nervous tension, fear, paranoia, churned up that orgasm stew, measured out the key ingredients. And she knows it. Which is why I make my final phonecall from the park.

"Hello?"

"Hi Cynthia."

"Hi . . . "

Waiting.

"I hope you appreciate what I did for you . . . "

Pause.

"I'm sorry, is this Tom?"

"Because it was all for you."

Pause.

"I'm sorry, who is this?"

"I think you're really sexy."

This pause is colder, a thin tension at the core.

"You shouldn't feel bad about your weight. Even fat girls can be beautiful."

Frozen recognition.

"And I think you're beautiful. Do you know how many times you made me come? How many dishtowels and kleenexes and pairs of underwear got all wet and sticky just watching you? Do you know how many?"

She doesn't hang up.

"I think I love you, Cynthia . . . What do you think of that?"

A deep, uneven choking, barely a whisper.

"I'm head over heels in love with you. So sexy. I come to you all the time."

Faint whisperings, first tears, anger as I hang up.

But isn't that what we all want from love in the end? Admiration and humiliation. Being pissed on and flattered at the same time — cause part of her was flattered I watched. I mean, no one was buying tickets before I showed up, and I doubt anyone will soon. I mean, christ, she's pretty fucking fat. And that's the problem with the world today: too lazy, too slow, too fucking fat.

I blame TV.

Also Available from *Canadian Fiction*

Northern Horror
Featuring Robert J. Sawyer, Nancy Baker, Nancy Kilpatrick,
Peter Sellers, and Edo van Belkom.
$19.95 CDA/$14.95 USA

Carrying the Fire
Featuring work by Douglas Glover, Tess Fragoulis, Lori Weber,
Nadine McInnis and others.
$19.95 CDA/$14.95 USA

Silver Anthology of Canadian Fiction Magazine
Featuring award-winning work by Leon Rooke, Rohinton Mistry,
W.P. Kinsella, Jane Urquhart, Barbara Gowdy and others.
$19.95 CDA/$14.95 USA

Cinematic Fiction
Featuring Cyril Dabydeen, George Woodcock, Elyse Gasco,
Tom Wayman and others.
$14.95 CDA/$11.95 USA

The Quixotic Reader
Featuring Meira Cook, Tess Fragoulis, Michael Winter,
Robyn Sarah and others.
$14.95 CDA/$11.95 USA

Cemeteries
Featuring Jill Robinson, Michael Mirolla, Francis Itani and others.
$14.95 CDA/$11.95 USA

Why Men Have Balls
Featuring Patrick Roscoe, Charles Foran, T.F. Rigelhof, Armand
Garner Ruffo and others.
$14.95 CDA/$11.95 USA

Order directly from Quarry Press,
P.O. Box 1061, Kingston, ON K7L 4Y5,
tel. (613) 548-8429, fax. (613) 548-1556,
e-mail: order@quarrypress.com